# I GOT TO KEEP MOVING

# I GOT TO KEEP MOVING

## STORIES BY BILL HARRIS

WAYNE STATE UNIVERSITY PRESS
DETROIT

# MADE IN MICHIGAN WRITERS SERIES

## GENERAL EDITORS

Michael Delp, Interlochen Center for the Arts

M. L. Liebler, Wayne State University

ISBN 978–0-8143-4593-1 (paperback);
ISBN 978–0-8143-4594-8 (ebook)

Library of Congress Control Number: 2018951989

Publication of this book was made possible by a generous gift from The Meijer Foundation. This work is supported in part by an award from the Michigan Council for Arts and Cultural Affairs.

michigan
council for
&arts
cultural
affairs

Wayne State University Press
Leonard N. Simons Building
4809 Woodward Avenue
Detroit, Michigan 48201-1309

Visit us online at wsupress.wayne.edu

*To Viola Brooks, Elizabeth Gay, and Carole Harris
for their courage and encouragement.*

"Life's sorrows can be borne if you put them in a story or tell a story about them."

Isak Dinesen

# CONTENTS

## PART 3. Kin—The Nettles

# Mardalwil County, Acorn, Alabama

# That First Year the Business Was Wood

## Caledonia/Acorn, Alabama, c. 1830s

Granny Celia and Grandpa Joseph were among those original hundred of what the Kimbroughs called the workforce. They arrived by boats on the Muskogee River. The old ones, in their own time between chaws or pipe sucks, took turns telling it. That is, they told what they could or would tell of it. All of it could not be told. Some of it was by then too distant, some of it was too cold in its cruelty, too bottomless in its ugliness to be remembered, or if remembered, told.

As to the exact year they arrived on Caledonia, they were not sure. They had no reason to know one year from another, because they were outside the significance of numbers such as those. Seasons and work—building, maintaining, plowing, seeding, weeding, plucking, and personal caring for—were measurements, by their reckonings, without value.

An event was remembered not by a date, but for itself: the time when such and such happened. The time the overseer was thrown by his horse, the time the mill caught fire, the time the barn caught fire, the time a Kimbrough had a heart attack. Births and deaths and selling offs had meaning, or when someone went into the swamp; these were occurrences worth noting and so were memorable.

The year Alabama had become a state, or Mardalwil had become a county, or Caledonia a plantation, or the town of Acorn was incorporated from Caledonia land—these meant less than two dead flies to them.

Of some, but minimal, import was what part there was about the Indians, who had been there long before them, and who were all gone but for their bones and blood in the ground and their spirits in the air, and only the last one of them, Red Stick, a Creek, who came and went at his will, was still there. Red Stick knew the part about his family and ancestors, but most of what he knew was too distant or deep or ugly for him to recall for telling.

The year the coffle of us of over 150 were bought and set out from a Charleston auction block and shipped south by sea down to near Savannah, then north and west up a meandering series of rivers, about ten fewer arrived than had begun the trek on some 2500 acres of woods and thick timberland and rich black Alabama dirt.

In the lead in the first wagon with Charlton P. Kimbrough was Missus Sarah Katherine Whitmore Kimbrough, the Old Man's wife. She was Missus Sarah. He never wanted to be called Master. Goodsire was what he said. Behind his back we had various names for him. Cloud Head. The Old Man, though he was no more than thirty at that time, still had a head full of wild cotton-white hair with a little tam 'o shanter, his blue bonnet, sitting on top.

Next in the line of Kimbrough brothers was Clay Monroe. He was in his late twenties at best guess. And then skipping behind like colts in clover came Thurso and Wick. They were twins, in their late teens or early twenties or so; neither of them or their doings is worth the telling. They were less than half a man, the two of them put together. They knew no more about business than a chinch on a chicken's ass. Neither one of them had sense enough to take his hand out of hot grease, nor did they have as much pride as crab grass.

That first year, wood was the business. The land was surveyed and we commenced clearing. Pines and maples and oaks we topped and toppled for shelter and for shipping and selling.

The trees whined like the axe blades had when we sharpened them on the trundled grindstones, and then again as we, teams of two axe men, whacked out wedges, and then we, teams of two sawyers, sawed through the timber's core before the splintering shriek and toppling crash, and we measured and bucked and limbed and hitched and skidded the trunks by harnessed mules to Kimbrough's Mill, that we had built first, about a half mile distant, at Kimbrough's Landing that we had also built, and then we scaled, sawed, edged, dried, planed, stacked, and bundled raw wood that was then transported by boat and train to market up or down the river.

We did that as we planted and farmed vegetables, and we built rough log shelters to house them and us as we tended the pigs and cows and sheep and chickens, and we built the grain mill, and we harvested more than enough to feed them and some for us, and we cured the wood and hauled it up to build the big houses for each of them, and we framed and we sided and we laid floors and we raised roofs: Highland House being Goodsire and his woman's; Pictland being Clay's; and Twin Oaks for Thurso and Wick, the twins, jointly.

Some of us ran off to the swamp after setting a fire or other mischief those first years and some of us got sickly and bled and died from consumption and cholera and pneumonia and pellagra and diarrhea and influenza and fevers and measles and mumps and all the animal poxes: cow, goat, horse, squirrel, and fowl, and we died from overwork.

Missus Sarah Katherine, Cloud Head's woman, who each Christmas called us all out and read poetry-rime stories from Scot-land, about wars between Vikings and all, and at times she called herself nursing us until she caught something and died.

Cotton was the second year's work: we uprooted stumps, cleared what had been forestland, and by March tilled and toiled, and we got the first cottonseed in the ground.

Next big thing was when the rail-road was finished up. Goodsire was big in that whole business, too. Like in every-thing.

Over that same time Clay Kimbrough, the one with the second-most sense, shut down the mill. It was a deal between him and the Old Man before they even got to Mardalwil County. He closed up his house and sold his acres for a profit to the Old Man and moved on off to New Orleans. He became a Negro Broker down there. But before then the Old Man quit, giving the twins credit and soon buying them out, four cents an acre. The fools were happy to get it, and to get from round him, and from Caledonia. They took the Northeast Alabama Railroad Company train, of which they had been at one time minority stockholders. Off up east they went. One later on turned out to be Esme's daddy. They say Wick, the other one, after troubled marriages died in a crazy house.

But all of that and all we did for them meant a heap less than what we had brought with us, which was our pride at having worked the soil of Carolina to death before it wore us out and killed us all. Knowing that even the ground out of which their cotton, that gave them all their power over us, could be defeated and depleted—that fueled everything we did.

It was inside of us. It was in our minds, *our minds*, out of sight of them even when we were in full view. The way we touched our children, our language of looks and nods, our rituals of no, the ways we supported each other with silence, a grin, or a lie.

It was the tellings of our surviving, and of our outwitting of them and their business, by not being who they took us to be, that occupied our notion of what was important for our marking of time.

It was in our ways of doing, in front of them—our walking, our wearing, our working, that sprouted from the seeds of our need to air our common yearnings and have them recognized and welcomingly accepted and understood as useful—whether any or all of those things were through strength; or by being sullen, daring, surly, dragging; or through shared wisdom or charms; it gave us confidence in ourselves and became storied examples in our ability to have an inside self, and therefore a belief in our spirit to continue.

It was in our singings, self-made or in chorus, and the rhythms (claps and pats and stomps) in our dances, and in little ditty-tunes that we put from the first suck as sustenance and anointment for our babies. Our offspring were given melodies to hum, little rhythms to repeat and remember. They were pacifiers and prompts and signifiers. If by hellish chance our ways parted, the children took with them airs to hum or whistle or think. And if by chance our paths recrossed or the broken arcs of our circle reconnected miles or years hence, and our names or our appearances were changed by time or lack of sight or circumstance, we would have a tuneful keepsake to certify our connection.

That larder or storehouse of instances, a collection of tellings stacked up like a vault of vittles, so we could continue to struggle up before light each day and face it, inspired by our being as much trouble as we could while having the gumption and grit to keep on until the world reversed its course or somersaulted, and snakes walked and mules flew and water turned to fire and wood to wind and then re-ordered itself again, and was back to some order we understood and understood us, so we could hold again without grasping, breathe again without panting, and get, grow, laugh unquestioned, wander, leave, have privacy, choose, be.

# Cretia's Gal

## Caledonia Plantation, Mardalwil County, Alabama, Saturday, April 1, 1854

It was cloudy that morning. It would be raining by that afternoon.

At the top of the hill inside Highland House, in the drape-shrouded parlor, Sophy's boy baby, Cretia's Gal's charge, crawled in random patterns through the thick legs of the pianoforte.

Cretia's Gal, 12,

*active, intelligent, ladies' maid, accustomed to cleaning, waiting on table, sewing*

sat, straight-backed, at M's Esme's shiny instrument. Her eyes closed, her dark fingers, choreographed by the echoing in her head, rollicked in the air above the keys in an exact replica of the capering patterns played last night by the French man.

Untutored, she did not know the melodies' names, their origins, nor their forms. Being under strict and direct orders from M's Esme, she had never touched the piano keys, other than with a feather duster.

Sophy's boy baby, Cretia's Gal's charge and inattentive audience, crawled in random patterns through the piano's legs and cooed.

&

M's Esme, bemoaning boy Jube's,

*Can not speak, good house boy,*
*Excellent gardener 13 years old*
*Well made, of yellowish complexion——*

stupidity, reprimanded his response to every order as they pruned and patted in the formal garden. She was unable to see for the life of her why she put up with the oddling little nigger. Whistling as if gabbing to himself; dumb as a fish; couldn't speak a word; never had as far as she knew. What she should do is send him straight to the fields, see if McCready could teach him a thing or two.

Maybe his muteness was why she put up with him. Meant he couldn't complain or lie like the rest of them.

Her constant wiping of her brow with her kerchief and the sleeve of her tunic had knocked her bonnet slightly askew. It tittered on her head like the cornfield scarecrows. The sight was enough to make Jube want to laugh.

She did not listen, Boy Jube thought. She did not listen to nothing, to no-body. Not even to her uncle Goodsire half the time, not to the Candytufts who wanted to be in the sun, or the Bleeding Hearts who did not, or the Foxglove who wanted moist soil, or the Fragrant Solomon's Seal who could stand dryness.

She had listened last night though. To that French man's drumming piano playing, pounding like the thunder of heavenly horse hoofs galloping out of the body of the pianoforte. His music stampeded out of the parlor and off in all directions: down the entrance lane, and off through the gardens and fields and orchards and forests and low quarters and swamp of the Caledonia's three thousand or so acres. She heard and listened to that pianoforte being played last night, all right, and instead of cooling with the mirk of night he could see it had simmered and re-rose in her, renewed with the graying dawn. She was still angry from it, snapping like a bulldog on a short chain.

Jube sat on his haunches. He patted dirt around the seedlings.

Earlier, as every morning, he was back from his ramblings, as they called them, and finished with hauling the cookhouse fireplace ashes and replacing the firewood, in time to see Cretia's Gal as she came down the stairs to empty M's Esme's chamber pot.

She had signaled to him that there might be trouble from the mistress because of last night.

The nerve of him, Esme thought, dark eyed man that he was, bringing that—she refused to call it music—to bring that—savagery into the parlor, extolling. It condoned the vile and the ugly instead of evoking tears and flutters of the heart. That was what music should be. Instead what had come out of the pianoforte pounded and thrust, heaved and throbbed, like something back of the barn in the middle of the night. Vile. It was an insult to music, an offense to civilization, contemptible to a White person's home. The parlor must be aired of it, the same as if a skunk had spewed its spray from corner to corner.

Uncle had no business bringing that dark-haired, dark-eyed man with the foreign name and fancy ways into the house in the first place. Bringing him from off, like so many of the other items, or gifts Uncle brought on his return from his travels away from Caledonia. They were never quite the right size, style, or shade, but all the same he brought them, proud as a cat depositing a fetched dead rat.

&

Cretia's Gal, unmindful of the quiet in the house, or the muffled reprimands of M's Esme toward Jube in the near distance, and without Cretia's Gal realizing it, her hands, weighted by the echoing music in her head, lowered themselves and made contact with the keys that she was forbidden to touch other than to gently run a feather duster across them once a day.

Her fingers ceased their air dance and were still for a moment, as still as the house, and then, to her surprise, her fingers began to move to touch the forbidden black and white keys, moving in the exact patterns that Mister Gottschalk's had moved last evening as she played exactly what he had played.

&

Esme felt a raindrop on the back of her hand. She had to will herself not to lick it off. Instead, she snapped at Boy Jube, contradicting her last order.

He silently did as he was told. Until, for an instant in the graying morning, he sensed all sound cease: the cheeping, peeping conversations of birds; the impatient worry of the sodden wind whispering to the young leaves about the rain to come and resultant rustle as it brushed past, and scurry and hunkering down in the undergrowth; the moist plop of the scattered *smirr*; the wanting fragmented lilt of distant field hand shouts; the sounds of work from the house; the lo and bark and whinny. When it ceased, Jube raised himself from his hands and knees to a squat. He tensed like a hound at the anticipated hunter's shot—and then sound again: the rhythmic pounding burst from the parlor through the window and doors.

Music.

At the first notes Esme looked up and around, her nose angled like a hound's at the smell of prey.

She might have pretended not to listen to the piano playing last night, Jube thought, but she heard it this morning, without pretense.

Esme thinks it must be a conspiracy of some sort. Cretia in on it. Snuck *Monsieur* Gottschalk back and inside to provoke her. After he and Uncle have arisen before sunrise to start off on horseback for the distant train and finally to New Orleans. This yet another attack on her patience by her body slave, this time direct rather than the usual nerve-racking slow grinding day-by-day insolence.

Esme spat a single word as she took off running, rushing, a raised storm toward the house as if lightening had struck the tail of her dress, and she rushed straight through the bluest anemones and India pinks, toward the parlor where the piano was.

The word was "Him!"

&

Cretia's Gal still only hearing the echoing sounds in her head was the only one in earshot of the piano not to realize it was she who was actually playing it. Playing for the first time in her life.

Polishing the pianoforte was her favorite household chore. Smoothing the oiled cloth back and forth about the dark wood: the part with its gold scrawled letters spelling Boardman & Gray, that her Mama

Cretia had taught her to read. The top that lifted to show the wires and little cotton covered heads of the hammers inside, the curved sides, the heavy carved legs, until it reflected her own darkness back at her. But never touching the ivory and ebony keys except to feather dust them with maternally possessive strokes. Warned about it by her mother. Threatened about it by M's Esme. To never fool with the piano keys. Never. Playing now, note for note, the music the French man had played the night before. With the same enthusiasm and volume. The same pounding rhythmic drive.

M's Esme, her bonnet clutched in her fist, her forehead wet from rain and sweat, entered looking about, stern and confused by what she saw and did not see. Jube was on the porch, at the open window, looking in at Cretia's Gal.

"Where is—? *Who?*"

Cretia's Gal stood, wide eyed as if shaken suddenly from a sound sleep. She stood looking at her hands trembling in spite of her tightly intertwined fingers.

There was a moment of almost hesitant embarrassment, as if each of them had caught the other engaged in a shameful activity, but neither of them, for the moment, knew what it was or what they should do.

"Where is he?" M's Esme demanded, unsure this time. She looked at Cretia's Gal.

Sophy's baby cooed and crawling on his hands and one knee, moving toward the woman, then stopped and plopped on his behind and sat looking from one of them to another, as he began sucking his right index and middle fingers.

"Who was playing that piano?" Esme asked.

Sophy's baby made a gurgling sound as he pulled his index and middle fingers from his mouth and pointed them toward Cretia's Gal as if he were answering the woman's question.

"You," she said to Cretia's Gal, whether or not she was convinced on the strength of the baby's identification. "Did you play that piano?"

The girl stood, looking down at her hands.

"Answer me."

The girl looked up at her mistress.

"Do not stand there looking at me. Did you play that piano?"

The girl didn't move.

"I want to hear you play something."

Still did not move.

"Do as I told say."

Cretia's Gal was confused, not sure that she had played, and if she had that she could do it again, and if she did, what she could or should play, nor what would happen then.

Sophy's baby rolled back to his hands and knees and scooted back under the piano as Cretia's Gal did as she was told and sat at the instrument. She closed her eyes and began playing not what the French man had played, but the tune that the woman staring at her from the doorway had been practicing for the last few days.

"No," M's Esme said almost calm, as if Cretia's Gal had misunderstood her request. "Not that. The other. Play like him again."

Cretia's Gal did.

Cretia, who had not been there, was in the parlor doorway.

"Who taught you that? Who? Her?"

"No-body, ma'am," Cretia's Gal said, her voice steady.

"No-body . . . ? Some-body." To Cretia. "Was it you?"

"Did some-body teach you?" Cretia asked her child, reassurance in her voice.

"You do not answer me by asking her a question," M's Esme snapped at Cretia.

"If you'll let me I'll find out," Cretia said.

"I'll find out," she answered. "From her."

"No-body, ma'am."

"Get me Mister McCready. McCready," she said to Jube. "Get Mister McCready!"

Jube looked to Cretia. Cretia nodded slowly, indicating for Jube to go, but to take his time.

Jube ran out into the rain.

M's Esme moved to the piano and grabbed the child awkwardly by the wrists. Cretia's Gal did not actively struggle nor did she passively resist. Her body, for the instant immobilized by fear, confusion, and dawning astonishment, was simply dark flesh, blood and bones, an object, with weight and form occupying space.

In M's Esme's attempt to pull the child away from the instrument the force of the girl's non-resistant but non-compliant mass caused M's Esme to stumble a step forward and hit her hip, first against the squat black instrument, and in a lurching half roll, attempting to regain her balance and avoid stepping on Sophy's baby crawling from beneath the piano, she caught her foot on one of its bulbous legs, and with a grunt, pitch headfirst, like a feed sack shouldered from a wagon bed, her left hand, nearest the piano, grasping at but hitting and dislodging the slanting vertical rod bracing open the angled piano top, opened last evening by *Monsieur* Gottschalk, striking it with the full weight of her forward fall and thus with sufficient force to dislodge it, causing the blunt force of the shined solid mahogany top to slam down with a gunshot-like report, as she, to break her awkward fall across the baby, jammed her wrist against the floor.

The wire strings in the instrument's shuddered innards raised a whining quiver, like the after-shiver of an axe stroke in the trunk of an oak tree. It droned in an eerie harmony to M's Esme catlike howl.

Cretia knelt beside her, gripping her non-injured forearm.

*. . . and Esme looked into the great twin pits and was consumed and sank deeper than the lowest hell into their burning blackness and the sorrows closed upon her, she was naked and empty, and in her distress she heard them say, there will be slaughter and overthrow, and all that is solid will perish, and the foundations will be compressed into dust.*

M's Esme swooned, her face as white as late May cotton.

In the few minutes later, M's Esme regained consciousness to the sight of Cretia's Gal staring at her. Her eyes. *Mal Occhio*, she almost screamed. She covered her eyes with her uninjured right hand and screamed, "Face her to the wall. Turn her away from me. Face her to the wall." Convinced of what she had suspected all along—the girl had *Mal Occhio*. The Evil Eye.

Cretia's Gal's just displayed sorcery of perfectly played passages from Monsieur Gottschalk proved that she was somehow connected with evil. It was the only explanation of the piano playing. M's Esme said she did not want to set her eyes on Cretia's Gal again until she had been punished, hoping that being whipped would drive the evil out of her. The gal had never, as far as she could remember, had a beating. That was what had let the dark spirit get in her. That and her sullen mammy of course . . .

&

The word went down: Bring them up. Bring them all up to Highland House after supper.

Just for the beating of a child?

Must be more to it to be called out in the rain.

When there was bailing out and patching up to be done.

Some: Let's just get it o'er with. So we can come back and get on with our doings.

Some: Just a child. E'en if Cretia's Gal.

Some: She needed to be taught a lesson. Same as ev'rybody.

They went: motley, sodden. Grudging.

The paths muddy, the grass slick.

Trudged up from the Bottom in twos and threes and random clots and clusters, nigh, they hoped, the chafing end of a galling day.

&

Esme wore the sling Cretia had fashioned from a piece of an old petticoat. The swelling was gone and there was no pain even when she flexed her wrist, but she had retied the sling as a reminder to herself and to them.

A lighted lantern on the table behind her, she sat in her second-story window seat and looked down on them as they slowly assembled in the yard.

Their coming together looked to be as resented and labored as her journey to understanding the thing that had, until the last few hours, preoccupied her life.

&

Cretia would forget, as they all did, Esme reassured herself. She'd mope and drag around a day or two—or hiss and strut, her tail up like a cat's. She'd have to be watched, closely, but she'd soon forget and get over it. They always did, no matter how they hooped and hollered, they always forgot. In the end they had little more feelings than the animals. It was their way.

So, that was that. But she still was not satisfied.

"Did you deliberately let her play that piano? To spite me."

"No ma'am."

"No, ma'am? Do not contradict me, you ungrateful devil. Aye ma'am, you mean. Well let me make it plain as pudding. See if this moves you, you sulky bitch. You have said your last goodbye to her while she served in this house.

"Maybe my uncle has coddled you so, letting you keep her too long. He cuts my dreams asunder. Would not let me perform, as I want to."

"Aye'm."

Cretia: These buckras ain't people.

Not contrite enough, Esme thought. Not nearly. Still under what she thought was the secret covering, that Uncle mistook in Cretia for nigger quality. Esme could see it now for what it was. Vainglory. Audacity. A flaming disdain that had been extinguished to little more than an ember, as she'd hollered *She's mine*.

Cretia: These buckras ain't no god's people, this one, nor Beasley, nor Goodsire too. None of them, not from here to any ocean.

"I know what's wrong with you. You do not think I mean it, do you? You think I'm just playing with you. You did not bother to control her because you take me for a fool. Goodsire is all you respect. You do not respect me. And you do not fool me. You may fool Uncle, but you do not fool me. I am not a fool."

She stopped, unsure about how to prove she was not fooled.

"No ma'am."

"Aye, ma'am, you mean. Well, the sun will never shine on your evil-eyed heifer in this house again—to look at me with that look of hers. Those *eyes*."

Cretia stood. Stock-still. She was stoic as a teaspoon in her saucer of sulkiness. "No ma'am," she said.

"'Aye ma'am,' you mean. But come dawn she will be in the fields just like the rest of them. We'll see how her well-fed insolence stands up under that sun. See how her eyes burn out there. And how yours look in here."

"Aye, ma'am," neither looking at her nor not looking at her.

"Do not you answer me until I ask you something."

"Aye ma'am."

As Esme adjusted the sling she had her second revelation.

The fields weren't far enough. Cretia's Gal had to be gotten as far from Caledonia as a slaver could send her, and as soon as she could be sent. She had to be sold.

&

"She's mine," Cretia repeated.

"We'll know whose she is when I write my name on her back," Mc-Cready said. Then to Asch and Caesar standing on either side of the girl's mother, "Now get Cretia out of my sight, and lock her down. Or I swear I will beat the skin off all of you, first to last!"

"Do not let him," Cretia said, a statement to anyone.

Nowhere nigh a proper plea, M's Esme thought. Ought to make her stay and watch. But something warned her not to.

"Whup me!" Cretia ordered. "Not her. Me!" As she is hauled away by the two mechanics.

"Hold some light here," Beasley, McCready's assistant, said. He had been handed the whip. "I want to see what I'm whupping. Don't want to waste my time whupping air."

A couple with lanterns moved closer, the rings of illumination bobbing like fishing lures on a black river.

Cretia howling like Biece's dogs, Jube, half bare thought, and we standing here. No better than bales of wet cotton.

Cretia's Gal sank to her knees and Moon and Odum laid her face down on the ground.

Seeing Cretia's Gal whipped, hearing Cretia's screams, Jube was, for the first time, and only for an instant, glad he had no parents to witness their child being beat.

During, Cretia's Gal remembered once, after a scolding by M's Esme, when Jube, whistling to himself, had seen her crying and had shown her what at first she thought was how to listen to plants grow—laying flat against the earth, each of them with an ear to the ground, until she had shook her head and admitted, No, she couldn't hear a thing, and he'd laughed and shook his head.

No. That was not it.

What then?

He had pointed at her then and wiped his fingers under his eyes and shook his head to show no tears. She had realized that because of his diversion she not only was no longer crying but had forgotten all about her hurt.

She had smiled at him.

He had nodded and put his hand to her lips to stop her from speaking, and at that instant M's Esme had shouted for her lazy bones, and she had turned and run for the house, but when she looked back before entering he was gone. Disappeared. As he could do. Leaving not e'en a silence where he had stood.

The drizzle wetting her lash wounds, Cretia's Gal laid, her face in the mud.

She listened for the sound of grass growing.

But e'en after the whip had ceased its snap and slash and Cretia had stopped screaming to bathe and salve Cretia's Gal's wounds, and to go to McCready's cabin and return to Highland House, they still heard her in their sleep, in the Bottom, in the grieve's house, and in the main house too. Screaming.

*She's mine!*

Cretia was weary. Slave weary. Too tired to spit or swat a wasp.

She had done what she could. Tonight, and the thirteen years that had come before, when each of those days and nights her primary purpose and thought was to get Cretia's Gal away to possible freedom. She did not e'en consider her good fortune in having had her child for that long to teach and give hope to. Many mothers did not have half that. Many had nothing.

*But was it enough? Had there been time enough?* Nagged like sore joints or dreams of flying. Was there an *enough*?

She remembered her own mother.

St. Thomas Caribbean woman, carried into southern slavery.

Cretia, born in slavery, but bred on her mother's stories of revolt in the Caribbean and of freedom in the north, stories passed on to Cretia's Gal in fact, parables, and sewing riddles as they had been passed on from Cretia's mother to her.

Would the child call on the lessons? Could she use them? Would they serve her? Be her guardians?

Once Cretia's Gal was gone, Cretia would never know. Had known that from the beginning.

Would never again see her. Or hear word of or from.

Who would she be? Where?

She would never know.

Never.

Never.

That was the way it of it. To be sold away was, for those left behind, a beginning that had no end.

Cretia was weary tired.

All she wanted now was quiet, and the strength to wait and to gather her strength, for when McCready came back from the slave trader without her child she would kill him, she would be strong enough for that by then.

&

Jube watched Cretia. He did not know what she would do. He did not know what he could do.

He remembered the sound only a few hours ago of the liquid being squeezed in the gourd and her word in the black of the cabin as she soothed the girl. Remember, was the only word she said, and something had passed between them, mother to daughter, something that he had not been able to see.

In the moments before their final separation they, with McCready and Jube in half shadow watching them in the lantern light of the servants' cabin, mother and daughter, had moved without looking at each other. It was as if they had long ago rehearsed the moment of their parting, and ev'rything necessary had been settled between them.

As McCready led Cretia's Gal out to take her to his cabin and then away, Jube was gone.

It was raining again.

&

Jube was crouched, hunched on his haunches at the edge of the cornfield. With his naked arms wrapped around his naked knees, he watched Cretia's Gal in the illumination from the faint lantern light from McCready's cabin. He marveled at how erect she sat on the surrey seat, waiting as McCready loaded his second satchel into the surrey.

Jube had been planning, as soon as he had time, to make up a secret language just he and Cretia's Gal could understand. It was to have been a language without words. Thought talk. So they could speak any time, whether they were together or not. She in the house, him in the garden, she on her pallet, he on his.

He closed his eyes and imagined it was in the morning, after the *pour*. He and Cretia's Gal are in the stable, watching a mama cat deliver a litter of six, as they had done one time, and in their secret no-word language he would say to her, What can go round the house and look in ev'ry window, but do not make no tracks?

She would smile at him, and without shaking her head would say she did not know.

Guess he would encourage her.

She would think some more, still smiling, would say-think she couldn't guess. What?

Then she'd hear him think-say: The sun.

Cretia's Gal would turn her head slightly, but still looking at him, and still smiling, admiration shining in her eyes.

Ask another one.

Then he'd say-think: All right, what goes all around the house and do not make but *one* track?

They'd go through it all again, Cretia's Gal looking at him and smiling in wonderment.

Finally he'd tell her: A wheelbarrow.

She'd wonder how he knew so much . . . ?

Jube opened his eyes as he heard McCready close the door to his cabin. The lantern was out. It was dark.

McCready's hound yipped once as its master hiked the surrey horse.

Man and girl rode off in the rain.

Cretia's Gal was gone.

Mud covered and naked, a beating in his chest like Ashe's hammer on the anvil, Jube blinked in the downpour, and licked the tears and raindrops from his lips.

&

A candle was in the center of the dirt floor.

Cretia and Jube were sitting cross-legged side by side.

"We've had it hard," she said, "from a baby up."

She told him about her mother's life in freedom in St. Thomas, and about her own life. She went on and on in the flickering light but all he could think of was moving through the dark after Cretia's Gal and being with her and dreaming about freedom they would run away to one day, e'en if they had to move through the darkness with her clinging to him; he was feeling freedom just thinking about it. Cretia saying she understood, she understood how he felt, could feel how he hurt because she had hurt, just like him. Telling him to let it go. Let the past be the past. Let it fall away like petals from a stem, let it go, or it would forever hold him down, telling him to be proud of the way he had learned to walk the dark. Be proud of the way he could help flowers grow. She was rubbing his hand and she was crying and he was crying, and they were crying together and he was breathing, breathing as if it were his first breath, as if he'd been slapped, had the breath slapped in him, and she was rubbing his hand, and he was breathing, and his face was wet but he was not crying any more, and his head hung down, almost to his lap, and he was breathing, just breathing, not crying, not hurting, his eyes closed, sleepy, and she was rubbing his hand, and he was as tired as he had ever been. She put something in his hand, smooth, round, and cold, and he clenched it in his fist. A bead.

Was that what she had given Cretia's Gal? He wondered as he slumped sideways and laid his head in Cretia's lap . . .

&

Cretia did not sleep.

Cretia looked up, as if she had been called. Not snappish like from M's Esme, but soft, like a butterfly, or a whiff in the air. She eased Jube onto the floor and moved to and opened the door. Listening. Alert. Trying to still her mind and concentrate amongst all the confusion of the past day. She closed her eyes against the night darkness and inhaled deeply, holding it as she felt her blood in her veins. She exhaled, thinking of rippling water. Lifting her face, eyes still closed, thinking of her mother, thinking of star glint. Motionless for a moment. Listening. For something beneath the night stillness, something softer than the silent pulse of growing, and sleeping for renewal . . .

She opened her eyes.

She nodded.

Yes, she thought.

She breathed easier.

But she did not sleep . . .

. . . Jube slept.

Dreamed honeysuckles. Growing out of his chest, and dogwoods sprouting from his mouth, red, orange, yellow, purple, and pink, and roots growing from his hair his fingers and toes and running away, faster than Bryce's dogs, to connect with roots growing from Cretia's Gal, and he thinks her name, and for a flash Cretia's Gal is there: a butterfly glimpse as she, darting from one room to another, smiles like the North Star. It is like the sugary dance of candy on his tongue, and he thinks her name, and she hears him in camellias and evergreens.

But when he awoke he lay with his head in Cretia's lap, the bead in his fist, and Cretia's Gal was there, but Cretia's Gal was gone.

# Macready

## Caledonia Plantation, Mardalwil County, Alabama, Saturday, April 1, 1854

West of Highland House, in the field, the hands hollered as they worked. Beneath their feet the chopped and plowed-under stalks left from last season's cotton harvest were sharp, the lumps of upturned earth were cool, and the worms, whole or plow blade- severed, were fat and slimy.

It was dark in the distance as it was overhead. Macready the overseer, or the grieve, as Goodsire called him, was anxious to get in the last day of plowing before the rain in the low rolling clouds began. As in the first days of every planting season, Macready thought, the field hands hollered like a sea of churning and whirring storm-stirred Atlantic brine.

*&*

The hands, in the endless cycle of another day too slow and work too long and hard, felt their joints and bones balk at acceptance of the rote drudgery. They hollered as they toiled under the watch of Macready, the man who worked for the man who had the papers on their life and labor, labor and life, and Beasley, Macready's deputy. Beasley, short little bastard, carried a long skint sapling, stunk like hell, and raised a whelp the size of a rope. Like a well-trained herding dog, working opposite Macready, circling, keeping an eye on them for the least little signs or signals of slacking.

Knowing neither of the men cared any more about them than a duck cared for a turnip, or than they cared for the work or the men. So to keep from falling down weeping, or taking off running, or standing there and losing their minds, they did their best to combat the senseless reality of it by doing what Macready and Beasley heard only as hollering.

Macready had taught them a song, a sea shanty—*Patty, Get Back*, his before Caledonia days on the sea.

> Adieu my fair young maidens,
>> Thousand times adieu
>> We must bid goodbye to the Holy Ground,
>> The place that we love true.

When they sang it he barely recognized the tune the way they stacked voice on voice and drug it out and broke it up.

> We'll sail the salt seas ov'r
>> But return again for sure
>> To seek the girls that wait for us,
>> In the Holy Ground once more.

It unnerved him but pleased him, because, he thought, the louder a hand hollered the more work he would do.

&

The Bottom hands hollered across and along the furrows and the fields, one to another, or just shouted out unthinking snatches of what weighed most on their backs and hearts at that moment. Their bondage, exhaustion, and longing for leisure were the subjects least directly expressed. Instead, the little annoyances, chips off the big block, were the difficulties foremost in their mouths if not on their minds. There were complications of love making, aching for lost ones, remembered slights, spites, nosiness, messages, bad times, and the good times at frolics. Their hollering was of no one type; it took no one form, just anything to keep them from being too, too, too dissatisfied.

The overcast morning fit their mood. The promise of rain, with its likelihood of being a downpour, or *teem*, or *pour*, as Goodsire said it, that would stop the work, would mean one more day of labor gone. One more day till all their days was gone. For their part they did not care if the *pour* came and did na stop falling until it drowned the world and ev'ry breathing creature with flesh, feathers, or fins, creeping, trotting, flying, or swimming.

&

And if there was a beginning, as if it really mattered, but for simply a place to mark, it was here, in their slow contentious and continuously steady cycle, like mill mules circling, sun to sun, season through season, grinding, monotonous, unavailing. They followed the ruts in the land. They hollered.

Arguing in their own minds, and with each other, with no more than a look or a nod or snatch of words as to how long it was going to be before Macready was going to have to signal to little Beasley to go and ring the bell to stop the work because of the coming rain and let them go on to the Bottom. It was going to have to be more than coming rain, it had to be a *pour*, and it would be, and the order would have to be given and the work stopped and they knew it. That was the kind of *pour* was coming. Ev'ry hoe hand, plowman, and water boy among them could read them clouds same as Macready could cipher a column of figures. And come this here kind of *pour* coming nothing Macready nor Goodsire nor no other white man could do to stop it. The hands took some satisfaction (though scant) in that.

Macready could feel them dragging, dull, and ferocious as they slumped, shiftless, slow, and mean in their gray homespuns. Damn them. The first day of the new season and already he wondered how he would be able to continue to stand the sight of them. Deceptive. Resistant. The hope of the threat of rain slacking them just enough to satisfy their animal stubborn need to be contrary without provoking him much more than they did simply by their blank, hangdog faces, empty except for their accusing, downcast eyes. They could be at once cowering and willful. Always testing, always wanting to get something without benefit of labor, as if they were somehow, by wordless contract, bound to have it.

Macready, overseer, or grieve, Goodsire's Scottish word for him. Responsible for the maintenance and well-being of all hands, livestock,

property, crops, and Goodsire's other interests on the Caledonia plantation. Sitting above them on Goodsire's sorrel stallion, and thinking how
what he does is as delicate a craft as a watchmaker's. Each little piece of
the mechanism has to be exact, in tune, to keep the instrument ticking
right along. He nodded at the appropriateness of his analogy. How to
keep them ticking right along—when to apply hard discipline, when
just a firm hand will do, when to read their natural sullenness for what it
is, like with Goodsire's spirited sorrel between his legs, when to ease off,
loosen the reins a bit and seem to let them have their way.

And, he thought, he was likewise a captive, languid, stubborn, slog-
ging, collared by contract for two more years, through the same mud-
slime as them.

&

The clouds, as bloated as drowned pigs' bellies, seemed no higher than
the treetops.

Eph, the jyner-carpenter, tilted his head back and sniffed at the air.

"Macready's harness ready?" Odum, who had just huffed up the hill,
asked Ashe.

Ashe pointed to the wall where he had hung the repaired harness.

"Had to wet your throat before the rain, huh?" he said, scraping at his
chin with the back of his hand.

"What you gabbing about?" Odum asked.

"Where you got it hid?" Eph was standing in the smiddie's doorway.

"Better gargle you some clove and peppermint water 'for you see
Macready," Caesar said.

"He smells that alcohol on you, he might send you back out following
a mule's ass in them fields."

"Don't worry 'bout me picking cotton. I picked all the cotton I'm
picking. Macready told me that his self."

"And did he na tell you to na let him catch you drinking Red Stick's
swamp water, too?"

"You do na know what he told me. And you better hope this harness fixed like he want it, or he'll be up here to see you three jackanapes his self."

"He do na like it he know where we at," Eph said. "And tell him do na get in the water he do na want to get wet. Now go on yonder finish slopping your cousins."

Odum looked at them and shook his head. He hefted the harness to his shoulder as he moved back toward the hog pens.

&

The rain was steady now, and would only get heavier and more intense. But it would be awhile, Macready decided, before he sent Moon running to ring the quitting bell. Instead he hummed along in his head to the babel of shanty-like laments and lilts they sang and shouted as they sloughed forward in their duties. The tunes and fragments reminded him, with a shudder as it did daily, of those sung by the long laboring crew of the *Buenos Aires* sailors, him among them, that caused at the same time the churning and whirring in his lowest bowel.

&

We do the work. When we do na work, work do na get done. Would na much get done today they nodded, smiling. Their field hollering over for the day.

&

As they were heading for the quarters, a boy brought a message from M's Esme at the big house for him to come, there was a child to be punished, and bring all of the hands to witness it.

&

Macready came. Dripping. Dour as the day.

They went: motley, sodden. Grudging.

The paths muddy, the grass slick.

Trudged up from the Bottom in twos and threes and random clots and clusters, nigh, they hoped, the chafing end of a galling day.

What had this to do with him?

It would be different if Goodsire were here, he thought. This was a household infraction, for Jonis to handle, but hiding his irritation, he accepted without question his involvement and the justice of it. The gal had to be punished. Aye. For causing her mistress hurt. Simple as that.

He could have reasoned to Goodsire that as dark-mooded as the hands already were, gathering them all back out of their cabins, in the rain, for them to witness the whipping of a child, was an inconvenience that would not pay long-term dividends. But it was what she'd ordered. And therefore it was his job, as it would be, according to the contract, signed and witnessed between Charleton Kimbrough, of the first part, and Michael (Mick) Macready, of the second part. And the sooner the stupid business was begun, the sooner done.

Macready knew the whipping would not be the end of it. For the next several days, at least, it would be on the field billies like a stink. Already unsettled by the rain and the prospect of its continued disrupting of their routine, they would, as if there was one mind among them, drag and grumble and give as little as could be offered without severe consequence. It would be another planting season bad begun.

All for a lesson to a child.

This, the whipping of negroes, among the sundry chores named in his contract; to perform all duties and services as required of a good grieve or overseer. He was responsible for everything, every coming and going, every facet of the control and managing of the property and Caledonia. It was his responsibility to rise before them and retire after them, and preside in between, with all necessaries guaranteed by him. Their labor, feeding, fitness, and confinement. His responsibility. Personally guaranteed. The maintenance and protection of all buildings, and property and fences, and the care and condition of all tools, livestock, and poultry. For the deliverance of a profitable crop.

With every intention to fulfill this portion of his duties, his mind had already leaped ahead to imagine laying the leather on her only enough to raise a couple of welts, without cutting the dark skin so it oozed red along the ridge, only enough to cause the whelp to writhe and whimper; enough for M's Esme, watching from the upstairs window, to be satisfied that he had personally performed another of his duties guaranteed to be performed by the conditions of his contract. Signed and witnessed.

But when she looked back over her shoulder at him as if wondering was there anything she could do to hasten this along, there was a glint from her eye, causing a whip-snap memory flash. A deep nicking, razor-sharp liquid flick that bit to his quick. Then a sudden dazzling of lightheaded recognition of the moment: the whip, the cries for mercy, the gush of his blood geysering through his body and brain, which in that instant he took for the sounds of rushing water. With M's Esme looking down from her window, like Sir Edward Handy-Webster, Captain, looking down from the fore deck of the slave ship *Buenos Aires*.

The earth rolled beneath him, the ocean of his blood roaring again in his ears, and then, the whip handle as blistering in his hand as if white hot from Caesar's forge. Macready did not swoon, but if he had not been so well prepared for it by previous distant and recent occurrences, he would have: where a sudden shift in the breeze, or a sound of a wheel against the axle, like that of a ship's rigging, or the snatch of a field-billie's song that echoed one of a ship's crewman, would cause him to start, or turn, or break into a sweat.

Beasley stood a distance from him, on watch, like a good guard dog. Moon the black driver beside him.

Macready head-motioned him forward and Beasley sprang forth with the eagerness of a retriever after a gunshot, Moon a couple steps behind.

The whip moved from a trembling to an eager hand. Do it, Macready said, as he walked away from their eyes: from the gal's, Cretia's, Mistress Kimbrough's, Beasley's, from all of theirs.

&

Macready's sleeping dog stirred a growl-groan in its furred throat.

Its master, his pipe clenched in his teeth, sat in the black of his cabin. He chewed a leaf of peppermint, trying to soothe the rumbling in his gut caused by the memory that had surged back in him like the gastric repeat of cold collards.

Macready knew what it was to be whipped. The scars that laced his back were testimony. The Master at Arms on the *Buenos Aires* had cited the 23rd Psalm as they sailed in the Atlantic sun, and he snapped the leather lash against Macready's young back. Cretia had seen the scars after the snake bit him, and she sucked the poison from him and then stood over him, her hand held forward, palm up, and said what she said.

Mr. Botkin, the Master at Arms, was born mean enough, they whispered, to spit out his sweet mother's milk and call her a whore, which she likely was, they whispered. For a lifetime he had marinated in the juice and brine of the devil's own black puke. All hands heeded and were still inadequate to the task of the *Buenos Aires*, a slaver out of Senegambia, which weighed anchor and set out that August for a Caribbean course. An undermanned ship with an overloaded hold: a combination ideal for profit, and for anarchy. The *Buenos Aires* was manned by a dog's dinner of old jacks, green boys, sops, sots, lubbers, misfits, and malcontents as ever swung in a hammock or from a yardarm. It was the least proportion of them had any sea experience.

Macready, fifteen, an able-bodied boy among them. In full flight from the constraints of Round Stone Bog. He was barely schooled in letters, social intercourse, church, civics, or the sea, with no more than an idea of how to distinguish the ship's magazine from the mess from the capstan, or fo'c'sle from the maintopman, or midshipman from the mawser, windlass, or keelson.

The first night under sail he awoke to the lurch and roll, lurch and roll to find a knot on his noggin the size of a coal lump, sick to his stomach on the rotgut grog freely served to fatten him up for the kill: shanghaied for lackey labor.

You bloody bastards, Mr. Botkin announced to the line of groggy boys and men in a forced formation on the foredeck, you have been pressed into the service of the Woodman & Brainbridge Company to deliver this load of African negars to St. Thomas. At the end of the voyage you will be paid and given free passage to the homeport of your choosing. In the meantime th'r'ill be order and discipline in the manner of true seamen. Do as you're ordered in a lively fashion and no harm will come to you.

In the name of a taut ship, no transgression or misstep was tolerated. No excuse accepted. Daily discipline of ridicule and corporal punishment was administered. The distribution of Botkin's wrath was as equally dispensed as it was random in its monsoon-ugly mood and intention. He had simply to whistle and two or more of his knot of crew thugs set upon point and the offender without explanation or restraint. Complaints of maltreatment whispered to officers, all of which reached his ear, were revenged by additional lashes.

The crew was little better treated or thought of than the cargo of Africans, who were dealt with like a kennel of snarling mad dogs that could only be kept at bay by foot, fist, blunt instrument, chain, or lash.

Mr. Botkin's every move was sanctioned by the sorry son of a bitch of a captain, one Edward Handy-Webster, uncle-in-law of Sir Charles Woodman, equal partner of Woodman & Brainbridge Co.

Profit from the sale of the black and woeful cargo was the voyage's purpose. Overhead was kept to a minimum. The cargo, from their confinement in the hold, cried out in desperation in a ceaseless chorus of howls and moans.

Portions of victuals, not fit for the maggots that infested them, were barely above subsistence level. Working hours were at Mr. Botkin's whim, and shifts tested reason and human endurance.

And after a few days at sea the heavens heard their cries, and an easterly blow advanced with it clouds and darkness and covered the good ship *Buenos Aires* like a cloak, and broke, flooding open its nether gate in answer. And the terribleness of it whipped the air and whirled the ocean, and the water pelted down. All that night, in the midst of the strength of the suck and swell of the sea, the *Buenos Aires* was tossed and battered as if it were no more than a shuttlecock. And as the waves chucked them up and swallowed them, only to vomit them forth again, the crew whined and prayed, and the blacks, battened, their air vents covered by tarpaulin, pled in muffled moans. And he, Macready, screamed his agony and curses as furiously and fruitlessly as they. Not for mercy, not for relief, nor e'en as a call for an answer or accountability, but simply out of the choice-less necessity of it. At least to scream and struggle would be the final sign of a short life lived.

But at the end of the long night, with the coming of the light on the water, there was barely a ripple. The cargo of captives were assembled and accounted for. And notice was taken that during the roar a corner of the tarpaulin, lashed down over the air vents as a precautionary measure, had torn loose from its mooring. On the one hand it had allowed some below to breathe and thereby escape suffocating, but it had also caused many, chained in the hip-deep water, to drown.

Macready, ordered down into the hold, pulled back. Mr. Botkin, driven madder by the fear and frustration, accused him of being less than a man, humiliated him, sentenced thirty lashes, and a combination of brine and pepper to be rubbed into his wounds. The count was ten when Macready relented, descended into the hot, rotten smell of the hold to unlatch and pass up the dead.

The creak and chafe of the ship's timbers, and the sway and slosh of the sewage of sea water, shit, sweat, snot, piss, tears, vomit, slobber, and blood awash in the vessel's bottom, were the harmonic undercurrent of the Babel of African simpering and moans.

Down.

A makeshift mask covered his face, yet the stench was a simultaneous blow to the budge of the nose and to his gut. Among the drowned he sought to unshackle were those that he guessed had willed themselves dead, and the suicides, their necks wrapped around with their chains. The living, in their grief, their anger, their illness, with their infections, ulcers, and whip-and self-inflicted wounds where they had gorged and torn at each other, their debilitation, their thirst, dysentery, diarrhea, their melancholy, were like scorpions in a box. As he crab-walked about the carpet of their slick black bodies, some, foaming at the mouth like mad dogs he'd seen in Surrey alleys, bit and snarled at him. He could not imagine Hell itself was any hotter, or its claustrophobic constraint closer, or its conditions more callous. He feared, with faint hope of help from above, that if he fell or fainted he would surely be eaten alive.

The gag and shudder of it, hundreds of kilometers inland, and a decade and a half later, were still branded on his brain. It still snatched him shivering and sweaty from sleep, or stroked him with its cold hand to lie moaning enfolded in its body's embrace. Its rhythmic inhaling and exhaling matching his.

# 4

# Eph

## Caledonia Plantation, Sunday, April 2, 1854

Usually Jonis awoke with a start before the roosters rose and cats crept in from the night, even before the others had risen to haul ashes from the cookhouse, empty the chamber pots, and build the fires, and so Aunt Amelia, heavy-eyed and dour, could set the coffee brewing. One second Jonis would be asleep the next he'd be as wide-awake and alert as a coon at the first hound's yap.

*So*

Jube was up even before Jonis. They boy placed the long-stalked Atamasco lily on the dewy spot where Cretia's Gal's had lain, her back welted, skin slick with rain.

Jube knew from watching and from being told long ago by Jonis, you did not get to be and then stay the grieve, the head house servant, by lulling and scratching your way awake in the morning. For the head of house to do his job for the master and for the benefit of the other servants, it was essential to be able to gather together bits and pieces of information—fact and figures, rumors and snatches of overheard conversation, looks, nods, moods. You needed all of that in order to be out-thinking your whites before they opened their eyes.

*So*

Cretia who had not slept stood outside M's Esme's door. Listening. She made a deliberate noise.

The sound that came back to her was like the sudden scurry of a scalded cat, followed by worried stirring. Cretia tiptoed away down the servants' back stairs.

Jube noticed Jonis was alert as usual as he told Aunt Amelia to have Sophy set the table (because Cretia's Gal was gone), then went about his regular Sunday morning routine.

*So*

Damnit.

The aftertaste of the Cretia's Gal news had moved like maggots or mealy worms through the grain of predawn and burrowed in the breakfasts of the hands in the Bottom. It had set the bile boiling in their bellies like hot lye bubbling in a wash kettle. It was barely daylight and they had to be mad already.

And now, their mood smut-black, they waited for Beasley. The little man who was in charge, because of McCready's absence. He was wasting their time by trying to get them strung out single file, like Christmas popcorn on a string, instead of just passing out their weekly damned draw of damned rations of fatback, molasses, and a little damn meat.

Any one of them could run it better. Hell, even Odum had more control over his pigs while slopping them, far as that went.

Shit.

Was not like this when McCready was doing it. McCready did it as he sat up on his sorrel, letting them lay about if they liked, while he checked them off in the ledger, a tick mark by each name, as Odum meted out their allotment through the smokehouse door.

At the pace it was going this morning it be time to hand out Christmas rations if Beasley, the fool, did not change his mind and nub-legged ways.

And ahead of them still stood the drudge of a Sunday of ditches and dredging and damming trying to drain the rainwater first from the fields and then the Bottom. And there was still their own Sunday work to be done.

Damnit.

*So*

Ashe and Caesar knew Eph was going to be mad, mad as a bottled hornet set on a sunny stump. Mad at Cretia's Gal's lashing. Mad at McCready who'd snuck the child off to sell her, mad at M's Esme for sending her off in the middle of the storming night to the broker in Mardalwil County's courthouse.

Cretia's Gal was gone, and they had not even gotten to wave goodbye. Aye, they knew. They understood why Eph would be mad.

They were too.

Cretia's Gal was gone.

Was stole off.

Middle of the midnight storm.

Stole off to the courthouse to be sold off.

Stole off to be sold off on the nigger-trading block.

Would the young Highland House widow woman who pounded at the piano and whacked at the weeds sell them off piecemeal and on a moment's whim too?

And whose chickens was it yet to do the roosting?

Oh, aye, there were chickens to come home and roosting to be done. Cretia's Gal was gone, but they knew it was not over, and wondered what Cretia was going to do.

They wondered what it was all going to mean, and worried how much they would suffer before the last egg was hatched.

They wondered.

They worried.

*So*

In the yards of the Bottom, young'n's Little Fred and Oscar sang back and forth and splashed in the mud.

"Ain't you hear that mournful thunder?"

"Roll from door to door."

"Did not it *pour*?"

"*Pour!*"

Punctuating the end of each line with a foot stamp in the mud.

"Ain't you hear that mournful thunder?"

"Roll from door to door."

"Ain't it *pour*?"

"*Pour!*"

"Ain't it *pour* last night?"

"Last night . . ."

"*Pour!*"

"Ain't you hear that mournful thunder?"

"Roll from door to door."

"See that fork-ed lightning?"

"Lash from tree to tree?"

"Calling home all lost children."

"We'll get home by an' by."

"Boy, did not it *pour*."

"*Pour!*"

"Did not it *pour* last night?"

*So*

With his rock-steady hand as practiced as the river's flow Eph shaved a curl of pinewood from the plank he held between his knees.

"I'm going to tell you why you're mad," Odum said to Eph.

As was usual for a Sunday morning the mechanics were gathered outside Ashe's blacksmith shed. What was unusual was Odum's tongue was flapping loose as the wings on a northbound goose, and his breath was smelling like the bottom of one of the peat-reek jugs he kept hid about the Caledonia.

He might be the main nigger at hog-killing time, and a high-stepper when McCready was around, but right then the crew—Ashe the smiddie and his assistant Caesar—thought, if Odum did not be careful with Eph the carpenter, Caledonia was about to lose its biggest fool.

They couldn't reckon what was giving Odum his false courage. Eph had already given Odum a lesson on the danger of letting his peat-reek-loosened tongue flap till it loaded more on his wagon bed than his axle could haul. They had thought getting jumped on had taught Odum to put a permanent hasp on his mouth when his throat was wet from that peat-reek.

It was the time Eph put it on Odum, so much so until McCready, the grieve *himself*, had to pistol-whip Eph off of the Caledonia hog man.

Not long before that Eph had lost his mind over Mae Lil, his woman on Hutchinson's Plantation. Odum got drunk and started gabbing about Mae Lil. Eph's jumping on Odum was the first sign that Eph had found his mind again.

Eph's mind left him when Mae Lil died trying to birth her and Eph's baby. She died and the baby died, and when the word of it reached from Hutchinson's Plantation, Eph lost his mind and quit. Quit everything. He did not *refuse* to be jyner-carpenter any more than he refused to gab or eat or follow orders. He just *did not* because he did not have a soul to care, or a mind to tell him to. Did not have enough mind even to respond to McCready's lash. And stayed like that until that morning the peat-reek set Odum's tongue loose and McCready had to break it up by almost splitting Eph's head open with the butt of his pistol. Was Eph had come within an ace of killing Odum. Was Cretia had to nurse both of them back to health.

With Cretia's Gal gone, Ashe and Caesar could see Eph had bad things on his mind. What they couldn't see was why Odum couldn't see it too, plain as day. They couldn't reckon what had got wrong with Odum would make him think gabbing about Cretia's Gal being took off to the courthouse to be sold would set any better with Eph than that other time gabbing about Mae Lil who had died. But sure as it was going to rain some more, Odum was determined as a terrier after a rat.

"I'm going to tell you why you mad, sure," Odum repeated to Eph. "You mad because now *ev'ry-body* know Cretia's medicine ain't worth a fart. Her working up to Highland House and had ev'ry-body scared of her. Even had Goodsire and McCready tipping around her. But come to find out she did not have enough mojo to keep her own child from being took to the courthouse and sold."

Ashe and Caesar wanted Eph to do or say something. But he just kept looking off in the direction of the river and the gray of Red Stick's swamp across it.

Odum thinking, Eph think he so good a builder, sure, he too good to be a slave. Got these other two fools thinking it too. Said, "And if hers ain't nothing your' ain't nothing neither. Since she's the one give you your mojo."

Eph looked up, but he didn't look at Odum.

"*Ain't that why you mad.*"

Eph was looking off now toward the distant stretch of cotton fields in the overcast morning sky. As if he was surveying Caledonia section by section.

Ashe and Caesar waited.

"What about Cretia's Gal? Do not she mean nothing to you?" Eph asked Odum, but still not looking at him.

It was not much but maybe he was leading to something.

"What I care?" Odum said. "Her head was ne'er going to lay on my pillow."

"I ain't gabbing about *lay*ing with her. That's all Goodsire and Mc-Cready was waiting on. That's all she was going to be for them, to tote their slops in the day, and some dark goodie in the night."

"She was not flesh of mine," Odum said.

"She was bright as a bumblebee," Eph said. "Tickled me to see her buzzing about. It was like *they* hadn't yet touched her. Like she was *still ours.*"

"*Ours,*" Ashe repeated.

"Seeing Cretia's Gal buzzing about put it in my head this ain't the only place or way for me to be," Eph said.

Odum told him, "Well you better get that *out* your head."

Eph asked, "Do not it ache your heart she's gone?"

"Ain't nothing a nigger among us can do," Odum said.

Eph picked up a curled pinewood shaving that lay at his feet. "You just do not know," he said. "But you will when I come back again."

Odum laughed. "Come *back*?"

"Stop what-*ever* I'm doing," Eph said, "and come back, see the hands lined up all around watching me throw dirt in Goodsire's face as he's being lowered down."

"Do not you know you got to *go some-where* before you come back?" Odum told him.

Eph *had* been some-where, Asch thought. And everybody knew it. He had been to Hutchinson's Plantation hadn't he? Many nights. Had gone the first time in the daylight to deliver a table he made to be sold to Hutchinson. McCready took the table and Eph with him in the wagon. That was when Eph first saw Mae Lil. Soon after started going to be with her at night. Many believed Cretia made him a mojo for him to get past Beasley's crew of Jack, Henry, and Moon, and the rest of the area's cadre of night patrollers and whatever other bogle-ghosts or witches there was in the night to stop him and the other plantation hands from escaping or roaming free.

Some believed Eph would have gone whether he had Cretia's mojo or not. However, he went. When he wanted. And he and Mae Lil made a baby. And everybody knew it. And McCready flogged him for it. And Eph went some more anyway, and Mae Lil soothed his wounds.

"But all that was *before*," Odum argued. Back when Cretia still could make a mojo that had some power ahind it. Cretia's Gal getting took off to the courthouse to be sold showed that those days were as long gone as last week's grits.

They watched as Eph, his head down, began walking in a slow circle under the workshop roof's overhang.

"Only way we get to go off is through the courthouse," Odum signified, "and that's to be *sold off*—like Cretia's Gal. And ain't no coming back from there!"

"You forgot you can *run off*," Ashe said.

Odum laughed. "Y'all heard Mr. McCready say, sure as sunup, he'd let Beasley shoot a nigger with running on his mind."

"McCready or Beasley shoot ev'ey nigger thinking about getting the rabbit foot," Caesar said. "Goodsire be out of bullets before he out of niggers."

Eph circled slowly, almost dragging his feet.

"And you see it ain't stopped Eph," Ashe said. "Nothing McCready *said* did not stop him. *Flogging* did not e'en stop him."

Caesar laughed and nodded his head.

"That's right," Ashe said.

"So," Odum asked, "you telling me you getting ready to *go* some-where?"

"Odum," Eph said, still walking, but as if they had not been gabbing all along and he had suddenly thought of something, "do not you feel like going some-where some nights?"

Odum was surprised by the calm, sincerity, and directness of the craftsman's tone. He thought of the time he *had* gone out one night, and shuddered remembering the screeching and hollering bogel-witch that had chased him until he almost run himself to death. He had never told them about that.

He shook his head.

"But do not you *want* to go some-where, because you ain't satisfied here?"

"I got my place with a pallet in the Bottom. That's all the where for me to go." Odom paused.

It did not seem enough.

"Same as Ashe and Caesar," he added. "Same as you." He laughed and looked to the others to join him. They didn't. "All other times I'm here, doing this work. *Same as you.*"

"You just *think* I'm penned up here with you ev'ry-day," Eph said. "E'en just this minute here I got freedom on my mind."

"I *think* you here because I *see* you here. Mr. McCready sees you here too. Would if he was here," he corrected himself.

"He would not see me here not more," Eph said. The quiet way he said it shushed them all.

"Cretia say you can be looking at the river and think you seeing it, but what you think you looking at is gone before you can blink."

"Cretia nonsense," Odum countered.

Ashe and Caesar were nodding. "You like the river, ain't you, Eph?" Caesar asked.

"Tell us," Ashe insisted. "About where you go."

"Off like the crow," Caesar said. "Do not you, Eph? Tell us."

Eph pointing, "Some days off to the North Star. Cool my heels till time to go cat fishing on the moon."

"Cat fishing on the moon," Caesar repeated, laughing and clapping his hands.

"And how about at night?" Ashe prompted. "You off like a owl, ain't you?"

Odum said, "Crow or owl or any-thing else, if you so much gone, how come you do not *stay gone*?"

Eph said, "Leave before your mind is ready is when they hunt you down and drag you back. My mind been ready. But you're going to know when I do take a notion and go."

"How we going to know, Eph?" Ashe asked, anticipating.

"By Biece's hellhounds howling."

Ashe and Caesar laughed. "Let me hear them howling," Caesar said.

Still circling Eph, he began impersonating the pack of bloodhounds on the scent.

Chilled at the sound Odum involuntarily said, "That's them all right."

Eph cupped his hands around his mouth muffling the yelping sound of his impersonation of the tired, distant dogs.

Caesar laughed. "Yeah, man."

"Red Stick taught me how to gab to them sons of bitches," Eph said. He demonstrated a conversation between himself and a bloodhound pack. "That's me telling them long-eared rascals goodbye. And them telling me how much they hate to see me go."

They laughed.

"And old Biece," Caesar said, "he'll be crying and shaking his head!"

"Tears size of goose eggs, 'cause he spent all that time raising 'em and feeding 'em gunpowder to make 'em mean." Ashe laughed. "And you done run 'em to death trying to track you down!"

"And where you at, Eph?" the smiddie's assistant wanted to know.

"*There*," Eph said. "I'll be *there*."

His tone stopped them again. They waited.

Odum did not like the silence. The tune they were taught as children ran through his head.

*If you ever break and run,*
*Mr. Biece's hounds get you just for fun . . .*

"Where?" Odum asked.

Eph looked at him and shook his head.

*Better na break and run,*
*Run you down by setting sun . . .*

"Cretia craziness," Odum declared.

"I e'en look like I'm reckoning on leaving," Eph told him "you better catch hold to my sark-shirt tail, else it'll be too late to holler 'Wait for me.'"

The crew laughed.

Eph circled.

"Mr. McCready hear you say that he'll fix your doings," Odum said.

"I reckon he do not need to hear him," Ashe said. "You'll tell him ev'ry-thing soon as he gets back."

"Ain't nobody said not' about telling nobody not,'" Odum insisted over their laughter.

An edge, like a fox burrowing its way under the chicken coop fence was working its way into Eph's tone. "McCready and all of them got they time to learn, hunting ain't no fun when the rabbit got the gun."

Ashe and Caesar threw back their heads and laughed toward the sky.

Eph continued, "McCready went off to do his evil doings, and you act like he standing watch up o'er you with his lash in his hand."

"Ain't nobody said nothing about all that," Odum insisted. He wished

Eph would stop circling like that. "Did they, Ashe? We gabbing 'bout something else. We ain't gabbing 'bout telling nobody nothing."

"Find hunting ain't fun when the rabbit got the gun," Caesar repeated, ignoring Odum.

"Unless it's some foolishness Cretia told you," Odum said. " 'Cretia say. Cretia say.' That's all you know, ain't it? You and Cretia. You and Cretia. Y'all thick as flies on *sharn*-cow flop."

Eph, his face expressionless, continued circling, head down, but not looking at his feet which were still moving with little more than a shuffling motion. Without raising his voice, changing the speed of his circling, or looking at Odum, Eph said, "I got other business on my mind, Odum. Otherwise I'd make you walk backwards through your shit again. Then thump your melon, see if it's ripe before I hang you in your smokehouse like a hog.

"That's another thing," Odum said. "I'm through being a push o'er. So do not think you can put your hands on me no more. Not without it costing you. Because I got *me* something now."

*That's it!* Ashe thought and looked at Caesar who nodded. Odum got himself a mojo from somewhere! That's what got him thinking he can tease rattlesnakes and pull the guard dog's tail. But whatever it is he got and wherever he got it from, this morning, fooling with Eph, it's liable to get him killed.

"I'm through being your dog, sure, I know that," Odum insisted. "Try me. See if I ain't got me something."

"Something McCready give you?" Eph asked without looking up, changing his tone or expression, or altering his pace.

"Ain't no-body said nothing about Mr. McCready, but you better watch your-self, 'cause Mr. McCready knows what you thinking. Know what we all thinking. All the time."

Though Eph's speed hadn't changed he was more determined in his gait. With each step his feet were placed more firmly on the ground. "McCready knew all he was going to know when he left here with that young gal," Eph began.

"Was not Mr. McCready sent her off to be took off to the courthouse to be sold," Odum pointed out. "It's M's Esme who bound Cretia's Gal for the block . . ."

Eph's eyes flashed like midnight lightning and still circling, his voice flat as a Highland House tabletop he had planed and sanded, he said, "McCready is gone! But little sawed off Beasley still around here walking. Run get him," he said to Odum. "I do not care. Be another test. Fair and square. Then we'll see whose hand meant to hold the flogging whip."

"Gabbing Cretia non-sense and death gab," Odum said. "Mr. McCready know . . ."

"Gabbing common sense," Ashe said.

"McCready know all he going know," Eph said.

Before he left here he was not but a white man following us around all day. Hell, what is that? That ain't nothing. Nothing. Just like him."

"Sure wasn't."

"I can out-do Beasley at *any*-thing. Let him name something and challenge me at it. Foot racing, hunting, fishing, building a cabinet, or chopping down a tree. Let him take a head start, and I'll still best him. Let us both walk off into the woods. See who come back."

Eph rubbed at his forehead with the heels of his hands as if he had a fever. "You keep gabbing about what *Mr. McCready know*." He stopped circling and squatted in one flowing motion. "What I know," he slapped the earth with his open palm, "is they all going to end up here."

Using the edge of his hand he began to scoop a small mound of dirt. "End up here, where Mae Lil and our baby at." Eph raked a fistful of dirt. "And I'll be back again." He pounded the ground with his fist. "Here!" He stood up. "And I'll be back from *there* to see it."

"How you coming back, Eph?" Ashe asked, anxious, but encouraging.

"With brass buttons on my jumper. Have a shiny crow feather in the band of my brand new hat! Be back so they, McCready and Goodsire and squat little Beasley and that heifer M's Esme, can look up out the ground and I can look down and I can tell all of them I been *there*. Let them *know that!*"

"Yeah," Caesar said.

*Back from where?* Odum wanted them to ask him. Back from *where?* Wanted to see him fix up his mouth and say it out loud. See if he had the grit for that.

*If you break and run*
*shoot you*
*shoot you down with his gun.*

Eph let the scooped dirt fall in a slow dry shower through the funnel at his baby finger.

"Going to see them all planted where they would ne'er sprout no more. And as I stomp the dirt down on their mounds, I going to do a frolic would bust McCready's and Goodsire's and Beasley's little peach pit hearts in their goddamn chests. Esme's too."

He did a quick, three-beat, dust-raising dance step, then clapped his hands together once and said, "Do not say nothing to *me* about what McCready know. I know what McCready *know*, and what he *will not see to know no more.*"

"What McCready know and will not see to know," Ashe repeated.

Eph clapped his hands once and began to gab-sing like those inching their arduous way along: the mule plowers and pickers, their backs bent double under the baking sun, their fingers bloody from plucking the thorny bolls. Their voices rising from them like shimmering waves off a heat oasis, open-throated but tense, as they shout-sang songs or sayings or messages to one another, along or across the rows, or hollered or whined some private, wordless, or coded musing into the air: jokes and anecdotes, tales and hearsay. Urgings, to stir slaggards on, or inspirit the weary, or still the tempted tongue, or tame the rising fury of the frustrated or angry. Accusations and curses and threats and denials, directed at each other. In every sound, but not a straight word of spite or bile or malcontent or displeasure at their work conditions or their masters or their masters' rules or wants. Some hollering. Some humming. Some moaning. Some groaning. Feelings too strong, too urgent, too bitter, too burdensome to wait for the seclusion of evening and home or Sunday. Every-one. Groaning. Moaning. Humming. Hollering. Anything. Ev'ry-thing.

Until the air was thick with it as May mosquitoes. Until they couldn't hear themselves think.

Until they couldn't hear themselves think.

Ashe's say-singing contained the same tension as the pickers, mindful as they were of McCready's proclamation, under penalty of short rations or the lash, against their gabbing directly of the misery on their hearts and in their minds. And so Ashe's shouting, like theirs, was like a hound's baying its plaintive *Why*? at an uncaring moon, or like restless roosters trying not *just* to crow *down* the loathsome sun, but to crow it down with such evidence and conviction as to keep it from ever rising on another day.

"Take Cretia's Gal off," Ashe moaned, "tears in her face."

"Oh, Mc-Cready," Caesar added, sing-songing too.

"Bring another one, take her place," Ashe droned.

Stretching the words out as long as the steadily fattening cotton sacks dragging ahind the hands through the long, narrow, rutted rows. Stretching sentence and syllable as long as the arc of the sun from dawn to dusk, as long as the season from seeding to harvest, as long as their lifelong bondage itself.

"Better not let Mr. McCready hear you singing no sad song," Odum said, more to take part than as a warning.

And then from somewhere he heard another wailing—it was Red Stick. Howling from some distance. Howling that Indian long note howling.

Ashe began to clap, harder and harder, the sound ringing sharp as lash snaps. "And you know when they leave here they do not come this way no more."

"Do not darken our door no more," Caesar added as he began stamping his foot, steady as axe strokes in an oak trunk, and alternately clapping with cupped palms, the sound booming like the stick-struck bottom of a water bucket. "Goodsire and Mc-Crea-dy . . ."

Odom backed away from them. Backed out of sight into the shadows of the smiddie shack. But not from their chanting or Red Stick's lamenting wail.

"Stole the black gal off . . ." Ashe said-sang.

". . . Oh, Mc-Crea-dy . . ."

" . . . stole her to market . . ."

". . . Oh, Cretia's Gal. Wonder where she gone . . . ?" Caesar pined.

The rain they all had known was coming back had returned. So gentle a *smirr* they hadn't noticed when it began.

Eph circling again but now his head nodding to a rhythm.

". . . middle of the night . . ." Ashe sang-said.

"Wonder where she gone?" Caesar countered.

"Know her mama in the Highland House hollering . . ."

"Wonder where she gone? Wonder where my child has gone . . ."

"Cretia's Gal gone . . ." Ashe chant-said. "Cretia's Gal, Cretia's Gal, Cretia's Gal, Cretia, Cretia, Cretia, *Cretia's Gal* . . . Wonder where she gone?"

"M's Esme and McCready stole her off."

"Know Cretia in the big house hollering"

"Wonder where she *gone*?"

"Wonder where my child is gone?"

Kongo mojo niggers and heathen redskin, Odum thought, apprehensively shaking his head.

As if angry with the earth, Eph began to stamp his feet as he continued once again in the tight circle. "You want to see a frolic?" He said, "Let me live to hear Goodsire ask me where I been . . . Then let them go where they belong, and wait for judgment day."

". . . Cretia's Gal gone . . ." Caesar said.

Nothing but mojo niggers clucking and frolicking in the *pour*.

Eph began pumping his arms. Bringing his shoulders into it, with quick jerks. His arms were glistening with his sweat and the gentle shower of rain. Finding a rhythm somewhere within that of his walking, Ashe's singing and clapping, and Caesar's clapping and stamping.

Odum touched the juju sack and backed farther away from the rain and the rhythm and the loudness, but most of all from the fuss Eph was raising. Mr. McCready liked it when the niggers was singing because they worked better singing. But Eph knew Mr. McCready did not allow no dancing in broad daylight. And Mr. McCready would know what Eph had done. Might know already, e'en off where he was with Cretia's Gal. Might know e'en there.

Eph: turning and clapping and stamping, finding a rhythm, as the rain increased. Clapping and stamping harder and harder, as if trying to stamp the hard, scarred rain and sweat-wet black flesh from his bones, as if, through his pounding, trying to embed his footprint on the earth.

Stomp.

As if to punish it.

Stomp.

As if it was a sign or warning in remembrance or revenge.

Stomp.

As if his heel could split the ground like a blunt wedge, or even better, like the keen, stone-honed edge of his axe; cleave into the earth to rend a fracture or fault or fissure as wide and deep as the distance between his desire and his reality, a crack rupturing to the core of the world, splitting it in two; a rift to run from his footprint in the work shed's yard, through the center of his rough and tumble shack in the Bottom, running then up the path to Highland House, splitting it all asunder until it toppled like Pharaoh's army into the Red Sea: Goodsire on his gray mare, and M's Esme in her buggy, and Beasley and the host of them, cast down in the rift, and drowning under the deluge of dirt rained upon them, like the dirt shoveled into Mae Lil and their baby's grave on Hutchinson's Plantation. Split, like the news of Mae Lil's and the baby's death had split him, forehead to breastbone to belly to balls, and his soul and his mind had tumbled, out, into the rift of the earth that was their common grave, onto which the dirt was heaped. And his mind flew off, and his soul, like a wisp was blown away, as with a strong wind blowing away a locust.

Helping Eph, Caesar and Ashe continued their singing and clap-a-tclapp-a-t-clapp-a-tclapp-a-ting. Circling him, slowly, as he circled, not to contain him, but to assure him he was safe within the ring of their guard.

Odum looking on.

It was getting faster and they were getting louder, and the *pour-rain* came down. Harder.

One thing to carry on like that in the night in the Bottom, or at Christmas frolic, but to do it in the broad open daylight. Loud enough, Odum feared, for Beasley in his shack in the Bottom to hear and be drawn to it.

Eph turned. Stamp. Stamp. Faster. Stamping harder. Then no longer just on one foot and then the other. Rapid now as running. Two-footed and one-foot leaps, with straight legs, then with bent knees. As if leaping on hot coals. Left one-two, right one-two-left-right-left-left-right-right-left-left-leap-leap-leap-leap-left-right-right. Twisting, shoulders one way, hips the other, head weaving like a reptile, arms flapping like wings, hands clapping, hands slapping his chest, his arms.

A rhythm, shimmering up his leg, would meet a rhythm that had begun with the shaking of his head and working its way down through his neck. Or a rhythm from his shaking shoulders answering counter rhythms from his waving arms and his clenching and unclenching hands. The spasms and jerks and contortions flowing together like torrents of water cascading down a falls into a swirling delta.

Tha-dump tha-dump tha-dump*a*tha-dump*a*. Clapp-a-t-claptap-clapp-a-t-clapp-a-t, as he stamped and spun and pumped, pumping, like his heart during his night rambles, like his heart when making the baby with Mae Lil, the combination of their hearts, drumming, combining with the drumming hearts of Cretia and Cretia's Gal, starting off to market, to the block, the pressure building like a blocked bellows being pumped, like the blood in his brain, threatening to burst out of him.

Remembering, Eph flung off his sark-shirt, and they could see where he had carved himself and where the flog marks carved themselves into his chest and back and arms. The pumping of his heart making him remember last night's flogging of Cretia's Gal, and he couldn't do no more than watch as the rain and the whip in Beasley's hand fell on her naked shoulders and back and buttocks and thighs. And the sight of the helpless hands, forced, or who forced themselves to watch, their tears falling like rain. But not enough to blind them.

And last night in the woods.

And Eph remembered it all and danced and they clapped and chanted, until they were all more exhausted than the work for their master had ever made them. And more joyous.

Until he subsided like a spent storm.

Eph was bent over, his hands on his knees. Panting. Water was raining on and dripping from his body, then spattering against the mud between his feet.

"Yeah," he panted, "I'll be gone. But I'll be back. *Again.*"

He saw, lying in the mud between his feet, the mojo hand Cretia had made him.

He said, "And when I walk up to that house and holler through the front door, 'Come out, get what you got coming,' and that man and that woman and little sawed-off Beasley ask me where I been, I'll tell them."

He picked up the mojo and held it in his palm.

"Tell them I been to freedom. And after I watch you die I'm going back again," he said with axe-edge bluntness and clarity and certainty. "Tell them I been to freedom, and I'm going back again," he repeated. "Then going to sit down and tell tales about how they done me wrong."

They watched him, waiting.

The rain had stopped again.

It was time. At last it was time. And Eph knew it. And he was ready. Ready to steal his body off. For good this time. Ready to try to find his self. See if he was a man in full.

*So*

# Mr. Wilcox

## Spring 1928

### I

Cotty hadn't slept good. He'd done his usual Saturday double shift and this was his only day off and he'd woken up early after he hadn't slept good.

Jenny wasn't for sure if it was the ache in that rotting back tooth again, or the grumbling of his stomach all night, but she was sure trying to pay attention to what he was saying while hurrying up to get the twins, Lollie Mae and Sallie Mae, dressed and ready for service.

But for right then he was satisfied with his coffee and his cigarette and going on about how he'd got slighted by Mister P. W. *Anderson,* who he couldn't hardly stand, and how close he'd been to getting him told for good, or worse.

She didn't remember from his telling now if P. W. Anderson was government or corporation, or which, but he was a high-up boss for sure.

"He's a white man same as me," Cotty circled back around again to what Jenny thought was his point, "but thinking he could treat me like I'm nothing more than some nig—some—schoolboy who'd showed up without his lessons learnt."

Sitting side of the bed, one foot pale as parchment top of the other, hair mussed, eyes red, but still a good-looking man, she'd tell anybody. The Mae's humming the tune quietly back and forth between them, antsy to leave.

And in front of the nigger, or niggers, she wasn't sure.

He had his finger in his mouth worrying at the tooth.

That in front of the nigger, or niggers, was new, she thought. He hadn't said that before, she was pretty sure of that.

The Mae's, being *too* fast, were giving her eye signals about going out of the door.

That just might put it in a new light about the niggers. She made a disapproving sound, but one he would know she meant as in agreement with his grievance.

The Mae's, each one looking more like the other one than herself, silently presented themselves to him in their new Mama-made dresses as ready, and he nodded his approval and smiled at them, which made her smile, as they told their daddy, Bye Daddy, like she told them, and he *Bubbbbbbed* through his lips like the Boogey man, waggled his stumped fingers at them and blew smoke, and they laughed, and she sent them to the porch with strict instructions, but he continued, not ready for her to go.

This was something about pride, she reckoned. Mister P. W. Anderson evidently must've had chastised Cotty, or *appeared* to, *just-like* he was some ignorant schoolboy who'd showed up for class without his lessons done, he repeated, clearer this time, his fingers out of his mouth, *and* had did it within sight or hearing of that nigger Mule, looked like he was snarling all the time, lip pulled back from his teeth like a mule braying.

"I'll tell you what's sad. Showed just how little Mister *Anderson* knowed about handling niggers. That was the *first* thing."

She nodded, waiting for the second thing, and listened to them being quiet on the porch.

"Rich *did not* make you savvy about handling niggers."

It did certainly not; she shook her head and looked at him.

Too quiet?

It most certainly did not.

At the beginning, Jenny knew, Cotty thought of it as a job he was glad to have, was even grateful for. And them, the niggers, they were just the necessary part of it. It wasn't his fault they were there under his watch. They may have been down on their luck or whatever, but they had broken a law. And he more and more realized he always had to be on his guard against their trying to shirk or slough off their duty, calling for stricter and stricter supervision, making his job harder, so he had, little by little, eroded any leniency he might have shown towards them, until, without even knowing it, he resented them to the point that there was no limit to his indifference to their welfare, because . . .

"If he wasn't scared to get his white shoes dusty," Cotty said, cutting off her thought, "and spend one shift seeing over them niggers, no, one *hour*, see what it takes to do what I do. Would be all it'd take to show him a thing or two, see how *his* belly churned after a night of that."

He wiped at his eyes and shook his head as if he was trying to wipe away the memory of his conversing with the boss man.

"Give him a chance to see exactly what kind of animal it is I'm standing shotgun over."

That had been Cotty's whole point.

The Mae's were out there humming the hymn, practicing, bless them.

And seem like, Cotty was saying, Mister P. W. *Ander*son didn't have no better sense, no race pride, he reckoned, no *respect* for what's proper before niggers, and what's common practice white man to white man, being betters before their kind. He didn't know what went on between white people up north wherever P. W. Anderson was from, but . . .

Jesus loved them, yes they knew . . .

"Mule tried to make like he didn't hear or see nothing, pretending, with that blind, deaf, and dumb nigger-do—now that's one thing they good at, hiding a lie and play-acting before white people, but they see everything, don't miss nothing, least little slip and they on it like a duck on a June bug, let it be the least little sign of lapse—"

His cigarette butt hissed in the slops coffee can by his feet.

Cotty said he knew the nigger Mule, who'd seen that Mister P. W. Anderson look like he'd cut Cotty off when he'd invited him to come back that night—would think that was what had happened—that it was intended on that Mister P. W. Anderson's part to be a slight, and that's how the snarling-looking nigger would tell it to the others when they got off to they-selves after lights out in the lock-down house. And his version of it was how it would be passed around between them, like it was a pint of bonded whiskey they'd lap their lips over and laugh.

Now Jenny had a full understanding of it.

He took a long look down into his half-empty coffee cup.

Because the Bible told them so . . .

"And whether it was like that or not, all that grinning, eavesdropping nigger needed to know was two white men was talking there. See that, know it's time to shut his earflaps down, time to turn his eyeballs inside out and be through with it. Period. Know that, and that I'm on top over him. Top-over-him. Was, is, and always will always be. Irregardless. Bible time Genesis, to Exodus, Leviticus clean to Haggai, Zachariah to Malachi . . . till today and tomorrow. Period. Mister P. W. Anderson needed to understand and respect that same as Mule, or they'll see what'll happen. Seen it already, mightily well told. Reason why he in them chains and I ain't. That is the nature of things."

She didn't want to be late, but neither did she want to hurry him.

"The *nature* of rules is, if you want to talk about rules, and you got to, because there's *got to be* rules. Or it's them or us. Some-body's got to rule and somebody's got to be ruled. And there was but two choices, the stick or the whip."

The Mae's scuffling around out on the porch were being as patient as they could be.

"That's the order of it. The superior *over* the inferior. See if when you go there directly he don't tell you your Bible tells you that. Proverbs. See, your laws, they've got to be enforced—otherwise, it's back to the law of the jungle."

Cotty knew Mister P. W. Anderson shouldn't be let to leave Kimbrough Works plantation without learning something he couldn't check off on a form, was what Cotty was thinking. If they would just once see them for his self, was what Cotty'd been trying to get him to see.

Let him see for his high-toned self; if only he'd come down off his high horse. Could show him better than trying to explain it in words. Then there'd be no question of the importance of the job he was doing or the talent it took.

When he'd invited *Mister P. W. Anderson* to see for his self, he'd said he was "disinclined."

Cotty was rubbing at his jaw, irritated.

What did *disinclined* mean? He would tell her what it meant. It meant hedging and hemming and muddy-mouthed is what it meant, and he wasn't no *business*-man, like Mister P. W. Anderson, but he knew that wasn't no way to do business. Period.

She needed to tell him that she needed to be going in a minute if she was going to get there in any kind of time for the Mae's to sing, them out there shooing the chickens by stamping their feet, her wanting to holler out at them about not raising no dust and dirtying themselves, but listening instead as he said he reckoned they'd savage and throat slash through the night, Mister P. W. Anderson had his way.

She nodded, reckoning so.

At least the Mae's didn't have old Sketter to chase and rassle at and worry any more.

He sighed. She sighed.

He still hadn't said it and she still couldn't go.

"Proverbs, King James, 13 and 24th," he said. Something he bet Mister P. W. Anderson'd never read in his life. Probably most of his time with nose in an accounts ledger never looked up to see what it took to get a decent day's work out of a squad of them—it wasn't by having them stand around listening at one white men tell another what Mister P. W. Anderson'd 's told him, that's for sure.

Skeeter'd been good at protecting the chickens and the house from other predators but then had taken to killing hens his self. Cotty'd tied a dead one around the dog's neck to break him of it, but it hadn't helped.

Cotty nodded and she took it as his sign that she could go.

She asked him to remember not—when he said, "Do you know what he told me? Had the flat out gall—?"

She didn't shake her head; she just looked at him, waiting. Knowing he was at the point of it.

"To go easy on them."

Their pause throbbed with indignation.

"And you know what he meant." It wasn't a question. "Spare the lash."

He closed his eyes and put his hand gingerly to his jaw as if cradling the aching tooth.

This was it. What he had been building to.

"It's my kind that's protecting his kind." He looked directly at her. "I'm the lean yard dog that was against the gray eyes and bared teeth at the edge of the night woods, watching after the fat sows with their snouts deepest in the trough."

She nodded, trying to ascertain her agreement with him. The rivulets had flowed together into the main stream.

"You have to treat a dog like a dog—or it'll all go to the dogs."

It wasn't his tooth that was paining him.

"He that spareth his rod hateth his son . . ." He paused as if he wanted her to recite it with him, but she did not know it. "But he that loveth him chastenth him betimes."

Mister P. W. Anderson hadn't—couldn't even look Cotty in the eye when he said "go easy on them" where that Mule could hear him—he'd said it like he was swatting away a gnat, a wasp.


# 2

Abraham, who hated being in harness, in a trot.

For the Bible told them so, the Mae's sang in their sweet, harmonious voices.

It was in the Bible, wasn't it? He had asked her. Well he would know better than her. Yes—far as she knew. Least she didn't know it wasn't in there. Reverend Rhodes would know—if she would ask him, but she wouldn't. Cotty'd said it, so—

Jenny did not know what she thought of it, his sparing the lash or not.

He hadn't told her anything of them she didn't think. No. She didn't think anything of it because she didn't know of it to think of it, which was fine with her.

It'd been that nagging toothache had him so he couldn't think straight. And that and somebody that high up in the company and from the headquarters up north surprising him like he'd done. Till Cotty couldn't say what it was at the core of his feeling. What it was was confusion. She knew. It was whether or no the slight had been intended, or was it just ignorance on Mister P. W. Anderson's part? Cotty hadn't said that was it, but she felt it for him.

The Mae's knew He loved them, they sang above the creaking of the wagon and the clopping of Abraham's hooves.

Jenny'd been a farmer's daughter. Her step-daddy Mister Morris'd worked shares same as Cotton Wilcox when she'd met him. Put something in the ground and pray it pays to pull it up, but Cotty'd never cared for farming and after his working at the mill came to no good, first and second knuckles of the last two fingers of his left hand whacked off, and the preaching'd petered out, and when the Kimbrough Works company job come open he did what he had to do—what was always done—what had to be. He'd took to the guard job like a hog to slop, and her and him and the Mae's'd been right happy ever since.

# 6

# The Mae's

## Spring 1928

Lollie Mae and Sallie Mae quiet out on the porch or stirring hushed in the yard and waiting on their mama to Please hurry up Mama, as they took turns looking at the closed door with arms folded, foot patting, face in a pout while the other walked in circles around the wash pot, but it didn't help, maybe because Mama was listening so serious to Daddy talking up a blue streak about something their little pitchers' ears weren't big enough to be hearing, or, because they were somewhat distracted by the faint sound, and ever worrisome smell, of the smoke and wet ashes from the fire up the hill and at the gin and saw mills from a long time ago. So long ago they didn't even know how long ago, but back, way back before the States' Rights War, back when all niggers were still slaves.

It was the sound and the smell, that nobody else but them could smell, that had to do with their never wanting to play at the top of the hill, which would have been a perfect place to play, weaving in and out of the burned columns, or to run up to the top and to roll down from, but they didn't, without even being warned against it.

The sound, loud enough on some nights to make them sleep with the covers over their heads and their hands over their ears against the jumbled nigger-like whispering and the low whimpering, and sometimes wailing of a white woman, like it was washing down from up the hill, or mumble rumbling from a long, long way, both in distance and time. Either the sound or the smell could come up so strong that, without a signal from either one, it would make them break out singing.

When the odor or the noise came didn't have anything to do with moonlight or seasons or weather conditions, or any pattern the Mae's could reckon. It could as likely be broad open daylight or sunset or a Thursday morning.

It was like when Old Skeeter used to just break out barking out at the dark when no-body else heard a thing and he'd keep barking till Daddy hollered at him to Hush up that yapping, Skeeter! And he'd give one or two more woofs like he was getting the last word in, or giving his last warning to what-ever it was he knew was out there—but old Skeeter had one on the Mae's because even though they heard it or smelled it or both they didn't have a clue what *it* was or why it was that they knew it was out there.

The Mae's had slipped and told of them once or twice but had learned not to speak on it too much, or at all if they could help it (but *never* about the crying of their would-have-been older brother that miscarried even though the nigger midwife was there in time. Mama and their daddy never spoke of it, though the Mae's knew of it anyway), but when the sensation did come to them their only defense was to sing, and when they were asked what they were singing about or why, they got that look on their faces like niggers who knew something but wouldn't admit to knowing it, wouldn't even, under threat of penalty, admit to knowing anything of it, no matter what.

Whatever, it made their mother nervous as a moth at a lantern, and their daddy go quiet as iron.

Haunted, hell! Some of the rough, barefoot boys at school cussed, bragging under their breaths. They went exploring up at the burnt-down big old house on the hill. Claimed they played tag among the blackened columns, burnt rafters, shattered glass, and busted bricks. The boldest, in direct contradiction to what they'd said earlier, claimed they'd discovered things of so scary and secret of a nature they couldn't tell, to protect those who didn't know of such things from the very horror of hearing them. Some nights it was full of haints and spooks, and other nights, niggers doing nigger-what-all up there.

Such as *what?*

Such as raising the dead, and casting spells on white folks. The carrot-haired one with the scabs swore he'd seen it and lived to tell it. The Mae's just looked at one another. That wasn't any more help in dispersing the smell or the sounds than when Mama tried to fan away the heat at church.

It was Mama had once assured them that what they thought they heard was just the wind in the trees or smoke from the fireplace. Yes, ma'am they said, thinking together that there was no wind, just like there was no trees anymore for a wind to be in, Mama. Just hundreds and hundreds of stumps their daddy said he had helped to cut down when they'd quit planting cotton, leaving nothing but little foot-high tables for sprites.

Nobody who couldn't hear or smell it could explain it or explain it away any more than they, Lollie Mae and Sallie Mae, had even a flickering notion of what they were on the fringe of, in the same way they had never put their ear to a seashell or heard the hum of electrical current through a wire, and wouldn't have had the words for it even if they had.

They waited. They wanted Mama to hurry up so they could get to church and sing their song about how Jesus loved them and for the preacher to preach, getting in after the devil (like old Skeeter used to snap after fireflies before he got so old, and Daddy said old Skeeter just went off in the woods and wouldn't be back), and Preacher Rhodes get them others to clapping and dancing and caterwauling and drown out the business of that from-up-the-hill crying and moaning and carrying on.

They waited and sang their Jesus loved them song a little louder, so maybe Mama would hear them, and hurry up please Mama please, hurry up.

# 7

# Ezekiel 28:2

A few, all women, stood applauding as the Mae's, faces flushed and split by their grins, holding hands, bowed, a third and then a fourth time.

"A-men!"

Answered by scattered amens as the Mae's joined Jenny, and the women resettled, found their fans, and watched preacher Roy Rhodes, proprietor of Rhodes Crossroads general store and postmaster, wipe his brow with his blue handkerchief and begin:

"Pride," he said, and wiped again at his forehead. "'. . . Let them be caught,' it says in Psalms 10 and 2 . . ." He paused, letting that soak in, or for them to try to remember the rest of it.

"Amen."

"Amen," he repeated. "But I begin to-day with the word from Ezekiel. 28. 2."

He began to read from the bible opened before him. "Son of man, say to the leader of Tyre, 'This says the Lord GOD, because your heart is lifted up . . .'"

"Amen."

"Amen . . . 'And you have said, I am a god, I sit in the seat of gods—'"

"Amen."

"Amen—'in the heart of seas . . .'"

A chill went through Jenny. She threw up her hand and shouted, "Yes," making the Mae on either side of her jump and look at their mother, who never said Amen.

Jenny was thinking of Mister P. W. Anderson, thinking *he* was in the seat of a god where he could lord it over Cotty, as the preacher continued, "'yet you are a man and not God'—"

"Amen," she shouted again, her mind racing to when she got home and told Cotty what he had missed about one person trying to put his self above another person.

*"Yet you are a man and not God—"* which is exactly what Cotty should have, would have said to that Mister P. W. Anderson, if it wasn't for . . . You mister, are a man *and not God*—not a prince, not a *chosen*, just some—boss from headquarters, up north or where ever it was, but all the same . . .

He was a—she couldn't even think what—*Lucifer*, fancying himself over and above Cotty and the worth of the job he was doing.

Preacher, like he was talking directly to her to help her remember it, was repeating the phrase just as she was repeating it in her own mind, *"Yet you are a man—and not God! For you have said in your heart, 'I am, and there is no one besides me.'"*

That was *exactly* what she was trying to think to say to Cotty when he had said what he had about how Mister P. W. Anderson had the prideful nerve to disrespect Cotty in front of them niggers. Cotty was a proud man and justified in it. The way he had pulled himself up. Quit drinking, found the Lord, good daddy—and that Mister *High and Mighty High Class*, in his pride thinking there was no-body besides him that mattered in the conversation, or the way of things here in Mardalwil County, Alabama. He did not have a clue about her Cotty.

And preacher went on and he went on working himself into a lather, from one side of the church to the other and front to back, clapping and shouting and wiping his face, going on about the foolishness and fatality of pride, and she, fanning with her hat, sweat running down her neck and armpits, repeated, *"Yet you are a man—and not God! For you have said in your heart, 'I am, and there is no one besides me.'"*

She, a Mae on either side of her, their hands covering their smiles, knew this was their favorite part.

Jenny rocked slightly back and forth and gave witness to the holiness of the Word, and she couldn't *wait* to get home and tell him what she'd heard. She wasn't even going to stay for the visiting after church. The Mae's would be disappointed, not getting to bathe in the praise for their song, but she had to get home as quick as possible to tell him the heartening words she'd heard.

"*A—*" said Lollie Mae.

"*—Men!*" said Sallie Mae.

# 8

# Witness

## Fall 1928

There so long that he, whose name was not remembered, was of the land. Saw everything. Quiet as moon's shadow cast through a shroud of cloud was present with no presence, but with predetermined purpose, always there, always there, seeing but seldom seen.

Said nothing but made himself known to those had the need to know.

Her wagon had clopped and rattled past, with her looking, as many of them did, more a widow than a wife, her face dry as husk, the reins in her lye-wrinkled fingers held as tight as her jaw was clenched. Of course she had not even seen him on the road shoulder. Why would she? Her twin gals, though, each the dead spit of the other, had, or thought they saw their own version of him without knowing what they were seeing, but hadn't acknowledged it to him, or to the other, from whom they kept no secrets, but still their hands held the other's hand, tight.

The wagon is out of sight when he leaves the road and cuts, without the crunch of footsteps, off across the parched hill bottom acreage of nettles and brambles, of what, in their time, had been the wooded approach to the hilltop main house of the Kimbrough Plantation. The land is now on the books somewhere as Kimbrough Properties, a subsidiary of Kimbrough Company Works. On it, an acre or so away, is the cabin the Wilcox woman left from a short while before. It, once looked down on from the house now char, is typical of its breed. It had been the overseer's place six or seven decades of seasons ago, and it is from which the overseer left one rainy night with the young girl beside him in the buggy seat. It has been rebuilt over time from the original one room to now house the Wilcox's, a family of four.

He stops short and leans on his skint maple branch walking stick. A colored boy he cannot identify by name but knows is a recent release from what whites call the convict lease camp is, his attention on the Wilcox cabin, alert as a bird dog in a bog, and doing a pretty fair job of moving and not being seen through the overgrowth of black bent grass and bottlebrush buckeye wide and high as the wall of a one-story building, going golden now as it does this time of year.

It is certain this is not his first visit around here under cover of the foliage, and it is certain also that neither is he here for chicken stealing or other some minor mischief. No. No, look at him yonder, he has other business on his mind as he, low-crouched, moves to squat out of sight within sight of the outhouse. Surveying it like a spider eyeing the weaving of its glowing silver and gold web. This young negro, still getting reused to walking without the leg irons, is here for business of a cold and keen-edged kind. Reckoning or redemption is his aim.

But by nightfall the boy who will soon leave without seeing if his prey has been entangled in the strands of his plot, will sit, resting, his back against the scaly gray trunk of a water hickory, halfway through the swamp, his wits about him, reading the assurance of the stars before dreaming a dream-filled sleep.

The boy could have set the shack and the sorry excuse of a useless barn afire; he could have snuck up to wait by the door and with a baseball-sized rock brained Blue Britches when he exited and tipped him down over into the well, but that would have been too much like a baptism, and therefore contrary to his intention; could have waited behind the outhouse and stepped around with the same rock and watched him, in his surprise, step back the way negroes had to do when a white passed, then hit him and watched with satisfaction as he dropped to his knees, face forward in the dirt—all of these, contemplated during the long hot days and short hot nights, the boy had harbored for all his time under the guard's dominion, but the boy's knowledge of what would have followed: the commencement of bedlam of a white man murdered and a negro, out of shackles, running, so that the remaining negroes would not, on his account, have to hunker down as the crackers rose up like devil dogs with bloodshot eyes and slobbering mouths, their tails ablaze, so no, the boy did none of these; instead, carrying a small sackcloth bundle, he leaves his hiding place, heading off back through the brush toward the river, and trots upstream.

So, the negroes at worship or on their porches or still in bed or cooking or just dragging in could continue without new threats to their oppressed existence on his account.

With his stick across his knees, he sat on a stump. He was like a shadow of the Groundsel bush at his side. He had a bemused expression as he waited with the patience of his age and nature. He listened and saw and felt the flurry of every living thing brought out and breeding abundantly in the business of the morning: the music of tweets, twitters, chirps, warbles of the titmouse's, chickadees, and blue jays that perched year-around; and the transient grosbeaks, bobolinks, thrushes, and towhees that soon after this coming Tuesday's rain, full of seeds, grains, beetles, wasps, and caterpillars, would, like the colored boy, leave there.

Directly Wilcox, dour, shirtless, exits his cabin, yawning and scratching, and carrying the overnight slops can, walking barefoot from his porch across his yard down the slight slope to the privy to open the off-kilter door and move inside.

He whose name was no longer remembered heard the sound and curses from inside the outhouse. He smiled and hummed a tuneless air like a warbler's trill. He moved off, purposeful as a bee, to pollinate through mind to ear to mouth to ear to mouth to ear, so by Monday, end of dinnertime, all coloreds in Mardalwil County, Alabama and further would know, beyond whites' authorization to stop it, detail by detail of the occurrence at the old overseer's place that yester-Sunday morning; so that, from that time forward, Mister Cotton Wilcox, Cotty to his woman, would go from being that rusty-toothed, blue britches-wearing, peckerwood camp guard who rode shotgun over the Kimbrough Works convicts on a company horse; daddy of them scrawny, devilish, coot-crazy twin gals with the angelic voices, and gaunt wife who thought her husband was the very picture of the hardest working, most family-dedicated man she knew; the one who had called that colored boy Mule nigger to his face for the last time, and who wasn't as smart as either one of them took him to be, or he wouldn't have squatted to take his Sunday morning dump on the one-holed plank of knotted pine that the colored boy, who had by this time crossed the river at the place described and recommended by one of the older men who had walked the woods and fished the river through there for years before being swept up by the authorities in a local raid and sentenced to a planting season of work on a squad with the constantly grinning boy called Mule, who that morning, had nigger-rigged the outhouse seat, cleverly enough so it didn't look meddled with, so Mister Wilcox sat and tumbled ass-first in full body flop down into the depth of his convict labor-dug privy.

# 9

# Confidential

## Acorn, Alabama, Fall 1928

Offenders were plentiful what with the shambles in the land even sixty years after the Rebellion. It was against the law for whites and coloreds to pursue their felonious endeavors as the Confederacy struggled to recover the civilization of its past. Or so politicians and merchants throughout Alabama had explained it to P. W. Anderson. So there was a ready supply, a surplus even, of those who could be arrested and convicted and imprisoned by the state of Alabama. The ones that the Cotton State did not use as cheap labor on its public works projects were leased out to private contractors. From the late 1800s until the present, the system fortunes had to be reclaimed or made in the private sector, and had been very beneficial in the rebuilding of the great state of Alabama.

Kimbrough Company Works was one such contractor. The accounting and the legal departments had expressed concerns that cotton, the golden goose, was laying its last batch of eggs. Suspicions were also expressed that the company representatives on the scene in Acorn, given their self-interests, might not be as forthcoming as they might be. P. W. Anderson, Management Consultant, from the home headquarters in Hartford, Connecticut, was on a fact-finding visit. There were indications that the system was ending its cycle of sustained profitability. P. W. Anderson was Kimbrough Company Works man in the field.

Anderson looked at the angel of the south in the bright yellow dress with the stenographer's pad on her knee and wondered—well, wondered how forthcoming she would be to direct questions about her job security, and the lengths she would go to ensure it.

He explained he realized it was Sunday morning and she had been asked at the last minute to come in to take his dictation. It needed to go out in tomorrow's mail. He also was to leave on the morning train, but he was not going directly back home. He had a side trip of a personal nature.

Miss Holden, he had been told, was her name.

"Eveline," she said, "or Evy."

"Evy then," he said.

"Ready when you are," she said.

He smiled. He began.

"All that I am about to dictate to you is strictly for the eyes of our corporate president in Hartford and officers of the board there." He paused, looking at her.

She, with her pencil poised, understood.

"People's positions, their jobs are on the line. Nothing I say must be repeated."

She nodded.

He smiled and nodded.

"CONFIDENTIAL."

She began writing, her eyes on him but her pencil making curlicue marks on the pad on her crossed knee.

"FROM: P. W. Anderson to the home office, Hartford Connecticut, etc.," he said.

She waited, ready to continue.

He complimented her on her perfume.

She thanked him.

He wondered how she stood this heat, and asked her.

She was used to it she guessed.

Yes, he could see how fresh and cool she looked.

He lit a cigarette with his gold lighter.

Did she like her job?

Yes, she did.

Did her husband mind her working?

She wasn't married.

Oh?

No.

He was sure she would have been.

She showed him her bare ring finger. Front and back.

He made a joke about the common sense of the young men in Acorn.

She laughed and shrugged. She waited, her pencil poised.

He imagined the heat was much more bearable in the evening with a cool drink.

It was, she concurred.

He stood and turned to look out of the window in order to refocus his concentration.

From the second-floor window, he looked across to three old men on a shaded park bench in the town square. They wore no jackets and the collars of their white shirts were unbuttoned, they wore dark trousers and laced shoes, there were two canes between them. They were city men, maybe retired city fathers. Not farmers. They sat as if chewing their cuds, but otherwise were as inanimate as the Confederate flag that hung limp in the breezeless heat adjacent to the nearly two stories-high bronze confederate soldier in broadbrim hat, canteen at one hip, bayonet at the other, bed roll over his shoulder and across his body, his rifle held angled up from his waist, stationary in a forward stride atop the Greek-styled plinth facing north up Nobel street. It was a memorial to the vanquished Grand Army of the Republic, glorifying a futile pursuit. He had seen its like in nearly every sleepy hamlet or busting burg he had visited or passed through from his beginning six days ago at the capitol on his journey's end in Acorn.

Others of Acorn's residents made their way about the slow motion business of going to church.

He asked Evy if she minded if he took off his suit coat. They didn't have this sort of heat or humidity in Hartford.

She pleasantly did not object. He was the boss. She watched him as he did and hung it over the back of what normally was her boss's, Mister Pittsford's chair. He turned back to the window.

He prided himself on his observational skills and fact-gathering techniques and being able to order and put them in logical sequence without the use of written notes. His dictation to her briefly and concisely recalled his observations and conclusions from his arrival in the Heart of Dixie, detailing the politicians and farm and factory owners he had met and their council and concerns.

He had recapped his journey to the point of his reaching the convict camp in Acorn yesterday.

When he looked back her pad now rested on her left knee. It had been on her right.

Was he going too fast for her?

No. No. She was fine.

He smiled. They were almost done, he reassured her.

She waited.

He hoped that it didn't embarrass her but he was pleasantly surprised at how well they were—getting along—and how thoroughly professional she was. First rate. As good as any of the girls from the secretarial pool in the home office, many of whom had gone to the finest clerical schools in the north and east.

(Had that been a blush?)

Did she get a chance to travel much?

She didn't.

She should. He found traveling really uplifting. The places you saw, the things you learned—people you met.

He smiled.

She returned it.

Where were they? Oh, yes. He apologized for the unpleasant nature of the details and opinions he was about to express.

He summarized that the conditions in the work camp were deplorable. They were below even the minimal standards that passed muster in this forsaken region.

He gestured to Evy to indicate, "Present company is excepted." Her head was down and she did not respond.

"There is a camp supervisory guard in particular who encapsulates the vices and what virtues there might exist here. His name does not matter. As to his manner, he typifies in mentality and civility an individual as lowbred as any under my command during my time in the service with the 1st Division in France in the Great War.

"I offer a direct quotation: 'A whipped dog is an obedient dog.'

"The supervisor's defense of his use of corporal punishment was reasoned and spirited. I have my suspicions, given my extensive military experience with this grade of southern soldier, that his argument to justify his prescription of floggings as a remedy for their transgressions had less to do with work-related discipline than with particular quirks of his inbred character.

"In summary, it is his argument that these workers, after being released from his supervision, are more likely to respect the law than when they came to him. There is no empirical data to substantiate that.

"As a sidebar, it was alleged by other guards that this individual engaged several of those in his charge in unauthorized work to improve the property that he rents from the Corporation, including the digging and construction of a privy. I suspect that this practice is also fairly widespread among guards, although I only have anecdotal evidence.

"Paragraph. The above has led me to four conclusions.

"Paragraph. First, throughout the state there is a single voice singing a single note: the white man must control the colored man because the white man is superior to the colored man."

Three stragglers, a lean countrywoman and her two scrawny daughters in cheap gingham dresses, hurried up the street toward the church.

"Conclusions. One. The agrarian south rushed headlong into a war with the industrial north and lost. This fact is lost on the vast majority of the population here. It is now trying to stumble backward toward some foggy memory of its antebellum nobility— that last word in quotes," he told her.

"Paragraph. Conclusion two," he continued. "On the face of it, they are right in their assessment of the inferiority of their Negroes—those last two words also in quotation marks. This paternalistic belief by whites, top to bottom on the chain of command, so entangles them in trying to keep their Negroes down, that they have fallen into a pit with them.

"Paragraph. Conclusion three. They are so ignorant in their half-wit worship of a soil-based economy that Alabamians are incapable of looking beyond the soon ending boom in cotton. This generation is not capable of leading Alabama into the next phase of profitability that Kimbrough Works is embarking upon. Therefore they are a burden. We will have to bring down our own people to manage things. The manner in which the natives here are involved should for the most part be limited to controlling the Negroes."

He stopped. A shaggy brown dog was trailing two young boys, each with a bottle of Coca Cola. The old men were still sitting on the bench.

He turned to her. It was to give him time to look at her and for her to look at him.

"Evy, let me ask you a question. Not as a very pretty young woman— but as—a girl of Alabama. If you don't have an answer just say so. I certainly won't think less of you."

He got a cigarette from his pack and lighted it, intending to give her time to consider his question and formulate an answer.

He sighed as if he wasn't sure how to phrase it. "What do you think of a people who from the topmost to the lowest down lack the foresight to put useless traditions behind them?"

He smiled and let the smoke curl from his mouth. "Remember this is all confidential, just between the two of us."

"I think they're fucked," she said. She flipped the spiral-bound cover of her notepad shut. "Just like you're planning to fuck me, you Yankee son of a bitch."

He was not sure if the twitch at the corners of her bee-stung lips was a smile or a feisty grimace.

He stubbed out his cigarette in the ashtray with the Kimbrough Works symbol under glass in its center.

"So now . . . " he said.

# Pearl and Son

# 10

# A Pint for a Dime

## Church Creek, Alabama, 1925

Pearl knew she was breaking her granddaddy's heart, and wasn't he, still, after all those years, trying to spit the taste of being a child in slavery out of his mouth, having suffered enough? But she knew in her heart it was her only choice, given her few givens.

Papa, her granddaddy, loved her as much, she believed, as he loved her grandmother, Mama, and he only wanted what he believed was best for her. But what he thought was best, she thought, was the second-worst thing in the world.

Papa knew when to plant and when to pluck; when to weep and laugh and mourn and when to hug. Papa knew how to talk to the white man. Papa knew about Farmer Moore. Papa said Farmer Moore had all of the qualities could be wanted in a husband. When the roll for heaven was called, Farmer Moore would be at the front of the line of the saved. Farmer Moore was stable as a rock wall and was as rooted as an oak in the colored community of Church Creek, Alabama. Farmer Moore worked his own land. He was a deacon in the church. He was a widower with a young daughter. Farmer Moore needed a wife.

Farmer Moore had seen Pearl at church and he thought favorably on her, Papa said. But being the decent, God-fearing man that Farmer Moore was, and being sensitive to the ways of the community, Farmer Moore had prayed on it and counseled with the preacher and the elder women of the congregation, and they had advised him that given his situation and the needs of the season, six months would be a decent period before he spoke to Papa regarding Pearl.

There was no question whether or not Pearl felt anything for Farmer Moore. She felt nothing for him, he who had been on earth almost twice her seventeen years. She thought what Papa and Farmer Moore thought of her was not as a person, but as an answer. Who could ride beside him in that fine buggy? Who could sit beside him in the front pew on Sunday mornings? Who could mother his young daughter? Who could cook his meals and wash his clothes and fill his bathtub and rub his feet and warm his bed? Who could be an extra pair of bleeding hands in the time to cast away stones and to plow and to pluck and to worry with him through the weighing in and the standing by at settling up?

The once-a-month preacher from Church Creek, who had offered guidance to Farmer Moore and to Papa and who had baptized her in the river when she was thirteen, hollered his warning against an afterlife of eternal agony in unforgiving hellfire against those who did not honor their Papa and Mama, and live long on the land given them, but how, she wondered in the pitch of the sweaty darkness of night, how could that not be better than where she was, doing what she had to do?

As Pearl saw it Lucifer got kicked out of heaven and his evil had landed on earth and took root, and cotton sprouted, and that was the birth of Hell on earth—and the next thing anybody knew Adam and Eve got kicked out of Eden.

Lord *Jesus* she wished that a snake would slither along and bite her, she hated picking cotton so! Even to think of it made her well up, made her tremble, near to nauseous. Starting at six years old, with Pa telling her to hush up that sniveling, gal. Gentle, but firm. You'll get used to it. It ain't that bad. But it was. Worse. Worse as worse could possibly be.

Razor-edged bolls pricking her stinging cuticles like peppered tips on the devil's pitchfork, digging clean to the bone, her sin-red blood dripping like an angel's tears. She hated, but couldn't spit out, the saltiness of her blood as she tried in vain to suck away the hurt. You wouldn't think a thing that small could cause that much pain.

Sharp as the little needles Mama used sewing stitch after little itty bitty stitch, sewing herself to near blindness in the kerosene light doing the handwork that white ladies just *loved loved loved* on their garments they strutted and bragged that their gal had made for them.

Many a Monday and Tuesday morning Pearl had a mind to just throw herself headfirst over into Mama's boiling big black tub of wash water right over in with the white folks' bloomers and drawers or fine cottons and linens, let somebody jab her down with the hickory stirring limb if she tied to rise up, till she just boiled away to grease.

Lord Jesus.

*And*, then too, there was the sun.

The always close, blinding, sweltering, blistering, strength- and soul-sapping sun, surrounding-close, the breath of the devil riding her back close, so she was trapped, choking, like during one of her lung-wrenching asthma attacks, trapped at the smoldering blueyellowred center of a burning lump of coal that would only burn itself, finally, to gray ash, like her mama had been; who while trying to teach her to tie her shoes, her dress tail was caught by licking, leaping flames in the fireplace, and who running down the road, a blazing ball, getting bigger, brighter, louder, maybe, hopefully, already dead when a white man in a wagon happened along and put out the flames with a blanket.

Lord Jesus!

The spirit had never touched her, not in church, not when she had been taken to the river and been baptized, not when they knelt at night and Papa prayed for the Lord their souls to keep, and not way over in the restlessness of those star-speckled deep country nights, yawning and sooty and bottomless and breathless black, her looking at a twinkling star then closing her eyes and wondering if her troubles would ever be over, then reopening them. She was never sure if the star she saw was the last one she'd wished on just before. She just knew she felt empty and small. Small and empty and about the size of one of the star pinpricks even as the country darkness expanded in her lungs and rose up into her throat in heaving asthma attacks.

Through those nights Pearl wept and sought support, but her dreams got taken hold of, and like Jacob she wrestled against thought and flesh and the powers of infallible light and erring darkness, until daybreak, to be awakened, exhausted, Papa shaking her in time to drag her slow self to the field.

If, as Papa and the preacher said, there was a God in heaven to help her have her way, then no child that *ever* suckled her nipple (or man either, for that matter) would be associated with picking cotton. Blaspheming or not, she prayed that to the memory of mama Aurelia.

One of the few things that sustained her was Beatrice.

Beatrice and Pearl were related. Cousins. Beatrice was a daughter of the son of Papa's dead brother. Beatrice and Pearl pretended they were sisters. Pearl didn't have a sister and all of Beatrice's sisters were gone and married, so Papa would let her to visit Beatrice sometimes, depending on the season, for a week or so, even after Beatrice married James.

Pearl loved to go stay with them because James liked whiskey and she did too.

For one thing it helped cut the phlegm in her asthma.

Around there it was against the law to sell whiskey to a Negro in such an amount that he could have enough to sell it to other Negroes and cut into some white man's profit, but James had a contact and he would go all the way to town on the mule and get it. They had what was called saloons in town but they wouldn't sell to him but he got it from his contact and brought it home.

It was in a jug, a gallon jug. But James could get whiskey delivered too. That was where Reece came in. Reece didn't care about drinking whiskey; Reece sold whiskey to make money. Reece would bring it to you, but you couldn't let the police know what was going on. He would bring James a gallon for two dollars and he would bring Viola a quart for a quarter, pint for a dime.

Papa said what-ever happened first or good for us (us meaning coloreds, coloreds way out in the country, miles from Church Creek), Papa said, with what sounded like the wisdom of Solomon, Farmer Moore would play a key part in it—said it to Ma, but so Pearl could hear it over in the row she was working.

The preacher said lazy hands made a man poor, but diligent hands brought wealth. Papa would say Farmer Moore's busy hands had made him prosperous, but Reece, if Papa had known of him, Reece, who during the day made it mostly by hiring himself out as a carpenter. He worked for white and for colored, whoever could pay him, as long as it wasn't related to farm labor. If Papa had known of Reece who gloomed at night, slipping from one side of the line of the proper and the legal to the other, he would have disapproved of his serpentine ways. Papa would have said Reece's hands were slothful, and because of that, Reece, in the end, would pay fourfold for the gains from his wickedness.

As Pearl saw it, Reece's hands were only lazy in God's, Papa's, the preacher's, and the white man's eyes. Bringing whiskey wasn't all Reece did you couldn't let the police know about. Reece gambled. He played cards and cast dice and committed other breaches. He didn't do it for fun, he did it for money. Reece, after the sun went down, was industrious as an ant or an owl or a bat. Reece told Pearl that his best money, his easy money, was made after dark, when God's and Papa's and the preacher's and the white man's eyes were shut and their hands were idle.

In turn Pearl told Reece, while they were sitting in the dark on a bottoms up tin tub in Beatrice and James's yard, whispering—Reece thought it was so the other couple wouldn't hear her, but it was so he had to lean close enough that he felt the humidity of her breath on his ear—It was way past time, she whispered, way, way past time that he dusted the Church Creek dust off his boots and went to where he could hone the razor's edge of his knack for skirting accepted conventions on the strop of some big city—bigger than Church Creek, Acorn say, where he'd bragged he had friends and kinfolk, and by doing, increase his possibilities and profits. And when it came down to it the only way, she explained to him, that those sanctified and righteous back country hypocrites could or would appreciate how smart and resourceful he was, would be after he had left them behind in the thistles and thorns of Church Creek.

At sunset on their day of elopement, a Five & Ten-cent store ring on her finger, Pearl was standing beside Reece on Nobel Street, Acorn, Alabama, which looked like it was long as a country mile. Along both sides of the paved street there were buildings with businesses of every kind. They were two and three stories high, with awnings over their entrances. Parked in the wide street there were wagons and horse-drawn buggies, as fine or finer than any that would ever be driven by Farmer Moore, and there were automobiles. Acorn was something to see and somewhere to be seen if there *ever* was such a place.

And Pearl was in it.

And, Bless Jesus, there was not a cotton patch in sight.

# 11

# Grits

## Acorn, Alabama, 1928

One of the big colored churches was having a camp meeting. The church was maybe half a mile away from where Pearl and Reece and their baby were living near Acorn.

Reece ordered some whisky so he would have it there to sell to folks.

So this particular night he went up to the church to put out the word to those he wanted to tell.

People were coming and buying pint bottles for a quarter and going on back.

A fellow, Bubba, came and bought a bottle.

Knock, knock, knock.

"Who knock?"

"Bubba."

Reece got it from the truck where he had it and gave it to Bubba. Bubba paid and went on.

After a little while, knock, knock, knock.

"Who knock?"

"Bubba."

Same thing. Reece got it and gave it to him and Bubba paid and went on.

Pearl asked, "How well you know him?"

"Bubba? Bubba all right."

Pearl didn't like him and told Reece so.

"You always think you know something. Bubba all right."

Some more people came and then knock, knock, knock.

"Who?"

"Bubba."

Pearl whispered to Reece, "Don't you sell him no more liquor. Because there's something behind it."

Reece waved her off and opened the door.

Bubba said, "Can I get some more?"

Reece sold him that third bottle. It had gotten late and Reece said he was going up to the meeting and find his brothers Champ and Perce.

His brothers were working at the Kimbroughs' place farming. They were rooming with Pearl and Reece. They had been at the meeting the whole evening. Up there trying to meet some girls.

Soon after Reece left: knock, knock, knock.

"Open this door, it's the police."

Pearl couldn't do anything but open it.

Two big white Acorn policemen walked in, looking around. "Where is that liquor you been selling?"

Pearl picked the baby up and told the police she wasn't selling whisky.

One of the policemen walked straight to the trunk at the foot of the bed where the whisky was.

"That's my whisky," Pearl said. "I'm sick. I have asthma and the doctor put me on whisky."

"You ought to know better than to lie to me, gal."

They took the four or five bottles that were there and left, saying they were taking the whiskey to city hall.

When Reece, Champ, and Perce came back she told them what had happened.

She said she thought it was because Bubba was a police spy and that he had turned Reece up. Reece didn't argue the point. He said he was going down in the country to his Uncle Johnny's to keep the police from getting him. He tried to get Champ and Pearce to go with him, but they said they didn't have any reason and they did not go. They were both a little high and they went on to bed.

Sometime after midnight the police came back. Pearl got up and let them in.

They police asked where Reece was.

Pearl said she didn't know.

When would he be back?

Pearl said she didn't know.

The police told Champ and Perce to get up. They were going to take them down.

Still laying in the bed Champ said, "I ain't going nowhere. I didn't sell no whisky and I ain't going nowhere."

The policemen were standing there with their big guns on their belts.

"Oh, yeah, you going."

Perce got up and said, "Aw, Champ, quit being stubborn. Get on up." Trying to laugh with the policemen. "He just mad 'cause one of them church gals wouldn't go off with him."

"You'll be all right if you go now, Champ," Pearl told him. "You'll be all right."

Champ and Pearce finally got dressed and the police took them out to lock them up.

Reece showed up late that next morning, Monday.

He had word that the people Champ and Perce worked for had gone to City Hall and gotten his brothers out of jail so they could go on back to work.

"I ain't got no white folks to stand for me," he said. "You got to pack up," he told Pearl, "we'll go on back home . . ."

She cut him off. "I'm *at* home."

"Naw, naw. We got to go back to Church Creek for a while till this blow over and then we'll see . . ."

Pearl said she'd already seen what she needed to see.

She was cooking bacon in a skillet on the stove.

"I am not going back to work on no farm."

"But I got to go back till this blow over, Pearl."

"What did I tell you when we left the country?"

He thought before he answered. "That you wasn't ever going back."

She forked the bacon over to its other side. She nodded.

The baby was crawling under the table by his daddy's feet.

"Did you take that for a joke?"

"Well I got to go back or go to jail."

"Going back'll be the same to me as me being sent to jail. I ain't. That's my last word on it."

Reece played what he thought was his hole card. "How you think you going to make it with you and the baby—without me? What you going to do?"

She turned to face him. "The same way I left the country is the same way I'll leave you. Now you want grits, or not?"

# 12

# The Flowers That Attracted the Bees

## Mardalwil County, Bantock, Alabama, 1933

She'd just shown up, saying she'd heard that Mr. Fong needed a washer-woman and chambermaid. They did not know she had heard it from some of the people had been around her sorry husband, Reece, who'd done some business of one kind or another for the Chinaman.

Pearl was hard working and bright and she'd brought her little boy with her, not that it was the proper place for him, or her, or them either, but he knew how to keep out of the way when he should, and how to make everybody's day brighter with his smiling and talking and everything while Pearl washed and swept and swabbed and emptied and aired out and listened.

Mistaking her for a wayfaring innocent, the girls—Victoria, White Mary, Iris, Sara, and Alice, and sometimes Ilene—took her under their ruffled wing. She listened to their stories of what not to do, paths not to take, temptations to avoid, and ways not to be in order not to follow their fate.

Then, after not too long, they listened to her and her story. Her husband. What he did. How she couldn't stand it anymore. How she got away from him but had no place to go. How she and her son were turned away from door after door of houses, businesses, and churches until they arrived at Mr. Fong's establishment and were taken in. They listened when she told them she wasn't going keep on being treated the way she had been, and added, they didn't either, far as that went.

What?

Then she told them who they were: they were the flowers that attracted the bees, it was their honey made the money, and although they only believed her a little bit they began to listen to her to save and savor as much as they could while they could, because they knew, in their innate knowing, that one day the mother and son would be gone, a long way from there, and not south. They didn't know how, but they believed Pearl did, and that they—Victoria, White Mary, Sara, Iris, and Alice, and sometimes, depending on the demand, Ilene—would still be in Mr. Fong's, or on the outskirts of some place worse, if they were anywhere at all.

They asked her things and got straight, commonsense answers that anybody else would have given them if they'd had anybody else to ask, not that they could do anything with the advice, being as they were stuck and sinking where they were, doing what they were doing.

Little by little they came to believe Pearl had more husk, was the smartest and maybe savviest and surely the least afraid of any colored woman they had ever known, and could do something they couldn't do, she could reach the Chinaman in his fewer and fewer moments of clarity in the cloud of dope smoke he floated in night and day. They believed she could make the Chinaman listen to her—and maybe even make something happen, and none among them might could do that.

It wasn't much they were asking, knowing it wasn't much they were going to get, but what there was, it was Pearl was their go-between, speaking on their behalf, taking their side, putting it so the Chinaman could see how it was to his benefit.

—What—?

A less contentious whore, she reminded Mr. Fong, was a harder working whore. She told him that fines for infractions rather than beatings, that an extra day for the girls' monthlies, that an occasional kind word would, overall, improve their dispositions. It would keep things from all the time being upset. He would have more satisfied girls, more satisfied customers, and more coins for his big boss, the Kimbrough Company's coffer.

It all must have made some sense to the Chinaman because he didn't stop her or the girls from any of their suggestions, and things quieted down and business picked up.

# 13

# Mr. Fong's Establishment

## Bantock, Alabama, c. 1933

Mud-moving motherfuckers; niggers so tough the mules was jealous.

Taming nature by force and the belief, come Hell or high water, they could do it with their grit and pig-iron toughness as they imposed their will on land and beasts, on each other, and Lord help them, on the snatch housed at Mr. Fong's two-story pussy emporium out at the end of the no-named road run back through the clump of red maples in that narrow neck of Bantock, Alabama.

Iris, lip bleeding, already hushed and rushed from her crib by the head woman who was standing there now, the lantern held face high in her left hand, the door flap draped over her arm. He saw no one with her to back her play. No man, no nosey whores, or curious others from his crew.

From downstairs the vet from the Europe war was bugling a slow draggy dirge he'd otherwise been tapping his toe to.

She motioned him back, back up against the wall. Naked from waist to ankles and manacled by his jumper and drawers, he shuffled the four steps back.

"She bit me," he said. He held up his left hand with the bloody teeth marks.

"Did you pay her to?"

Her right arm out of sight behind her, a pistol in her hand sure as dog shit.

"No."

"So she bit you 'cause you hit her."

Well the house woman wasn't the only one with a weapon. Thing was, his razor, effective as a pistol up close, was in the breast pocket of his jumper, his jumper in the tangle around his muddy boots.

He'd been mad since early noon. It was all Big Pepper's fault.

"She's got soft feelings and is sometimes nervous," the woman said, talking about Iris, "but she's eager to please, if asked right."

Her voice so low he had to strain to hear her. She nodded for him to pull up his clothes to cover himself.

"Either way," the woman continued, "I'm all the discipline Iris needs."

He had seen her signal to cover himself but still stood, unbending.

Mad at Big Pepper for causing the delay. Mad at Walking Boss for sparking a needless strain for some outcome not worth the purpose. They knew Walking Boss was the Boss; the knife-edge of the system's sword that hung over them by a thread. It was a lesson learned when the birth blood was being washed from them. They knew they were the two-legged mules who made possible the advantage and wealth given to whites but denied to them. They needed no reminder, like they needed no help to reestablish the lost rhythm Big Pepper caused. They knew how to stack up sufficient sandbags of numbness to wall off the individual and collective unconsciousness, and turn *themselves* back into the coordinated, single-purposed beast, unburdened by the nagging consideration of the uncompensated nature of their labor.

But still Walking Boss made it worse by putting it into words. Saying he stood for no woman-weak, drag-ass niggers in his crew!

Her telling him she hoped he'd enjoyed his time with that child, because if he raised his hand inside Mr. Fong's establishment again, Iris's would've been his last dip in some snatch. She didn't limit her prediction to Mr. Fong's.

The time didn't seem proper for arguing with the house woman on the fine distinctions of it, but Iris, with her mule-muscled flanks, and her knowing when to Gee and Haw was a far piece, in years or ways, from being a child.

Big Pepper was ass-dragging, true. And, interdependent as they were, it *didn't* take but one of the twenty-odd of them to throw the whole business off just a hair, just enough to pull them out of the rhythm: skiff loaders piling dug up bottom clay, for the skinners to cart up the embankment, for the dumpers to pile, for the graders to form into an artificial breach against the future of the rising of the Daddy of Rivers, fickle as a pretty woman. On the orders of somebody in a suit in an office somewhere the decision was made to corral the mighty river to man's puny desire for control of its flow and floods. And against all sense, the way they do when they get something in their minds, that anonymous white man's order moved through the boards, committees, and panels of federal, state, municipal, and private agencies; was mapped and charted and graphed by cartographers and engineers, was parceled and with sufficient palms greased; was awarded to the Kimbrough Company, and finally, down through their board and committees and offices to the Walking Boss. And it trickled down to them, down to the levee niggers, clothed in mud, head to boots, to get it done. For somebody's reward, but sure not theirs, sure as hell not theirs, to—season after season, from near light till near black—block, divert or dam the river's natural run: a human-plus-mule machine, clicking and ticking, all hands moving forward, with the regularity of a high-priced Elgin watch, or the switching hips of a black gal under her washed and bleach-thinned cotton summer dress.

The levee niggers took pride in their self-controlled effectiveness, like a close-ordered army unit. It was one of the few prides they could strut, and Big Pepper *was* dragging, dragging ass and throwing the whole mechanism off. And Walking Boss, who was a watchmaker when it came to the regulation of the labors of his crew of mud daubers, was about to make an adjustment; fine-tune his muscle and blood apparatus when *something*, some sorrowful thing in Big Pepper sprung loose.

Maybe he was sick, or, maybe the hardest rolling of their hard rolling crew was, God forbid, tired. Maybe sick and tired, and that caused his breaking the rhythm, or maybe the rhythm just broke, the way the river just crested and overflowed, and the break allowed his mind to wander, off back home, and the un-dammed thought was so sweet till *whooo*—he just couldn't make himself pretend like he was satisfied.

*Ooooowhhooo*—for never being able, one time, to walk in and slap down a wad of dollars on her dresser, tell his woman it was *hers* without condition or fret, or for missing the sight of her boiled white under-things sun-drying on the line, or for a son he could make a meaningful promise to and keep his word, or lack of a cold drink whenever one crossed his mind—for the moment, or maybe till kingdom come, he just couldn't make peace with the truth of his life and prospects. And that set off the hair-triggered humming from deep inside him. More holler than hum, *Oh Lord*—more moan than holler—*Lord*—and longer, *Lord Lord*—as if being squeezed out of him like sweet potato meat from its skin, wavering up from his bowels through his belly, up his windpipe, and out his mouth and nose.

Big Pepper wasn't holy-roller-tongue-talking like the sanctified, his humming wasn't sent from On-High, but dredged from deep below the layers of earth and clay they skinned and moved. And they knew what he was feeling even without the words.

"Oooooooooooooooooooooooo-*Ooooooooooo*," wavy as washboard tin.

"Whew*hoooooooo*, ummmmmuu*ummmmmMMM*mmmmed."

More yowling like a bobcat or yodel than just a holler, and the others, the hard- muscled, hard-eyed, hard-fisted crew couldn't listen, and they couldn't not.

Wailing wailing wailing for all he was worth, for all the next to nothing he was worth. Which between Jim Crow, the commissary, and the walking boss came to just a, a gut-language humming nigger on his knees—grunts and groans strangled—from deep, deep, down, down in him by a system with more constricting arms than an octopus. Something ignited in him like a slow-burning fuse from the end of his umbilical cord, tiny sparks giving no warning, as it smoldered along its length till it exploded, or imploded in Big Pepper.

"We do business here," the woman said. Her point was that beating on one of her girls wasn't prohibited, but its execution was, necessarily, negotiable, as was everything; it was never the possibility that was in question, it was the price.

He was still standing full up, jaybird-naked from the waist to his ankles.

This fore noon, he thought, if he'd had that pistol she sure as shit got hid behind her back, he'd've snapped one off in that cracker Walking Boss; no maybe drawed a bead on him and said his name and give him time to be clear on who was doing the saying. Then squeeze the first one off, *POW*! Open a nickel-sized peephole between his milky, peckerwood eyes; see who whistled coconut head then.

Drawing blood costs extra, she explained. Seventy-five cents.

Him taller by shoulders and his head than her, and her only a couple strides from his callused, big-knuckled fist, but, he thought, a pistol behind her back, or his name wasn't Oscar, and the Mississippi wasn't muddy.

Grave-silent as all noises had stopped: the song-hollers and hooting hoopers and curses, men grunts, mule brays, suck of boots pulled from the mud, exhortations of the bosses, creak of trace lines and whinge of clay-loaded scoops hauled up the quay.

Silent.

The only sound was Big Pepper whose only words when there was a break in his hollers—"*Too much, too much . . .*"

Lying there rag-lank, without whim or wheeze, too pitiful for even the bosses to beat.

Coconut head nigger, Walking Boss said, calls his-self a levee man.

He shook his head in disgust and whistled for them to heft and haul him off, and for a twice-sized nigger named Natchez to step in Big Pepper's place and to keep the rolling going, keep the rolling on.

Walking Boss reigned his roan into an about face; and its tail swishing back and forth, ambled with a steady gait on up the road, a ways on up the road.

It came to Oscar, as ashamed of it as he could be, that the bile of the memory of Big Pepper was no longer *as* sour on his palate. The gorge of the sight of his work mate lying curled like a baby, the sound from deep down wretched out, or worse, shriveled inside him, was swallowed now; only an after-collard green's acidity lingering at the back of his throat and an acidy slosh in his upper gut. Getting some stank from Iris had been his maybe too easy antidote after the forced witness of the sand run out of a man.

As a way of introduction, "My name," he said, not that she cared, "is Oscar Ashby. What's yours?"

"Pearl," she said offhanded.

"I tote my share of dirt yonder to the levee."

Trying to tell her something about himself—about the self-betrayal he felt for, one, the work he did every day; for two, having near douched Big Pepper out of his mind so quick; and for three, for just now, with that big-hipped whore he'd hit. But no, the house woman with the pistol didn't care anymore about him or his name than Walking Boss did; damn if he stayed, double damn him when he was gone.

"I don't know what got wrong," he said, the sound of bugled blues oozing up through the planed pinewood flooring.

"I didn't come with mean intentions. Reckon that was just the fool in me."

There was something in the hallway behind her, moving, something small. Had it been there all the time?

Oscar Ashby didn't have the time or the words to say his sorrow at having hit the gal. Neither was it in his disposition to linger too long or too deep on his concern for Big Pepper. All notions of unease or connection along fraternal tributaries had to be blocked. Just as he had to dam off considerations of that part that was in him that might admit to being brother to the river—free as the water spirit, seeking its own free way—but channeled, leveed, rerouted by his brute effort in concert with Jim Crow, toward intentions not the river's own. Neither did he let himself think that was what Big Pepper, who had been the hardest roller on Kimbrough Company's crew, had thought or questioned that morning, and that was what breached the barricade and broke loose the still water deep inside him. And Oscar Ashby did not consider that not asking or insisting on the need for an answer was the difference between Big Pepper, *God knows where he was*, and him, feeling fine, fresh off a prime piece of Mr. Fong's cooter.

Even the (after) thought that he was probably not going to be with Iris again—not at regular rates if at all, it wasn't so much *her* but who she reminded him of—his future way blocked by the woman with a pistol, probably cocked, who had him standing before her like a schoolboy who hadn't learnt his times-twos. Hell, it'd be a bedtime story in camp to laugh at when the darkness got too quiet. How he had to stop himself from saying Yes ma'am.

Something short behind her. Still. Maybe it was a midget, no, maybe a toddling child.

Talking, almost making conversation now; for the tone of it, they could've been neighbors in a front yard.

"You roughneck levee niggers don't know moderation," she said.

A smile blew across her mouth like a breeze over a dandelion. She nodded at his Johnson. "Properly used, poking poor Iris with that pike should've pained her enough to suit you."

His pride rose as he bent for his drawers. The bugle playing downstairs like she was playing with him. Was she letting him off the hook?

His drawers up. She was watching him intensely, but with the pretended ease the bosses sometime used late in the shift.

He smiled as he pulled his overalls up and hunched his shoulders in the straps.

"Money on the wood," she said. Her way of confirming that his evening in one of Mr. Fong's cribs was over unless he wanted to force something, and if he did the consequences were his to bear—with the odds, as always, favoring the house.

He reached with slow deliberation into his side pocket, trying to show he meant to incite no more punishable harm to the whores, management, or property. He fished out his last three quarters, leaving him a nickel and a dime, and laid them on the chair seat where she indicated with her nod.

Mr. Fong's policy was for his customers to leave his establishment with nothing but a smile, she said, referring to the fifteen cents.

He wasn't much for drinking, and as far as gambling, he wasn't worth the change from a penny.

The way he'd messed that up in here with Iris, she said, might signal his luck was pointing in a new direction.

He declined. Too many limber wrist magicians with them dice to suit him. And that pig piss passed off as whisky wasn't to his south Alabama taste. So, jellyroll was the prime attraction for him there, and look like he'd fucked that up, so he reckoned he'd hump on back to camp, if it was all the same to her.

She told him he might want to see to putting some iodine on his hand, there being no telling where Iris's mouth had been.

As she stepped back to let him pass, the dark creases the lamplight etched into her face from the distance disappeared and he saw she was not much more than out of her teens, if that. Younger by years than Iris or him. In her moving back, the lantern light swept the hallway. Behind her he saw it was a boy child'd been doing the moving, maybe four, five years old. Head tilted to one side, cocked like a coonhound waiting on his master's command. His face was only illuminated for a second; only long enough to glimpse what looked like burns and scar tissue across his closed eyes. Maybe it was just a trick of the wavering coal oil light.

By way of farewell and explanation Oscar Ashby said, "I had a shitty day."

"Bout like mine," she answered.

The child moved out from behind her, but still in her shadow.

"You feel bad," the child said. Said it in a man's voice, in a voice that sounded as if it was inside Oscar Ashby's head, as if it was rising in a rush, rising.

"What?"

"You feel bad about what you did."

It was his own voice coming out of the child's mouth. And he heard it above the sound of the rising in him that was about to break.

"You *need* to say you sorry."

Oscar Ashby turned from the young woman. She couldn't be more than twenty years old, he thought as he rushed off down the dark hall. Pass the tarp-covered doorways. To stagger, step by pine plank step, one hand on the knot-holed wall to steady himself against a non-drunken stagger, down into the room below, where he was called by that bugled blues being tooted by that nigger from the Great War in Europe; down, away from the young woman; down, away from that voice, away, before they witnessed the flood breaking in him.

He made it to the door and out and skulked off outside to some shadowed pocket of silence, his back against the knotty wall, and let the slurred and stretched blue notes thunder out of that battered horn and wash down, wash down on him, down like mud-making clouds of rain.

# 14

# The Hopper Hotel

## Ernestsville, Virginia, c. 1934

It had all happened so unexpectedly fast. Giddy fast. And Rachel Ann was still in the center of it, spinning, as when she and her sister, Catherine Ann, had held each other's hands and spun themselves around and around on the front lawn, leaning back, faces up to the sunny sky, spinning, a top of sisters, until they were so dizzy they stumbled around like drunk uncles after a cotillion and collapsed laughing like hyenas.

The suddenness of the proposal, the rushed civil ceremony presided over by his first cousin, the justice of the peace of Acorn—people would think they "had" to get married—whispered Aunt Rose to Aunt Emily, and then moving away so suddenly—all because her beaux Whitmore Charlton Kimbrough, of the north Alabama Kimbroughs, had been promoted to go to Hartford, Connecticut to take up the new position of vice president of Kimbrough Properties and had to be there by Monday noon to sign some paper. So they were in a two-car caravan driving through the night, Rachel Ann in the backseat of the Madam X Cadillac Sedan next to Pearl, the dusky young gal of about Rachel Ann's age. Pearl, Rachel Ann had learned just that afternoon, was to be the author of Rachel Ann's night of deflowering.

Southern Belles, blue-veined women of the south, were in their honored and privileged place by God's dictate and the efforts of all good, true white men. That notion, like sweet tea, had been consumed by Rachel Ann all of her life. Everything that was done below the Mason-Dixon line was done for them. And she understood that her part in it was to be, first and foremost, appreciative. To let that appreciation glow through her every waking gesture, word, thought, and act was her recompense. Surely that was little to pay for the enormity of the gift that she of the blue veins had so lovingly and totally been given. Surely.

And just as surely, and blasphemously, she was a hostage of her own power, her cherished virginity, and was therefore, in her blaspheming, prayerful that there was a way *out* of the crystal box she and her kind had been imprisoned in by southern white men's need to be thought of as their women's protectors. Those men, their men, said she and her kind— mothers, sisters, aunts, nieces, cousins, and brides—were treasures loved above all else, held higher than all other, to be guarded against the possibility of defilement with every fiber from the vile desires of any male other than their kind. So it was ultimately not about the women for themselves, that their men protected them, but because the women were the procreators, the bearers of the seeds of the next generation of men. It was not wild desire, licentious love, impious lust for the women that drove this protectiveness; it was vanity, conceit, and calculated, iron-fisted possessiveness, like the ownership of valued land or livestock.

Rachel Ann had overheard some negro man say one time to another colored man of a colored woman passing on the square that, She was the kind of woman turn water to whiskey, turn tin to solid gold, and if she would just let him get a *sniff* he would bargain with the devil about his sinning soul.

Rachel Ann had turned too late to see the woman the man was talking about. But secretly, that was the kind of woman Rachel Ann wanted to be. A new kind of southern white woman. Not trashy, but not either like the proud, devout white women like her mama and Aunt Emily, and her Aunt Rose and dear, sweet Aunt Alma. Sapless, superior ladies concerned with pure and proper and *de-corum*, looking down on every-body and everything from up on that top roost where her daddy and her Uncle Earl and Uncle Wallace had put them, and where spinster Aunt Alma got a boost and hand up from her sisters. Put there to get them away from the men so that they, the men, could go where they could quit being cavalier gentlemen, and do what men did in as much peace and freedom and privacy as they could enjoy without the presence of their burdensome cackling women, who were like clothes with cockle-bur linings.

Rachel Ann wanted to be the new white woman who showed her new husband (and the Yankees), a new non-maidenly southern woman who retained her mystery of eternal virginal-heroine-hood that they worshipped, and yet to be the other side of her—the dark pleasure, fire-desire.

Rachel Ann contended that her one possibility, the one stone that would kill two birds, the escaping of her societal role and the gaining of individual recognition from her guardian benefactors, was the way of sass and all its possibilities, as practiced by the colored minxes that nurtured her and her mother and aunts and grandmothers back to their beginnings in the cradle. The outwardly cheerful, ostensibly devoted colored women who cleaned, cooked, and raised the children of the whites. Seemingly loving them.

Setting out W.C. had said, in the way he said everything, without thought of the possibility of contradiction, "the boy will ride in the lead car with me for a while, so you and Miss Rachel Ann can talk." Driving the Madame X with Rachel Ann and Pearl was Willie Dink Crawfoot, W.C.'s chauffeur, the unpleasant-looking negro who secretly tried to listen, but knew not to let his eye linger too long in the rear view mirror as the two mix-matched women, their heads together, whispered like best school chums.

Rachel Ann wondered if Pearl and Willie Dink could communicate, like night creatures, through unspoken colored telepathy. As she was being driven away from the only home she'd ever known toward the wilderness of the north, were they plotting for Willie Dink to suddenly swerve the big car down some cutoff, eluding the lead sedan being driven by her husband, and leave her, laid waste in a ditch, throat razor-cut from ear to ear, to roar off to the first big city and lose themselves in a black bottom forever?

But as titillating as that idea was, even the thought of it was not half as exciting as the scandalous knowledge she was receiving from Pearl.

Even with the faith of a true believer, there was no telling the nature of the reply to a prayer. Now Rachel Ann, through her carefully negotiated union with Mr. Whitmore Charlton Kimbrough, was the salvation of home and hearth and the preserver of her family's social and economical place and dignity, and was being initiated into the secret world of women. Not women like her dear mother. Silent, secretive as a saint, as Catholics said, but bless her, for all her bearing and decorum, she was flighty as a hummingbird, and deaf, dumb, and blind as her daughters were on matters that mattered.

That night in a hotel room in Ernestville, Rachel Ann would enter her honeymoon chamber. On that first stop of their two-car motorcade she would exchange her virginal blush for full womanhood. It was at the insistence of W. C. that she was, in the back seat of the Madame X, being tutored to enter not as a retiring southern flower but with the sass of the world of women such as Pearl.

Rachel Ann and younger sister Catherine Ann, when they were little more than hairless newts, whispering, their heads together, like with Pearl, shared nervous giggles at their tales of white knights with unscabbered swords, handles encrusted with jewels captured by his forefathers from a faraway land peopled by the likes of the exotic Scheherazade-ian girl seated beside her, with the exotic scents of the lusty wenches who opened themselves like morning glories to seduce and please the men who were the masters of the civilized world.

Rachel Ann, at W.C.'s request, had to be privy to the secrets of those feisty, brazen women, so he would be pleased and assured that he had gotten his money's worth, if not more.

*What*, Rachel Ann had long speculated, *was* the source of colored women's sass? How were they are able to stand up to their men (and some of ours) and to make them accept it! Mama never made dear daddy whistle or sing to himself, or feel low down as a snake's belly in a wagon rut, like the colored women could make their men do.

It was their sass that allowed them to be un-ruled and unruly, and to not care about work or responsibility. Because of their sass—she meant what she saw in the freedom of their movements—they invited being looked at and were free to acknowledge or ignore those looks by their choice, unafraid of opinion, good or bad. Their men were attracted to them not for their family name, or what they had—for they *had* nothing but *themselves*, their bodies and their laughter, the toss of their heads, the shine in their eyes. It was the sassy, sap-full women that seduced men to endure what *we* demanded of them—men who never had enough, as far as she knew, to spoil them.

She thought of them of a Saturday afternoon on the thoroughfare in scrap cloth head rags, knotted at the nape; dresses handed down from their employers; shiny, bare legs; or in store-bought frocks or worn dresses little more than Crocker sacks safety pinned together—but such garments seemed to transform their wearers' attitudes. And especially in their starched Sunday whites, white stockings on slim legs and polished white shoes; still, in the churchyard, with enough sass to, as she had heard them joke, make the preacher lay his Bible down!

The way they stood, hip thrust out, or one dusty bare foot upon the other, with hand or wrist on their waist, or wearing their hats angled in a way that if any white woman was to duplicate it she'd be called a common strumpet to her face.

Even at common tasks, there is a sass about them in the ease of their motions: chopping cotton or churning; stirring clothes in a wash pot and hanging them on a line; at the stove or ironing board; flinging corn to chickens, a baby on their hip; or, stepping aside, slow as sorghum, and defiant, as she passed.

It almost made Rachel Ann weep to think how much had been sacrificed to be better than them.

Pearl did not seem the domestic type. She was of another breed. Of the ones who were somehow able to support themselves with minimal or no contact with whites, at least the level of whites with whom Rachel Ann associated. Women who wore their pride like dime store perfume dabbed in secret places, proud not of what was set aside for them, or given to them, but because of who they were in the world, however narrow that world might have been. In her eyes it made Pearl all the more exciting and qualified.

She had not asked, let alone insisted, that Pearl fill in details of her background. Rachel Ann had heard only that she was a widow, she had a son blinded by an accident involving his father, and she had an encyclopedic knowledge of the mysteries of intimacy not even hinted at in Rachel Ann and her sister Catherine Ann's hot-eyed readings of Sappho.

# I

They had stopped for the night at a roadside inn in Ernestsville, Virginia.

Miss—Missus Rachel Ann, the night-new bride, had followed Willie Dink, toting the second load of their luggage, into the hotel and up to the Kimbroughs' room. Room 206 in the rear away from the highway side.

Mr. Whitmore Charlton Kimbrough and Pearl Moon, as she called herself, still stood in the circles of light beside the gas pumps in front of the Hopper Hotel. Her hands clutched around the top of the purse as if it were the rail of a sinking ship.

Three days ago Willie, who said he was Mister Kimbrough's chauffeur, showed up at Mister Fong's establishment saying he had come to fetch the Chinese man who ran the place. Mister Kimbrough wanted to speak with him. Pearl told the Negro, in his black suit, white shirt, and little black leather bow tie that Mister Fong was not well enough just then to see anyone, let alone be taken anywhere. Any messages to be given or rides taken were to be handled by her. She and the chauffeur went back and forth until she turned and walked away, leaving the room with him standing in it until she returned, putting on her coat and hat, telling a woman she called White Mary to watch her child for a bit: she was going for a ride, talk some business.

Mr. Whitmore Charlton Kimbrough, who managed the company heading the levee project, had asked and Pearl responded that mostly what was required of the women in the place his company provided for his workers' pleasure was that they be breathing and have a snatch. But yes, she added quickly, guessing at the intent of his conversation, yes, she could teach a young girl a thing or two. Thinking that he had spotted some young gal that he all but owned, and wanted her to be tutored in the rudiments that he had described. Her mistake was that the pupil he had in mind was to be his bride. She was the youngest daughter of the Sayres, another old Alabama family.

He'd asked how long would it take Pearl to be ready to accompany them to Hartford?

Long enough to collect her son and wake Mr. Fong up to say she quit.

He'd motioned for her to get to it.

And now there they were standing, at half past midnight, on the roadside in Ernest, Ohio, at the end of their first night's trip away from Acorn. Him in the center of the dull yellow circle of light from the hotel fixture on the porch overhang, her on the shadowed edge of it, and he was asking how her—conversation—with Missus Rachel Ann had gone.

Fine, she told him.

Willie Dink, back from toting the suitcases into the hotel, stood at the edge of the porch at the top of the stairs, silhouetted against the lobby light. He was wiping at his forehead with a soiled white handkerchief.

Mister Kimbrough stepped on and ground his cigarette into the concrete, then moved up the two steps, stopping beside his chauffeur to say a few words too low for Pearl to hear. Dink nodded, looking toward Pearl. His boss then walked into and through the lobby without acknowledging the clerk behind the desk.

Pearl moved into the dark off toward the left side of the hotel. After only a couple of steps forward, she opened her hand from her grip on the purse with the pistol in it. The boy, who emerged from the darkness behind her, extended his left hand and found hers. Without a word they fell into step with each other and moved down the passage between the hotel and the café toward the shack at the bottom of the hill near the railroad tracks.

# 2

And so it was in room 206 of the Hopper Hotel.

Rachel Ann had seen, yes, her eyes were *opened*, and she saw, in an instant, *the* final instant (his, W.C.'s, eyes closed like fists, his loins and thing in her up to their hips, shuddering) the flashing of a thousand emotions across his face. And then his eyes half opened. They were dark and dumb as a cow's, and in them in a flash was surprise. And joy. And fear. Joy that comes from the surprise of a hope fulfilled. And fear that came from the same source. As if it was not only his, her new husband's, first time seeing *her*, but his first time *seeing*. And he had tried to say her name but only managed a thick-tongued, teeth clinched grunt.

She did not wink or weep or acknowledge his astonishment, nor take it for love. She was stolid as a judge, but when he rolled away, fighting to find his breath, she turned out the lamp—which she had insisted remain on—to hide her insistent smiling. His body twitched like a dreaming dog's as she wrapped herself around his back, cradled him as he slept. There was an exhausted whimpering in the pit of his throat as he in his stupor relived the throes of their initial post-nuptials meeting.

It was all she had hoped and more. She could not imagine that war heroics, or religious conversion, or financial or political domination or any other power could possibly match what the colored girl with the blind child had blessed her with.


# 3

The desk clerk wanted to take the telephone off the hook and watch the rising sun, in its own time, light and then enshadow the red-orange limestone of the courthouse across the road.

The clerk also wanted a drink and why not?

There was a knock at the side screen door. Sharp, but not heavy, knuckle raps.

One-two-three-four.

The clerk did not look up. It was the colored woman. The clerk was expecting her. The clerk knew she could see him through the screen, leaning on his forearms against the registry counter.

The bottle of bonded whiskey and the glass were right there within reach under the counter between the stapler, a box of cloves, the envelope, and the box of tinted picture postcards of the attractions of Ernestsville: the hotel, the square, and the factory. The dark amber was at the halfway point in the bottle. The label facing away from him, its back turned like a coy lover.

He wished the doors were shut and locked.

Have a shift as empty of guests as his glass was of the bonded.

Shut out the flow, north to south, south to north, with its predictable seasonal surges and ebbs of asphalt-blind, road-weary loners; Old Money vacationers; average Joes and Janes; the anxious and grief-gnarled rushing to or fleeing from tragedy; families, their nerves raveled after hours of confined travel, arriving isolated from each other as back road billboards; salesmen with satchels and jokes and (hated) cigar smoke, some regulars; some roving scrapers-by asking about cut rates; the pitiful parade of those on the bum looking for light work, or a handout, or a night's flop under a roof. Sometimes, depending on the depths of their humbleness, or if they were vets and not cocky, the clerk might let them sleep in the shack out back, down where the colored woman and child had stayed the night.

What each visitor needed, in varying degrees, regardless of their circumstances, was a civil welcome, some reassurance or condolence, and rest. Like a pharmacist dispensing pills and serums, the clerk supplied information and, if pressed, recommendations. Where they could eat (next door at Hubbard's diner—well, the clerk preferred the meat loaf, second the liver, occasionally the beef stew; or if it was fancier they wanted, a block down at Blakey's Fine Dining); the stores (Shorter's general store for gas and auto service, travel needs and notions; Dominic's barbershop; Ruth Maria's beauty parlor; the post office, and the churches by denominations; Doctor Morgan, Attorney Timmons, Sheriff Merritt, the pawn shop.

They had arrived last evening about an hour after his second shift began. A gray Ford Coupe driven by the white man with the colored boy as passenger. The second car was a new black Sixteen Madame X Cadillac Sedan driven by a colored chauffeur with the white woman and the colored woman as passengers. Both cars were dusty and bug-spattered from their time on the road. Their names and Alabama tag numbers entered by the husband into the registry ledger. Young couple. The white couple were old south money on both sides the clerk had guessed. Mister and Missus she had said, smiling, as the recent groom signed, her saying it as if she were sampling the first sip of a chardonnay.

Mr. and Mrs. Whitmore Charlton Kimbrough formerly of Acorn, Alabama, and staff.

Their coloreds, the woman and child, had stayed outside while the colored driver saw after the luggage. The woman had been just discernable in the gray, darker than ghostly gas and morning fog, beyond the glowing circles of the lights and hotel sign. The driver and the servant girl hadn't looked to be a couple; she, even out in the dark, looked young, was good looking. He looked too old for her, but they were only domestics traveling north with their relocating employers, and they stayed in separate rooms, but you never knew.

Mr. and Mrs. Whitmore Charlton Kimbrough had reserved ahead. Or some flunky from some office in Alabama had.

W. C. Kimbrough, party of two plus colored staff and child, written in watery blue-black ink on the 3 x 5 card by Willard, in his loopy hand-writing, too florid to be a man's. But that was Willard for you. He was off to drive his uncle, Uncle Oscar, up to Eudora. That was the reason for the clerk having to do the double shift, instead of spending the late afternoon in his shades-drawn room with the redhead. In his chair his feet up, clearing his head until his usual 10 p.m. or so.

The colored woman didn't knock again or clear her throat. She knew he had heard her, and knew better than to be too pushy.

He pictured himself reaching for and setting the glass on the counter, then reaching for the bottle of bonded, uncorking it, pouring a hair-of-the-dog drink. Drinking it. Instead he said, "Yeah?"

She asked if she could come in.

Fallen arches had kept otherwise able Willard out of the war, that and his uncle Oscar, three-time mayor of Ernestsville, and manager of the factory, who kept Willard sheltered from the French trenches and gas and smoke and memories of it.

He signaled.

"You coming in or you staying outside?" she asked back through the screen door after she entered.

There was no answer but the screen door opened and the boy stepped inside.

Be-Jesus.

The boy was thin as a reed, probably tall for his age, knees knobby in his short pants. He was going to grow to his feet. And his face—black around the eyes. It was like they had been seared shut by a hot poker. The boy was blind. There was no attempt to hide it. No smoked glasses or cap pulled low. And he carried no cane to tap along in front of him. His steps were measured but sure. He moved forward without swinging his arm back and forth in front of him the way he would do if he were in the dark in an unfamiliar place or—. He moved about sort of sensing things without touching or rubbing up against them. Like a cat, was the closest the clerk could come to thinking of it in words.

The clerk turned his attention back to the colored woman, the mother. They were both fresh clean and looked like they were used to it, rather than like two creatures that had wandered in out of some back woods. The boy was moving silently around the brightening lobby.

The clerk said, "If you're looking for the people brought you in they're gone." He had been thinking of different ways to say it.

There was a pause.

She didn't react the way a woman should—a white woman, even the redhead, was prone to be hysterical or dumbstruck. A white woman would get a worried look and before long the teary question would come up of what was somebody going to do to help her? Your average colored woman would first pray for mercy—then do something to make you feel sorry for her. Not this one.

She turned to the boy standing by the purple chair, stroking its arm like it was a cat. He turned to her.

"You were right," she said to the boy.

"They left early," the clerk told her. "About an hour or so ago—little after 5 o'clock. It was still dark."

"You don't know," the child said, "who you'll see again when you think they're gone."

"Anyway," she said, almost as if it was a joke, "they brought us farther than we could've walked in the same time."

She turned away from the boy and was looking at the clerk, her head slightly lowered, sizing him up. Her manner was steely as a Kraut bayonet. She was judging whether or not he could be trusted, if so when and/or how much.

"They left something for you," the clerk said. "*She* did," he corrected himself. "The husband was against it, but he let her. The young woman asked if I had stationary and an envelope. She sat at that desk there while he, her husband, drummed his fingers and tapped his foot. She brought it back sealed—with a name on it." He fetched the envelope and held it, the edge of his hand resting on the counter.

The boy moved next to the desk. Stood.

"Pearl Moon," the young colored woman said, almost smiling. "I'm she."

The clerk had held it up to the light after they drove away. It was money. The clerk was sure of that, but no more than four or five bills. The clerk hadn't been able to make out the denominations of them.

He held the envelope out to her. She stepped forward and thanked him as she took it. The clerk could have demanded identification if he'd wanted to.

"Work for them long?"

"Looks like it was long enough to suit them," she said. The clerk wasn't sure if she meant it as a joke. You couldn't always tell with them.

"That's a more reasonable reaction than I'd have had they left me stranded without prospects," the clerk said.

"Mister," she said, "our noses have been deeper in the mud, and our behinds higher in the sunshine." She tore about a quarter of an inch off the end of the envelope, held it edgewise, blew it open, and eyed inside. "And being a woman alone with a child," she continued, "I've learned to anticipate what people might do, and to position myself accordingly."

A tone to it but polite, still there was something about it he didn't like.

Seeming satisfied about something the boy moved to stand in the sunshine again.

"I've had guests leave a pet dog and drive off, but never people, colored or white," an edge to his tone.

"Did you know Gabriel, Mister?" The boy asked.

"What'd he say?"

"Gabriel," the boy repeated. "He was in the army, too."

"How'd he know I—?"

"The 369th colored troops," the boy said.

"Does he think I'm—?" Enunciating, "No. I was in the 38th Infantry. What does he know about me being in the army?"

She smiled. "He's special, Mister. He knows things sometimes. Don't ask me how. He doesn't think he's ever met a stranger." There was pride in her voice. "You have children, Mister?"

Before the clerk could answer her to say, *bring them into this world?* the boy said, "No." Meaning he didn't. He didn't.

"He's truly a gift," the mother said, the envelope nowhere in sight. "He's going to do great things one day, Mister"

"Gabriel told me about the 369th."

"There was a war vet where we used to be," the colored woman said.

"He was overseas fighting the Germans," the boy said.

"Gabriel saw a bad time," the colored woman continued, "shell-shocked, maybe. He fared hard—"

The boy disagreed, saying, "Gabriel was okay. He understood what he had to do."

Looking away from the boy she said, "Gabriel wasn't his real name; it was the name we called him because he had an old cornet that he could blow it so it sounded like he was talking through it."

The boy hummed a few bars of some tune. The clerk'd heard it before but couldn't remember where.

"Gabriel told war stories about fighting in France and being in the band," the boy said.

The clerk said, "I was in France—but there were no colored troops." He looked to the young woman.

"He listens, figures things out," the colored woman said with a shrug, "Little pitchers have big ears."

The boy laughed at that.

"I was in the 93d Division," saying it quickly to get back to some point he thought had been lost.

"The 369th was in the battle of Rheims," the boy said. "You didn't know Gabriel, did you, Mister?"

"You've got it mixed up," the clerk said. "I was with a fighting unit. East of the Rheims. The 369th—the colored unit—I never heard of them."

"They had their own regiment," the boy said.

"Must've been stevedores, digging our trenches, building roads for us . . ."

"They were fighting men," the boy said as if stating a fact. "They fought with the French because the French let them be soldiers. But fighting the Germans, just like you. They captured the village of Sechault, Gabriel said. Never lost a foot of ground to the enemy. And Gabriel was in the band too. They were led by Lieutenant James Reese Europe. They were called the Hell Fighters from Harlem," the boy said in one breath. "The Black Rattlers."

They quit talking and stood facing him. For a moment the clerk wished he smoked. It would have given him a minute to get the pack from his pocket, shake one loose, find his matches, light it, inhale, hold it, while he had a chance to think. But smoke reminded him too much of the conditions back in the trench in the French woods that night and that morning.

"That's what Gabriel said, didn't he mama?"

"You know what he said. You don't have to ask me."

Smoke and mustard gas, dense as darkness—that finally lifted to the spectacle of sprawled corpses: doughboys and Huns and horses, mangled, strewn like garbage in a field of blood and mud.

The clerk didn't smoke, but he did drink, and he wanted one. He said, "We'd billeted down in the Lorraine but moved up to Rheims."

The little mockingbird boy didn't argue. He waited, his head cocked, listening as if to check the clerk's facts.

The bottle was sitting right there under the counter. Its back to him.

"Our unit, 38th Infantry regiment, was part of the regular army, 3d Division. We advanced into the Rheims-Soisoons-Chateau-Thierry pie wedge, northeast of Paris by 120 Ks. Was Death's triangle, as it turned out."

Why was he telling them? "It was no farther than it is from here to Miller."

Realizing only after he said it they weren't familiar with the local layout. At least the clerk didn't think they were. There was no telling what the little burnt-faced one knew. Was no telling either why he continued telling them his war story.

"Men and boys, we were part of an American force quarter of a million strong. The Rainbow Troops they called us. And there's no black in a rainbow." The clerk half smiled.

"We were commanded by Black Jack Pershing, though," amused at that fact for the first time.

"Listen to the man," the boy's mother told him. She said to the clerk, "He'll argue with you if I let him, and he won't back down."

The clerk didn't care about that. "Our tactic was we would take their blow, let them think we were falling back, then when we're back to our line of resistance take our stand and give them all we had."

They stood listening, waiting as if they didn't have anything to do or worry about after being abandoned by the people that had left them there.

All the clerk could think of to say was, "The Huns ordered a push— If the 38th, our unit, doesn't stop them, the next thing you know Krauts are planting the Kaiser's flag on top the Eiffel Tower.

"Their strategy was to slaughter us. We meant not to be slaughtered."

During that night there was a light-show barrage of heavy artillery, and the flash and whiz and bark of machine gun fire. He'd felt others around him, some, sweating in the canvas and glass confines of their gas masks, hysterical, giving up, preparing to die. Some were so dumb-struck with dread they felt relieved that they would soon get theirs, and it would all be over.

Sometimes when he was in his room he would look up and the red-head would just be watching him and would accuse him of being asleep with his eyes open.

"Beginning about 3 a. m. It was toe-to-toe," the clerk said.

"Us, raw as a rutabaga, bone cold, muddy, sore, mangy, and hungry, us against the Prussian Guard, Kaiser Bill's favorites. It was an eye for an eye against the best of their best."

He paused. They waited, ahead of him. The only sound was of an automobile—mercifully not stopping, heading in the direction of the factory.

He'd tell the redhead no; he hadn't been asleep—just—daydreaming.

If the clerk's nerves had been like hers, like the colored woman's—steely as a bayonet—in the French trench when the fog lifted that morning and they clambered over the top, he'd've . . .

It was becoming close in the lobby.

The boy whistling the same tune before he said, " 'Cake Walkin' Baby from Home.' When Gabriel blew it on his horn we could tell—"

"Tell what?" the clerk asked.

"Who was trouble and who wasn't. We watched the ones who didn't hum or pat their feet. You—"

Enough! The clerk stood, pushing the stool back with his foot. It banged against the front of the service wall behind him. "Outside," the clerk said.

The boy did not flinch but stood as still as a cigar store Indian. "You—" the boy was about to say something.

"Outside!" the clerk repeated, as the colored woman was saying, "He's fixing to tell you something."

The clerk said, "Guest'll be stirring directly."

"Mark what he says," the woman said, as the clerk continued.

"I could get in trouble for letting you wait in here." The clerk didn't want them to talk anymore, or for the blind boy to tell him anything. Not even where he might've heard that tune.

The son and then the mother exited in step through the screen door. They had told him enough about Black Rattlers and Gabriel blowing his horn. The clerk glanced down at the bonded whisky bottle and turned away from it, following them.

"Those white people had responsibility for you but they left you."

He too was outside in the unpaved passageway between the hotel and the restaurant.

"If I'm seen carrying on a conversation in there with you, I could be out of a job," the clerk said. He stood with his back against the screen door. His face felt red.

The boy and his young mama stood, side by side, as if in formation near the wall of Hubbard's diner, watching him. They were patient as posts.

They had to listen.

He smelt the frying bacon and the coffee from Hubbard's.

To their far right at the front corner of the frame building was a red and white COCA-COLA sign. It was as faded as the paint on the wall it was nailed to.

The clerk never ate breakfast. Mornings his stomach would not even let him entertain the notion of it, but the smells from the cafe made hunger rise in him like the sun warming its way along the flat of the wall, white as the redhead's shoulders as he, in his stale room, slouched, his drink balanced on the arm of the worn, once plush chair, and she, stolid, sitting on the bed, knees up, her slip rucked around her hips, drinking too, or standing, or leaning on the sill, her broad back to him, stared across the tracks as night fell on the factory's rear wall.

The mother and son stood as if for their picture to be taken. To their left, over their heads, behind them was a newly posted handbill touting

ROYALE & RHYMES' MINSTRELS

ALL COLORED ALL THE TIME

Shell shock was a white man's disease. Coloreds were too happy to be shell-shocked. If they were any ways sad they just sang a blues until their spirits picked up again, or they packed up and picked up and took off up the road.

30 PERFORMERS & MUSICIANS

The colored minstrels that the handbill advertised were set up in the field behind the factory near the railroad tracks. They had been there for the last two nights. The redhead had told him she saw them on her way to his room.

The smell of bacon was making the clerk lightheaded.

On the poster there were rows of ovals of the black faces of the minstrel performers and musicians.

Where had he heard that tune? His stomach was gurgling like a running toilet.

"What happened to your boy?" The clerk heard his voice like a phantom's speaking from deep within the forest of his mind.

"Nothing, he's all right."

"Looks like hot barbed wire got run 'crost his face."

"Accident," she said, with a tone that wasn't apologetic, assertive, secretive, or revealing.

The clerk's head was swimming with the aroma of frying bacon, his belly sizzling. The craving in his belly made itself heard.

"He wants to tell you something," the woman said.

The clerk shook his head.

It was that first feeling—more than a feeling—knowledge, that ignited in him, bright as a shell burst, causing even worse heart-skip and gut wrench; that even though he went over the top with all the rest and did what he had to, like all the rest, he would forever not un-feel how he had felt in that moment when the order was shouted. It was not the feeling of a man. It was an emptiness past fear, a vacancy, and could only be erased—not by music, not by sex or religion—by nothing but drink. That any revelation or exploration of it or suspicion of its having been was—what? The clerk did not know.

"What's your boy's name?"

"He doesn't have a name."

It must be a nigger joke.

"How do you call him, when you want him?"

"I don't have to call him, Mister. He knows when I want him."

Was it a joke? All of it? Had Willard, Willard and his uncle, somehow had something—?

The clerk could sense her impatience with him. It didn't make him mad at her. Not like it did with the redhead.

She was just a steely-nerved colored woman with her scarred, blind child. She wanted to get on to whatever path they had to follow.

"He'll name himself when he needs one," the young colored woman said.

It made just enough sense not to pursue it, or was just colored-crazy enough not to follow it for fear of the worthlessness of the outcome.

"What's it like to be blind?"

The boy turned his face to his mother.

"He just sees different," she said.

The clerk didn't argue. It didn't matter. None of it mattered.

"You're lucky you're blind," the clerk said. He meant it. Lucky as that son of a bitch Willard, he thought. Said, "You won't have to go war."

"It helped Gabriel that he had his horn to blow," the boy said.

What mattered was to dismiss them. Then telephone the sheriff to alert him to their being in the vicinity.

The colored woman looked over her shoulder to follow his line of sight to the handbill.

The clerk looked away from the handbill and to his left across the road, at the courthouse the color of the redhead's hair, where the sun in its stubborn journey eased dark angles before it.

"It's 6:30 now," the clerk said. "You have until 7."

"My boy might can help you, before it's too late," the woman said, "but you have to listen."

The clerk turned and went through the screen door and closed both doors behind him.

He imagined the young colored woman and the boy slowly walking away, trying to decide what to do.

# 15

# All Colored All the Time

## 1937

Mister R.W. Boone was how he always introduced himself to colored or white, adult or child. It was ever just his initials or only his last name. R.W. Boone, like it was a single name.

Ralph Waldo. R.W.

They knew what he stood for. He stood for the race. The Race. Mister R.W. Boone was a race man from the top of his head to the soles of his feet. It was colored first and last with him. Anybody knew him knew that. Race man. *And* a ladies man. That was a close second. Close as his next heartbeat. When he stepped down off the lead car in a new town, he was either escorting a woman down who'd been with him for a week or so, escorting her across the track, a ticket in her hand to send her on her way back to where he'd picked her up, or he was being met by some other woman waiting on him to let her ride along with them for a week or so until he escorted her across the track, a return ticket in her hand.

Boone's rules: 10:15! R.W. put his index fingers in the corners of his mouth and whistled his loud, shrill note. Time for the morning meeting. Be there or be fined. Too many fines, be fired. That was his first rule as any day opened. Boone was quick to say he didn't give a fat goddamn what they did or with who or what, long as the consequences didn't include the law, come out of his pocket, or keep them from answering morning roll, or the call for places at showtime. Whatever it was they'd done, he offered as general information and not boasting, he'd likely done it or seen it done and it hadn't killed him, so it wasn't nothing to get the big head over, or be too shamed of, and wasn't nothing to damn anybody else about for doing it, or an excuse for being late. And he didn't want it, whatever the hell it might be, to cause him any upset.

Boone was known, he thought, for being fair, giving everybody all the room he could for them to be themselves. All he wanted was for his operation to run like a business, on time and professional. Not like a family—he'd come from a family (that was all anybody knew on that subject), and he'd seen how a heap of other families operated and they were, to the last of them, lacking in the necessary harmony to turn sufficient profit to pay fifty plus people a living wage. Royale & Rhymes was a business and he was the head of it. Everybody had an assigned job and as long as they did it in the way expected it was all good and greasy. But mess up in a way to bring in the law, or so it came out of his pocket, or kept any one of them from answering one of the two daily calls, and they'd likely be left on the side of the tracks quicker than a cat can lick its ass.

At the very first it was thought by a few (Clara and Martha) that she was his latest *traveling companion*. Traveling companion being only one of the behind-his-back names they (mostly Clara) had for R.W.'s women.

Clara: His one a weekenders, his bed warmers—

Martha: Bosom buddies, close associates, playmates—

Pearl Moon this new one called herself. She didn't fit the pattern. R.W. liked them young and long-legged. Of the two she lacked the long legs. But it wasn't only the legs— there was the boy, and blind to boot. R.W.'s women never had babies with them. It wasn't that he wasn't known far and wide to have sowed his seed far and wide. Johnny Appleseed didn't have nothing on him, they, Clara and Martha, joked.

That was attested to by the short stack of envelopes he mailed off monthly each addressed to a different woman up and down the lines and each with a handwritten note and support money. Not even a race man, one who was a Lothario, would take on a woman with a scarred, blind boy. It was against his nature and his rules, as Clara and Martha knew them, but he had taken the two in, the young woman and her son, scarred and blind.

The night-black southeast Indiana landscape rushed unseen outside the train coach windows. She wasn't fooling no-body, Martha low talked to Clara through the smoke of her last Old Gold before bedtime. Had a whole heap of airs trying to cover up pinch of substance; if you asked what Clara thought. The smoke shooting from her nose like from a dragon's, she fixed her mouth as if that was all she had to say on the subject. Martha hadn't asked, but knew without asking, what Clara's answer and attitude would be on the question of the new one and her blind boy. Like, she wouldn't beg for mercy, Martha said, if Lucifer had dragged her for a solid mile. That was true, Clara thought. Pearl Moon wasn't an easy woman to like, by women or by men, but she didn't take no stuff. And that boy, Martha continued, gesturing, her fingers dancing like fairies through daisies, he so blind he can't see whether he suppose to sit down or stand up to pee. She ought to quit, Martha was told by Clara, who almost doubled over with suppressed laughter, knowing Martha was, if anything, just getting started.

R.W. was a rooster all right. He sure liked women. And they sure liked him. Picking up their conversation the next morning at breakfast, Martha did believe R.W. would hump a burning stump. R.W. and every other man God delivered through some poor woman; Clara laughed in agreement.

They'd both slept through their predawn arrival in Eutassee. Slept through the three rail cars containing Royale & Rhymes' Minstrels rolling tent and equipment, instruments, show props, and crew. It had been switched off and deposited in the old Southern Rail yard and coal chute, an industrial branch line, weedy from recent disuse, spur and near the Sullivan Gin Mill and Warehouse, once thriving when cotton was still king. Where at harvest time bail-loaded wagons had snaked clear back to the county limits. The Northern yard, with the proper passenger depot where buyers had arrived in droves, was across town nearer the city center. Royale & Rhymes' troupe would layover there for the two days while they set the three-pole tent and perform that evening and the next.

Now, with the bottom busted out of the U.S. economic barrel, and times being tough as mule meat, Eutassee was like almost every town

Royale & Rhymes went to, and they played them all: big, middle-sized, and little, colored and white. And to all in distance of a railroad line and were lucky enough to have some change in their coin purse to purchase the pleasure of an evening's performance from the All Colored All The Time performers.

And sure as the moon and the sun, somebody in practically ever berg and junction they hit was interested in joining up with them. Be it a farm boy with an itch for some form of excitement that tending a cotton crop could not offer; the budding local beauty being circled by hard-eyed but empty promises to make her satisfied; the swamped by a bad situation and all the signs saying it won't be no better soon; and any of the hundreds of others lost and looking. So despite his being a through and through race man, if he took in or took on every stray with a reason to get away he'd have a parade strung out behind him as wide and long as the Mississippi. The couple times they remembered he'd done it years ago, the strays'd found just how long and lonesome that road was they had dreamed so much about that they couldn't get whatever they'd left behind off their minds.

"Ain't everybody can live the life we lead," Clara said. Martha slowly nodded her head—turn tail, or just as likely, chaff, under the unaccustomed rule of a colored man, and, after a few nights out, good riddance, they'd run or wander off.

Clara and Martha paused, chewing. If R.W. let them all tag on he'd look like Moses leading the children of Egypt. But Royale & Rhymes' manager prided himself on leading a top-notch professional outfit. When the colored and white paying public entered the Royale & Rhymes tent, they knew they had walked through the flaps of the finest colored entertainment outfit their money could buy. The troupe's reputation was at stake every night. If all they offered were ragtag amateurs with no more talent and excitement than the locals could produce themselves on their own porches or parlors and never regret the cost of admission, then we deserve to go belly up, R.W. said.

"He's something, ain't he . . . ?"

The slight forward tilt of his bowler matching the dangle of his cigarette, his white shirt, bow tie, three-piece suit, shined shoes.

Martha sucked at the salty-sweet bit of bacon rind stuck between her canine and upper right bicuspid. R.W. was looking at his pocket watch. The morning meeting started at 7:15 sharp. Clara's elbow was crooked on the table, the steaming cup at her lips. Still tongue-worrying the gristle, she slowly wagged her head.

"Ain't a white man in America can do what R.W. does better than him."

The two trombone players thought R.W. Boone wasn't so much an alchemist as something they didn't have a word for. An alchemist had something—cooper, brass some earthly element to tinker with to start in his quest for gold. R.W. Boone was whatever you'd call it that came *before* alchemy. That somebody who took *nothing*, if you could call pure need nothing, and turned it into something. If there was a name for that then, they thought, that's the tag you'd have to pen on R.W. Boone.

Martha on her second Old Gold and first cup of coffee of the morning, and Clara with her hot chocolate watched R.W. talking to Carpenter and the boy. Now there was a pair.

Even the ones who considered the boy a nuisance or claimed they couldn't stand his ways or the sight of him took some time with him. Amused by his determination or impressed with his willingness to try anything, they'd take a minute anyway to direct him or instruct him. Hell, they'd say, he's trying, and if somebody doesn't tell him something or give him a guiding hand he'll kill his young fool self.

But he had something, him, and his mama, too. Grit or backbone or sand, or whatever it was, it wasn't every day that, satchels in hand, combinations like them came walking in.

In the span since the two arrived, Clara and Martha'd had sufficient time to observe and speculate and to piece the whole thing together—to their satisfaction anyway.

The mother and the boy'd come that first night and seen the show. She sought R.W. out and told him his troupe had talent, that what they lacked was style. Their costumes were raggedy as a billy goat's ass, she said. Telling him people performed up to the way they looked. Clara and Martha hadn't actually witnessed the meeting but they could imagine it clear as Miss Ann's crystal.

Pearl Moon standing there with Royale & Rhymes' boss man, looking dead at him like she did, making her bargain with him. Like two men, two white men. Saying she could see the pressure was on him running the show and all. Him saying she hadn't seen him long enough to know nothing about him but how tall he was and what kind of suit he wore, and how his pocket square draped from his lapel pocket like a silk-tongued beagle's. Her standing there letting him say it, waiting on him to finish. That was probably one of those moments, Clara and Martha surmised, when she, Pearl, put that pause on him. When she just looked at you in a way that stopped time so what you'd just said bounced back at you like you had shouted it against a stone wall, and you didn't hear the echo of it the way you'd meant it when you said it, but how it must've sounded when you were trying to sass or lie to your mama, or escape by some lame excuse to somebody with dominion over you or the situation.

Another of her tricks was you'd say something to her and your voice wouldn't come back at all—just fall down a well with no bottom—and you'd stand there wondering if you'd really said anything at all or only thought you had. And if so why you'd bothered. Still another was what Pearl Moon did with those eyes of hers. She saw sharp enough for the two of them, her and her blind son, and she had a way of looking at you when you thought she was through with you, patting her foot, her bent wrist on her hip, or even if she walked away and you were to look after her, she'd glance back over her shoulder and a chill would run over you like somebody'd opened the back door of Alaska.

That was how they imagined she had looked at R.W. that first time they met and negotiated. Then, they imagined her saying, You trying to do everything yourself. Some of it you good at, some you ain't. She could see he knew business, he didn't know style is what else she could see. She did. Knew style. That was her business. She knew why the customers came and what they wanted when they got there. What he ought to do, they, Martha and Clara, imagined her, Pearl, saying, was give her a budget, let her take on the management of the updating of the costumes and such, freeing him up for his booking and other company running duties like picking the towns, supervising, making the payroll.

R.W. must've, they surmised, argued with her about how she thought he'd turned Royale & Rhymes from a sad-ass floundering minstrel troupe into a three-car attraction, employing thirty-odd people, and holding its own in tough times against cutthroat competition, if he was as lacking in whatever it was she thought he was lacking in.

They could imagine him too, looking back at her with her attitude as brassy as a San Francisco whorehouse bar rail, and not only listening to the gist of her business proposition but mulling it over: what if he let her concentrate on making his performers live up to their potential? If after a couple months he didn't see an improvement in the performance and revenue, then he'd leave her and the boy by the side of the road where they'd come from.

R.W. took a chance. He announced who Pearl and the boy were and said they would be with them for a while, time period to be determined.

So Pearl and Son were joining the Royale & Rhymes All Colored All the Time traveling show with a company of thirty-one permanent members: comedians, singers, musicians, dancer; box office, concessions, and maintenance staff. She would be helping out.

The train slowly picked up speed, its ruff-ruffs were like a medium-sized dog issuing a half-serious warning. Ruff-ruff-ruff.

At full speed you could feel it rushing forward with slight shimmies, sudden eruptions of rhythm surprising, rolling right or left, that accented but did not interrupt its determined hurtle forward. On steady stretches it toot-tooted like a high-powered automobile. Was the whistle, he wondered as they swayed through a curve, a language, its code rolling out over the land, was it a message to those who worked or went on their way as it called to them?

Pearl and Son sat together, son now asleep against his sleeping mother's side as if it was the first good sleep they had had since Moses came down from the mountain.

When they awoke Pearl nodded and spoke when nodded and spoken to. Even Clara waited. They had been on the road a spell was as much of a story as either one of them would tell. They could have been from Mars for all anyone in the Royale & Rhymes Company knew.

Once in Dawkins, Georgia when the crew and the hired locals constructed the tent, joining the canvas sections, raising the poles, hammering the stakes, hoisting and tying off, Pearl and the boy went into town with R.W. and came back with a trunk-load of materials and notions. She went to work making and reconstructing band costumes.

Sewing, Pearl said, was the skill she had picked up from her grandmother who'd been a seamstress for some white ladies. That was as much information as she volunteered.

Pearl worked hard, nobody couldn't say she didn't; the sewing machine clacking when they got up and when they went to bed. She even took in laundry from a few of the company to pick up some extra money. They weren't sure if it was the constancy of the work that made her manner sometimes chaffing and fire-spitting, or what, but there was a rough patch with them getting used to her ways.

But openly admitting it or not, Pearl's improvements were a shot of tonic. The beads and rhinestones and sequins and feathers and gold braid and shiny buttons she bought and sewed on their costumes did make the show flashier. And look like their energy perked up and their timing got sharper. And at every stop the yokels' jaws dropped. Martha and Clara knew the audiences couldn't've been any more knocked out if they'd've bammed them between the eyes with an axe handle when they stepped inside the tent. Pearl Moon had those costumes so shiny they almost didn't need the kerosene lamps. There were standing ovations just for the female performers strutting costumed out onto the stage. Like the All Coloreds were a bonfire, a pyre burning hard times and Jim Crow signs. And, not that the performers saw an increase in their pay envelope, but revenues were up and there were equipment improvements.

The word had gotten out on Royale & Rhymes' new look. It was worth the price of admission was the word that spread ahead of them by railroad men and solo entertainers and preachers, the way colored news took to and moved through the air like dandelions seeds and Caribbean moss.

R.W. had, for some time, even before he realized it, wanted to find some way to shed some of the weight on him regarding the running of the show. He had listened to Pearl and was cautiously hopeful she might be of some help, even if not in the way she proposed. But what it was that he had seen, what had set his showmanship instincts flaring up like an allergy, and the deciding factor for taking them on that the trombonists Clara and Martha hadn't reckoned, was the boy. R.W. talked and listened to the mother and he watched the boy. The boy was a curiosity. A mama's boy and unschooled, but he was razor smart. Out of the ordinary, like his mama, and like her, with flair. Too soon to say if it was special—as she declared, to whoever she met and whatever she meant, whether he was gold dust, or just an oddity—but the potential was there. Properly presented people would pay to see him.

Without declaring his intentions R.W. gave him little chores around the minstrels to gauge their reaction to him and him to them. The boy was willing. Within his limits able. And R.W., who knew women and talent, saw he had music in him.

Carpenter told a different story to everyone who asked about the loss of his hand, not arm as everybody incorrectly said—always pretending (especially with women) to be reluctant to tell it. One time it was the war overseas, the next a factory accident in Alabama, then a run-in with a white mob in Mississippi.

Separate or together that Carpenter and the boy got anything done was thought by many to be amazing, the quality of the work they did do through planning, and detail, and patience was a near miracle.

"You just have to figure out another way to do it," Carpenter said.

Oh, it could be funny to watch, but at the same time, it was some kind of satisfying to see them working together.

From the first Pearl Moon told R.W. to tell them all, as she would do over time by word and example, "Don't baby him (too much). Treat him equal. Let him get his scrapes and bruises. He's special, but he ain't no pet. Don't baby him. He needs to be strong. Let him stumble let him fall. Get him used to what's ahead. I won't be around forever. He's got to know that, and be prepared."

Opinions ranged from he better not get in my way, to give him a chance, to he's one of us now. They saw how hard he tried. He worked hard. Worked as hard as his mama, who outworked an army of ants.

R.W. gave strict instructions: Son was not to get involved while the gangs of canvas men and constructionists erected the tent.

So he shambled about. He thumped and stumbled and slipped. Blundered, reeled, toppled, sprawled. He groped and staggered and got turned around. He tripped over, lumbered, or fell into; or lurched, bumped, teetered, scrapped, or tottered; tripped against people, poles, walls, into ditches, boxes, trees, rocks, ruts. Pratfalls that Nicodemus and Snuff, the black-faced comedy duo, would have been proud of and did in fact study for pointers in the naturalism of the boy's comic flops or plummets. He'd give a week's pay to see him on a bicycle, Snuff whispered one morning as the meeting was breaking up.

Undaunted after a fall Son scrambled up, licked his palm to wipe his knees, licked again if it was blood-sticky, then swatted and slapped off the dust and dirt and went on. On the train and inside the tent was easily memorized and navigated because it was always the same. The constant challenge was their continual moving, a new town usually every five or six days, strange terrains, unfamiliar topographies, foreign footing on each new lay of land.

Early on there was some mocking behind his back and to his face—careful not to let his mama or R.W. or especially the carpenter catch them. But it wasn't too long before, through the combination of her insistence and the boy's being able to do what was asked of him, they got used to him and the scars. Among them it was an unspoken policy that other people's business was just that. Nobody wanted to be questioned themselves, so they tended to respect that in others; tended to, but with their intentions longer in taking effect in some cases than others.

Carpenter was the first to take the boy under his wing.

Martha hunched Clara as she gestured with her head and laughed. The boy and Carpenter, the only one-armed carpenter any of them had ever seen, were repairing a rickety section of bleacher seats. All around the camp as troupe members moved about they snuck looks or just stopped all together to watch the two of them, the one armed carpenter and a blind boy as they went about replacing plank sections. Carpenter was precise in his construction, in spite of the fact that he never drew a plan or work with a blue print. He'd just see it in his head, complete, down to the last miter angle and nail, and then build it to fit that vision. So his instructions to the boy were exact.

Bring me a handful of them nails in that box on the ground behind you there. And you can knock over that saw horse about four feet to your left on the way if you want to, but I wouldn't.

Or, Hold this 2x4 for me right here where I got it. Now take this nail right here and hold it right there, like that. Hold it true, get your noggin' out of the way so you don't bust my hammer.

Where without the boy he used his stump to hold the board with the nail held between his big and second toe of his right foot.

Oh, it could be funny to watch, but at the same time, it some kind of satisfying to see them working together.

An oatmeal box Carpenter had gotten from cook. Antenna wire. Coil of copper wire. Ground wire. Carpenter explained what each piece was as the boy fingered them. Crystal detector. Earphones. Telling the boy about how the air was full of radio waves sent out by radio stations located all over.

"Like there are thoughts everywhere in the air," the boy said—or in his head, he wasn't sure which. "And I just pick them up, huh?"

Carpenter tapped the boy's forehead. "Yeah, I guess you got a noggin like a crystal detector."

They laughed.

"Now, the antenna"—the boy found it on the tabletop. "That's right. That's what picks up the signal sent out from the station, and it flows between it and the ground wire—that's right. You tune it to the station with the detector. Yeah, that's the detector." His hands were guided through the assembly process: wrapping the copper wire around the oatmeal box. Wires connecting from the oatmeal box to the ground wire and the earphones and detector. Wires connecting the box and detector and antenna. And when it was done and the antenna was strung out and in place, Son put on the earphones.

"You do the adjustments," Carpenter said. Fiddling, his face scrunched in concentrating.

"Something scratchy."

"Static."

"Oh, static."

Adjusting.

"Anything?"

Son was shaking his head.

"Keep trying."

And after a few minutes he jumped with delighted surprise. "A tingle," he said. He turned his head slightly. A smile butterflied across his lips.

"What?"

"I hear it."

"What?"

"Music." His hand trembled at the knob. "Somebody is talking—"

"—and—?"

"—More—*Music!*"

"Just so you'll know," is what R.W. said to the boy that first evening before Professor Smith's downbeat, and the Royale & Rhymes All Colored

Minstrels, led by Eggs Isbell, as Mr. Interlocutor shimmy-wiggled on the stage, and before the first act finale of Son's debut.

"You know by now," R.W. said, "I don't assume anybody knows anything I haven't said to him or to her, so if I'm telling you something you already know, stop me. I know you and your mama've traveled some, and seen a thing or two, but, so there'll be no mistaking who these people are who pay to sit in my tent, and how you're to think of them, I'll tell you. They are the hardest-lucked, poorest, most backward-ass people anywhere. Nobody gives a damn about them other than what can be wrung from them. And when they're sapped dry as cow chips, they'll drop where they stand and the landlord won't miss them, and they know it. They're trapped."

The minstrels Pete Ratliff and Billy Faddis as their characters, Nicodemus and Snuff begin their routine with the drunk, Nicodemus, who stumbles into the mortuary by mistake and tries to wake up the corpse laid out next to the napping mortician.

"Their lives," R.W. continued, "won't get a bit better and neither will their children's or likely their grandchildren. They are never even going to get in sight of pulling even, let alone getting ahead, and there is nothing they can do about it."

The nature of the establishment into which Nicodemus has blundered is slowly dawning on him. The audience roars.

"If it wasn't for some jook off at the end of some dark road, a church on Sunday morning, and us once a season—"

The ghastly enormity of Nicodemus's mistake is compounded when Snuff, as the mortician, awakened by the commotion of Nicodemus trying to find a portal, any portal of exit, sits up and speaks.

R.W. looked at the boy, his head cocked slightly.

Son's face cork-blackened beneath the white bonnet and blond, curlicued Shirley Temple wig. He'd been painted with big red liver lips and two large white buttons for eyes. His mother had sewn his costume: a calico dress and white pantaloons. With black patent leather Buster Browns.

Shirley Temple acts were big in the movies and vaudeville houses. There were Little Eva and Mary Pickford and adolescent white girl imitators everywhere. With Son, R.W. saw his chance to put a spin on that kind of attraction.

"They know all that without question," R.W. continued. "And still they keep on. Why? Because they're stupid? Because they're no better than beasts? No. Because there is nothing else they can do—until Jim Crow catches a cold and croaks, or one of us catches him off by himself and chokes the living evil out of him. Until that happens we are the only things outside their world they have to look forward to that doesn't, in the long run, cause them more pain. That includes the next planting season, Christmas, falling in love, childbirth, and death. But we roll in, and for two hours under this canvas we put on a show that has to last them maybe for the rest of their lives. That ain't to be taken lightly."

"No sir," Son said without pause.

"They file in through that flap like they're entering St. Peter's gates. And we have to respect that because they're paying for our supper. You hear me?"

"You hear?" his mother asked, laying her hand on his shoulder.

"Respect," the boy said.

He heard.

"Ladies and gentlemen, Eggs announced, boys and girls, for the first time on any stage anywhere—"

On cue and the release of his mother's hand from his shoulder, twirling his parasol, just as they had rehearsed it and rehearsed it, he skipped straight down the hard-packed earth aisle between the folding chairs and onto the step-high platform of the stage in the center of the tent. It was Bessie Smith's tune. He had heard it since he could remember. Those first few piano notes pounded out like a couple of hammers striking in the last coffin nails, before easy rolling into a slow, barrelhouse blues. It seemed like a Negro couldn't have a Victrola Talking Machine without a Bessie Smith tune spinning on it. Even when it was electronically reproduced, her big voice was hot and bright as the sun, and chilling as the sky around a winter moon. When Bessie sang she was declaring her presence as their spokeswoman. Helping get all her listeners told on the true matters of the world.

> There ain't nothing I can do, or nothing I can say
> That folks don't criticize me,

The opening of *T'Ain't Nobody's Business If I Do*. First put out by her ten or fifteen years before. Son didn't even know he was singing it the first time R.W. called it to his attention. It was a near perfect imitation of the Columbia records singing star.

> But I'm goin' to do just as I want to anyway
> And don't care if they all despise me.

Son had not even known he knew all of the words until R.W. asked him to sing it through. And the second time when Professor Smith was called over to listen, and then when Bobby Collier on drums, Bump Reynolds on bass, and Professor Smith playing piano, and then Peck Morgan made music behind him. And he rehearsed it again with them for the next couple days.

For the longest time R.W. had wanted a child act as a part of Royale & Rhymes' roster. He was missing a good bet by not having one of the most popular type acts in vaudeville. On stage far back as R.W. could remember, portrayals of Little Eva from *Uncle Tom's Cabin*; to Mary Pickford, the girl with the curls as Snow White in the moving pictures; to Shirley Temple, singing and dancing and being cute on screens all over the country every night—all brought in the big dollars. They often did adolescent white girls' versions of colored dances and music and people loved it an ate it up like ice cream.

From the first he had considered the possibility of creating a spot for Son on stage. The boy was personable, self-assured, and had a raw, unexplored talent. Hearing him absentmindedly singing the blues caused the idea to click, like a cue ball's perfect point of contact with the object ball that propelled it into the called pocket. A parody of the parody of a prim little white girl doing colored material.

Before his mama released him she asked him if he thought he could sing with people listening; would he be nervous? He asked if it was important if he wasn't. It was. He said he wouldn't be.

Not on that first night, or any after, was there anyone among the audience who did not know the lyrics. At first they responded as much with the joy of hearing the song as with amusement at a child singing it. The tune was, true to Bessie Smith's attitude, a full-throated statement to any and all—family, lovers, friends, white folks, preachers, and any damn body else walking and drawing breath—that what they did was something they owned, something they strutted, something private and personal as their heartbeat, and something, maybe the one thing, they had couldn't nobody else touch.

It was only after a line or two, once they'd recognized the tune, that they could feel the spirit. From her throne as the Empress of the Blues, Bessie was speaking unto them through the mimicking voice of a blackened-faced child in a kerosene-lighted tent in a field yonder from the train tracks.

> If I should take a notion
>> To jump into the ocean

Just like Mistress Smith, in her royalty, drawing out then holding selected words, like a mule straining in its harness against a hidden root.

> T'ain't nobody's business if I do, do, do do . . .

Royale & Rhymes' audiences didn't come to sit back and be pulled along on a buggy ride like white folks behind old Dobbin trotting to church on Sunday. They came to grab a handful of mane, sling their legs over the back of the wild buck of Royale & Rhymes' Colored Minstrels, and hooping and hollering hang on while they spurred it forth.

> If I go to church on Sunday
>> Sing the shimmy down on Monday
>> Ain't no-body's business if I do, if I do

They shouted praise when pleased and catcalled when they weren't.
The boy's singing—what'd Mr. Interlocutor call him?—Little Mizz
Eva Topsy—because it was coming from a child—or maybe, due to
the feeling behind the words, maybe it was really a midget posing as a
child—no, it was a child—a boy?—a girl?—belting it out:

> If my friend ain't got no money

Bessie's song. Their manifesto.

> And I say "take all mine, honey"

Felt deep and wide as a 4 a.m. prayer, coming out of the big red water-
melon mouth of a child:

> T'ain't nobody's business if I do, do, do do . . .

Then that spoke to the width and depth of Bessie's message.

> If I give him my last nickel
> And it leaves me in a pickle

If a child could be made to feel it, then Lord have mercy!

> T'ain't nobody's business if I do, if I do.

It lifted them. It filled them up. It emptied them out. Throats lumped.
Tears rose, glistening. Laughter exploded like dynamite blasting at the
taproot of an oak blocking their path to betterment.

> One day I'm goin' crazy
> Get me a shotgun and shoot my baby . . .

Shoot 'em, they holler.
Shoot 'em one time for me!

Ain't nobody's business . . .

No-body's business, amen-ing in the face of the look-the-other-way
Lord, the hot-cold barbed wire clutches of the law, and every coldhearted
white somebody from there back to Timbuktu.

I said it ain't nobody's business . . .

Lord, have mercy, they sang ahead of him.
Lord, have mercy, it ain't nobody's business,

Hey! what I do
It ain't nobody's business what I do

Nobody's!

Their pocketbooks opened like a Kansas plains cloud black as the
ebonies on a standup front parlor piano. Pennies, a few nickels, and a
dime or two rained onto the stage like they didn't have to worry, didn't
have to grieve. He understands.

Listen at him! They hollered, he understands, Bless 'im, and He ain't
*nothing but a child.*

The show went on from there, but not before he had to sing Madam
Bessie Smith's blues again. And twice a night from then on.

# 16

# Going to Town

## Smith's Crossing, Georgia, c. 1938

Under Carpenter's supervision the crew of locals were rigging the bleachers and raising the tent.

Peck, first cornetist, was smoking a ready-roll he'd bummed off Napoleon Hampden. He was standing with Son. They'd rehearsed and were ready for their opening that night in Ford's Bend. He was watching Jasper Graves, Royale & Rhymes' advance man, who'd just come in from placing handbills on posts and walls in town and window cards in local businesses, and was talking to R.W. Peck could just barely overhear them.

"You aren't going to like it," Jasper said.

R.W. waited, not liking it already. "Another show posted over Royale & Rhymes' handbills all over town," Jasper told their boss.

"Who done it?"

"You ain't going to like it," the thin, wavy-haired, light-skinned, hazel-eyed man said, stalling the bad news. "It was another minstrel outfit."

He didn't think it was a damn opera company, R.W., said, but whoever in the hell it was he wasn't going to blame Jasper for bringing the news *if* he told him what the news was sometime before sundown and time for the damned show.

Jasper, only slightly less anxious, said, "They're a four-car unit down at the other depot."

Peck could see R.W. rifling through his mind for troupes with four train cars.

"They white. Robben's White Smart Set Minstrels out of New Orleans."

"Any sight of them?"

They hadn't set up at the pavilion in the town square when Jasper'd left. But they were expected to any time soon.

Stepping into the sunlight out of the shadows of the tent, Professor Elmore Sawyer, the band director, sensing something, joined them. What was wrong?

Jasper repeated his report in a rush, adding, "and you know the smoke ain't hardly cleared from the last lynching they had around here."

"That was over in Nelson County," R.W. said.

"Y'all all right?" Peck, joining them, asked, his hand on Son's shoulder.

"You think lynchers don't cross country lines?" Jasper asked.

Graves asked if they ought to pack up, citing R.W.'s number one rule about the possibility of trouble and the law. He had a bad feeling.

"We were here first," R.W. told him.

"But they here *now*," Graves countered, "and this is a mostly white town. When they get a scent of blood . . ."

That didn't make any difference, Sawyer said, as Bump Reynolds joined them.

"What's up?"

Professor Sawyer explained.

"Them crackers got to learn," R.W. concluded as he fetched his 21-jewel railroad model Waltham from his vest pocket. An 18-wheel steam locomotive hand carved into its gold top. He thumbnailed it open with a soft pop.

"Time for school," he said. The watch closed with a click.

Son asked, "We going to town, R.W.?"

"Yeah, Son, we're going to town."

At the end of his long list of orders rattled off like Bobby Collier's snare drum paradiddles, they knew who was going, and those who were staying in camp were to continue with the set up and to be ready for possible trouble.

The band went in led by R.W.

Peck could see the boy, with his hand on R.W.'s arm, could feel the calm and the excitement. There was also Professor Sawyer, and a cadre from the band: two cornets, two trombones, clarinet, tuba, and snare and bass drums. Heading toward town, dressed in their red-coated uniforms with the polished brass buttons, with gold epaulets and braided floral designs across the chest and down the sleeves. Bunched together they crunched along beside the tracks, the cinders and gravel sharp under their feet. They could have gone around skirting the business district and come up behind the square, but R.W. led them across the tracks and walked the three blocks up Logan Street to the corner of Main by the Post Office, where they could hear the faint sounds of "*Doing the Uptown Low Down.*"

To Peck's ear the white minstrels were well trained and strictly rehearsed. Their execution was as precise as the wheels and cogs of R.W.'s 21-jeweled Waltham. The white musicians knew the tune but that was about all; Professor Sawyer's glance and head gesture confirmed his similar thought to Peck. It had as much feeling as a stone at the bottom of a cotton sack. Their tempo dragged like a cotton-loaded wagon creaking behind a sun-besotted swaybacked mule. The best could be said for Robben's band was that they sounded fit for a society orchestra playing for swells in tuxedos and dolled-up dames in sequined gowns. Well, that might have been how it looked on the sheet music, and okay for that kind of crowd, but this was a town of scuffling, raw-boned Swamp State crackers, rough as the trunk of a palmetto tree, and plagued by the low level of cornmeal in the barrel compared to the numbers of mouths had to be fed.

As R.W., Son, and the musicians moved up the street, Peck heard the six brass, four reeds, and drums from up the street. Sawyer signaled his band into formation and they were at the ready, marching in step, in place, at the corner by the boarded-up People's State Bank and across the street from the Gulf Gas station. He called number twenty-eight in the book. "*Doing the Uptown Low Down.*" The same tune the Robben's White Minstrel's band was working their way through.

"All right boys; let's buck 'em," he said. He counted off. There was a bass drum boom and a glissando from the tuba, then a slow, dampened, rat-tatted dirge-like tempo on the snare. Willie Bump Reynolds's tuba's deep boom-thundering aftershocks threatened to undo the nails holding the boards over the failed bank's windows, as well as any loose teeth, earwax, and idle thoughts within a radius of several blocks; or set clanging the bells atop the wedding-cake-looking steeples in the array of churches about town.

Peck and Napoleon Hampden's cornets, playing as one, took the lead. It was mournful, but bright. It was steady as the sun's heavenly arc. They could be heard with clarity down the four or five blocks to the pavilion in the town square where the Robben's Smart Set musicians, ringed by townspeople, were doing their best.

Son carried the printed placard on a staff.

> ROYALE & RHYMES' MINSTRELS
> ALL COLORED ALL THE TIME
> ARE HERE!
> Nelson's Pasture
> 7 pm

Son was guided by Boone's hand on his other shoulder. Up the center of the street they marched, between the parked cars and buggies and mule-drawn wagons angled parallel on either side. Past shops: pharmacy, barber, women's ready-to-wear apparel, manned by assistants left behind while the bosses had moseyed to the square to hear the white minstrels play a tune or two, or by benevolent merchants or proprietors who'd released their help for a brief, end-of-the-week reprieve. In the second-level windows, there were heads and shoulders of stay-at-home women who lived above the shops.

A few men, women, and children stepped in behind Royale & Rhyme's musicians, following them in. The crowd standing or lounging on the lawn around the pavilion or seated on the benches, beneath the statue of the war hero, started to turn toward R.W.'s band as the white musicians in blackface and dressed in red, white, and blue satin outfits, and red pillbox caps with black patent leather bills, strove valiantly to keep playing the tune in their tempo. Their effort, against the vigor of Royale & Rhymes' lead unison cornets was like a rooster on roller skates. The twin punches of Clara and Martha's trombones goosed the tempo steadily forward and higher, but still holding it for the back beat.

It all proved too much for the Robben's bandsmen. Man by man the white minstrel musicians shut down, despite their conductor's admonitions to the contrary. They laid their instruments on their laps or stood them on their thighs or knees, and they sat still as cornerstones, as the colored musicians reached the end of the circle around the bandstand, still playing, their sound and rhythm washing over the crowd like Noah's flood, and then circled the pavilion again, following the boy's and Boone's lead, the **Royale & Rhymes** sign bobbing on the staff with the boy's clogging but sure-footed march step. The Robben's White Minstrels watched, their expressions hidden by the grease or burnt cork, but their postures lacked starch, and uncertainty hung on them like gray moss. The colored musicians circled them again, as they brought the tune to a climax, and enthusiastic applause.

Scattered, like a half handful of black-eyed peas around the edge of a bowl of rice, were town Negroes and Negroes in town. Domestics. Handymen. Street vendors. Each of them was aware of the others—in case—for the good it might do, and each in their caution—you had to know it to see—concealed their delight, pride, appreciation, and even apprehension. Peck and the rest of R.W.'s musicians saw it, soaked it up like flowers in the sun.

Professor Sawyer called the number of the next selection. Number thirty-three, "*Russian Lullaby*," a popular, sentimental tune of the day. They played it in a plaintive tempo. Drew Toomer's clarinet played the melody over quiet drum rolls from Bobby Collier. The crowd's light applause over the introduction voiced their recognition and approval. The trombones and cornets and clarinet offered a counter melody based on "*Brother Can You Spare a Dime?*" The crowd stood, hushed. Some swayed slightly, half smiling. Some dabbed at their eyes with sleeve handkerchiefs or knuckles or backs of their hands.

The all colored band began to exit the pavilion area along the sidewalk they had entered on only moments ago. Clear of the main body of the crowd and back into the street, Sawyer clapped his hands, indicating a doubling of the tempo. Peck's cornet solo was from the melody of Gounod's third act devil's aria from Faust. *Translating and transcribing as he played, its brassy brightness cutting the air like a scythe*:

| | |
|---|---|
| C'est l'enfer qui t'appelle, | That's hell calling you, |
| C'est l'enfer qui te suit! | and that's hell behind you! |
| C'est l'éternel remords, | It is the blues for now, |
| C'est l'angoisse éternelle | It is the blues forever, |
| Dans l'éternelle nuit! | On the longest night you'll live! |

The longest night you'll live! On the band's exit there were, on both sides of the street, more people in doorways and on the sidewalks than there were on their entrance. Some who had trailed them on their march up Main now followed them back, plus late joiners in tow, smiling, cutting a step, or trying to: the elderly, the idle, maids on errands, mammies pushing their wards in straw strollers, barefoot schoolboys, young toughs, clerks and assistant managers returning to the shops from supper with heads nodding or bobbing with the beat and against it.

There was no one not aware of the Sawyer's band boys and girls in their bright red coats, sweat streaming down their shiny faces.

Peck eyed the colored people, their joy now as hard to hide as a bull under a blanket, as they grinned, snapped their fingers, and bobbed their heads. Some smiled and looked whites in the eye long enough to acknowledge and be acknowledged. Some, along with various whites, followed them as Boone extended the route out of town a few blocks more, past the Baptist Church at the proper end of the old business section, and by blocks of two-story frame houses and then down that stretch of Cotton Lane.

The tune now was "*Keep Your Hands Off My Mojo*." The crowd had dwindled to a few, mostly boys on bicycles and on foot, and a barking dog or two. By the fields of twelve-cent-a-pound cotton, R.W.'s band went, still in formation, by the idle

Sullivan Gin
& Warehouse.

They stood, out of formation, clustered in the dirt road, the air alive around them. The band was fidgety. They paced like thoroughbreds cooling down after a hard ride, pacing, snorting, pawing the earth, as they caught their breath, regulating their hearts.

Their instruments were at the ends of their arms like unacknowledged faithful dogs or smoking guns. Their breathing: some full-chested, some snorts, some swallowing. *Hummhuphnnph* of throats cleared. Dry coughs, dry spits. Feet: shuffling in place, scuffs of dust, a step or two forward, back, or to the side. Their bodies humming like new strung telephone wires. But there was a difficult-to-define uncertainty as they milled about. Like schoolboys at a dance: anxious yet eager, fretful yet cocky. Still, necessary for that moment, in close proximity.

Initiating the ritual of group smoking, Peck bummed a cigarette. The snap of the top of a tobacco tin, crinkle of a cigarette package, scrap and *tszzzt!* of a safety match. Flicking scent of sulfur.

*Muum* of thanks.

Naw, ne'mind, I don't want to be the third, let me get a light from you Drew. Mild indignation at having to ask.

"Damn, Peck, you want me to thump you in the chest too, to help you inhale?"

"In the rush I forget my smokes, *all right*? I'll give you one when we get back if it means that much to you."

"You'll give one back—that'll be a first."

Then the inarticulate quiet of the after excitement of what they'd just done.

They didn't know what to do.

The smell of rain a rumor from the west.

Bobby Collier, his drum on its side between his feet, drumsticks under his left arm, blew his nose, the knuckle of his index finger closing one nostril then the other. Sniffed. Wiped with his red and white handkerchief.

Peck had to pee. He crunched off through the scrub for privacy. Martha and Clara, their trombones angled against the shoulders like rifles, turned their backs. Napoleon Hampden crunched off to sneak a swig from his flask.

There was a swallow's quick, sharp, trilled single note wheet-tweets; a wren's rapid, high-pitched chattering.

Jasmine sugar-sweet in the nose.

Standing in high brown grass Peck noticed Son. He could see the boy whose head was turning quickly back and forth like a hound trying to catch a scent. Peck could see the boy had never been around the musicians when they felt like they were feeling then. Peck felt pretty much the same way. Anxious. Out of sorts. They were as restless as if they had unexplainably forgotten who they were. As if they, only minutes ago, had slipped back, to before Son knew them, to before they joined to work for R.W., to some point where they were only themselves—John Henry, Bump, Napoleon, Bobby, Drew, Clara, Martha—individuals, and not R.W. Boone's Royale & Rhymes' All Colored Minstrels All The Time Band, under Professor Sawyer's direction.

Peck shook it off, zipped up. Crisp, drought-dried stalks snapping as he high-stepped back through the weeds and wildflowers. Son moved toward him, reached, touched, and tugged Peck's sleeve. He whispered to the cornetist.

"*Cakewalkin' Babies from Home*," Peck called out, smiling. He had been thinking the same damned tune. It was as if it had come to him and the boy in a flashing, prophetic, two-pronged revelation. His bandmates, relieved by the simple logic and rightness of it, formed a near circle, raising their instruments to the ready without an upbeat, and launched forth at the Professor's snapping head nod of a downbeat. They played the opening choruses, the trombones answering the cornets, the riffs from the reeds signifying like cawing crows.

Martha and Drew began singing, trading lines:

"Here they come, look at 'em, demonstrating," Martha began.

". . . going some, ain't they syncopating?" Drew followed.

"Talk of the town, teasing brown, picking 'em up and laying 'em down . . ."

Son was in the circle, he was, in rhythm, high-stepping in place, in a slow clockwise rotation.

"Dancin' fools, ain't we demonstrating?" Martha sang.

"We're a class of our own," Drew answered, throwing his arms wide to them.

Martha, wagging her finger, "Now the only way to win is to cheat us."

". . . you may try," Drew sang, shaking his head.

". . . but you'll never beat us!" They ended together, laughing.

The horns and drums took over with all their might. The music played not for the sparsely clouded high blue sky, or the shuttered gin off a ways, or the dilapidated three- room shack back by the clump of scarlet oak, the moss over-layering it all like a widow's veil, or for any stray fice or livestock or fowl. The brass band, with the twelve-year-old blind boy's stamping feet setting the lick, were playing only for each other.

"Strut your stuff, boy!" R.W. encouraged as Son waved his arms over his head still marching to the beat.

Playing their jubilation at being who they were: R.W. Boone's Royale & Rhymes' Minstrels band under the baton of Professor Elmore Sawyer, euphoric exaltation at their capacity of expressing it and their being their only competition.

*"You're the cake walkin' baby from home"!*

For the first show that night, the crowd clambered out like there was going to be free money. It was thick as bees in a hive, as ants on sugar. *First* show because Boone added a second to accommodate the overflow, the sheriff increasing the license fee by half. Coloreds and whites separated by the rope. For the second show, which went past midnight, the rope was moved, the white section being smaller by half than from the first.

Surprisingly, Boone told Peck later, there was no attempted reprisal from a disgruntled faction within the white minstrel camp. Had any attempted reprisal proven the case, everyone in Royale & Rhymes' Minstrels had some defense, a tent peg, razor, hammer, sickle, rail spike, or pistol at hand.

There were several from the white minstrels in attendance at the second show, incognito as possible.

Peck could see, even in the shadows of the yellow-gray light of the kerosene lanterns, the white musicians' postures, like pointers at the hunt, eyes darting, taking mental notes.

Nicodemus and Snuff—Pete Ratliff and Billy Faddis—did their skits, under Boone's orders, without blackface. Pete Ratliff, urged forward by Billy Faddis, protested. Boone told him if he blackened his face his pay envelope would have less green in it.

Described it to the boy with the pictures he might have missed, filling in for him, and others who had not heard, or wanted to hear it again. "We took them fire today, Son," R.W. said. "And they didn't have the water to put us out. Posting over my goddamn handbills trying to say we don't exist."

"Or," Peck said, "like we don't goddamn matter."

R.W. wouldn't stand for that even if they were announcing the second coming of Jesus Christ.

The boy was sitting opposite him, Indian style, his ankles crossed on the seat. His elbows were on his knees, his face in his hands, his head thrust forward like an automobile's hood ornament.

"A word was not spoken and our stride was not broken," Professor said. He and the others were standing in the aisle, or seated nearby. Listening as the train pulled away with a lurch, entering its slow acceleration toward gaining traveling speed.

Boone hurried through or skipped the parts where the boy, despite his excitement and fighting sleep, nodded rapidly, indicating he knew that part, his whole body rocking with his pleasure of the memory and connection as the train rocked and swayed and the night deepened, Baba—deba—

daba-deba-daba—

dah-dah-daba, sounded the whistle. And there were the first sprinkles of rain against the windows, as the train rocked and swayed toward Smith's Crossing and the state line.

# 17

# The Redhead

## Ernestsville, Virginia, 1934

The early shift guy got there at 6:51.

By 7:02 the clerk, the bottle in a brown paper bag in his hand, walked step by rote step to his room.

There, he drank.

When the redhead came he would not, in the rise and blur of days, break the silence with a mention of the colored woman and her blind, scarred sapling of a son. And the two of them would drift from him like the sight of his chilled, huffed breath on that trek in France, marching through mud—concentrating on each step, each step, sloughing, sloshing, the hup, two, three along, abandoned kilometer after kilometer through the void of cold and dull throb of weapon and kit weight, hunger, lack of sleep, dragging, step by rote step, or like smoke . . . when whatever belief he'd ever had evaporated.

God did not know what He was doing. There was no reason for things. No order to His blessing or punishments scattered in dibs and dabs or in floods or flames. Take what comes. And wait. In the pig muck trenches in Rheims-Soissons, or behind that counter, or in a room . . .

And one evening, when from a room down the hall the smell of burnt biscuits floats under the door of his room, the clerk will, in the silence, choke the redhead until her tongue, red as her hair, lolls like raw liver . . .

Clara thought R.W. would get around to telling them one day. Out of the blue at morning meeting, or when the train was pulling out, while they would think they were on one subject, it might be a month, six months, a year, but in his own time he would say something about

Pearl—whatever her name really was, and Son, whatever his name was or was going to be, and their leaving. Clara thought they'd been fired. Martha thought they had quit. Until they knew better they had to wonder and hypothesize.

Everybody had their own firsthand version they heard from somebody else secondhand. According to Bump, Pearl, showing the other side of herself, had got in it toe to toe with R.W. about how much or little they were being compensated for their contribution.

Pearl'd said, Bump said, she thought as little as R.W. paid people the only reason they stayed with him was because they didn't think they could do better.

Clara humphed.

Whereas, Bump continued, Pearl'd said she thought if she couldn't do better then she'd just jump over in somebody's river and drown.

Let her, Clara humphed again.

Rather, Bump said Pearl'd said, than be underpaid and underappreciated she'd just as soon go back to doing what they were doing before them joined up. And to prove it they were leaving his cheap behind.

The way Pete Ratliff told it, Pearl had to pull a pistol on R.W. to get him to pay her what she thought was fair. R.W. said, Pete Ratliff said, he would do it this one time but the budget couldn't stand it on a weekly basis. So be it, Pete said Pearl said, but this one time at least Son was going to get his fair compensation. R.W. didn't see that insults were called for, Pete said, they were just talking he said. No. They were talking about money, Pearl, according to Pete Ratliff said, which was negotiating she said. She thought she held the upper hand because the draw from much of what they were discussing was because of Son's being in the show and singing his little blues. She said in so many words Son was the golden egg and she was the goose that had laid and hatched it. She knew, she continued, repeating his phrase, we all just trying to make a living, but she had to look out for herself and her son. He understood that. If she felt like they weren't getting out fair what they were bringing in then something had to change. He didn't think she was bluffing and he told her he appreciated all they had done—she cut him off saying the only appreciation she gave a damn about was the green kind she could put in her pocket. Right then he said he couldn't see his way clear to do any better by them than he was already doing. She knew when a bluff was a bluff. He had set his stakes in the ground, marking his boundaries. She told him then that was the way it was. They shook hands like two white men. That was Pete Ratliff's version of it.

"She was going to miss us a sight more than we do her," Clara said. "We a world on this train."

She and that boy going to do all right, Martha predicted to herself.

"Our own universe," Clara continued, warming up. "They won't never be in another organization like this again. Not colored from root to top branch to limb tip. Proving night after night Jim Crow is a lie."

For her part Clara was glad Pearl and Son were gone and said so to R.W. and any and everybody else she wanted to say it to and could corner long enough to say it. Martha on the other hand didn't say it but she was sorry to see them go. Not so much Pearl, though she liked the way she'd stood up to everybody, including R.W.

Martha had spent little time with Pearl. Alone only twice she could remember. A costume fitting, having strands of fake pearls the size of peas tacked onto the red velvet dress Pearl had made. Martha listening as Pearl, a staggered row of straight pins in her mouth, not so much talked as kind of hummed, words but unconscious ones. It was in response to something Martha had asked, trying to sound casual, but probing for information on the mysterious seamstress and all else she was. Not understanding every word, straining so as to be able to give an exact or at least a reasonable word-for-word account to satisfy the grilling she would get from Clara when next they met.

Pearl: "I met the Chinaman. He took me in. He had his reasons, but I had mine too. I learned—about me, what I could and would do. Learned how *to* do. How to run something. How to do with people get them to do what was needed. That was good. Good to know *that*. It got me though. Made me see what it took."

With Clara afterwards, Martha couldn't interpret *what* had been good to know. What *that* was.

"She didn't say, Clara! Didn't say *who* the Chinaman was, didn't say *what* people, or what she got them to do."

Martha listened, as Clara complained that she knew less now than before Martha'd told her what'd gone on.

"I didn't want to say nothing," Clara said, afraid Pearl'd realize she was being overheard and stop.

"Oh, she *Pearl* now, is she?"

"That's her name, Clara."

"It's the name she go by."

Martha laughed.

Clara would've found a way to get some answers, she said. Them little scraps Martha'd brought back was useless as hen shit against a hurricane. Martha'd smiled and didn't argue. Martha hadn't told Clara the last thing Pearl had said that day, said directly to her, mouth free of the pins pushed back into the purple ball of a cushion on an elastic band around her wrist. Pearl holding up a looking glass big around as a straw hat, for Martha to approve the repair.

"Son says he likes you," said direct and as information, not in passing. "Says he likes you because you're nice."

And anyway, it was Son Martha thought most about; especially him with the dreamy look on his face as he listened to the crystal radio him and carpenter had assembled. And the way him and carpenter worked together. It's a sorry hen don't think her chick'll grow to a peacock and prove to be a rainbow for the world. But Son had something special about him a non-mother could see as well.

Agreeing with Clara about how tough it was going to be for a woman on her own with a blind child, Martha in her silence rooted for their wellbeing.

"They call me one-armed," Carpenter said as he was saying goodbye to Son, "they wrong as usual. I got two arms. It's a hand that's missing. And since we been together you've been that other hand for me, and a good one. And if they'd thought big enough to ask us we could've found a way to build the Taj Mahal or the Great Wall of China. They just didn't have sense enough to ask us.

"Everybody is what they called handicapped, boy. Yours and mine's just more obvious, but that don't mean nothing."

"Yes, sir."

"It has been a pleasure working with you," Carpenter said.

"You too, sir."

"I'm going to hear about you some day."

"I'll make it something good."

"Deal."

"Deal. Thank you for teaching me."

# 18

# Two of Your Old Friends

May 2, 1938

Dear Peck,

Baby, you will never guess who showed up out of nowhere
and is rooming here at 560 now. Two of your old friends
that you wrote about. Pearl Moon & her boy! They've been
here two days. I see what you meant about them . . .

V

Honest to Jesus, it wasn't that Vienna *wanted* to know everybody in 'lo'
Dunbar's business. It wasn't even that she was that interested, except
maybe to have some gossip to speed up the time in the shop, and to write
to Peck about. Most everybody heard what she heard, and maybe more,
including 'lo' Dunbar's barbers, bartenders, pool hall men, funeral parlor folks, bootblacks, hustlers, and who knows who all else, knew most
of what there was to know about most everybody anyway. Same way the
domestics, chauffeurs, yard boys, workers out at the plant, janitors who
crossed Dunbar Avenue day to day into the white folks' section, even
out to the Henderson District, got to know their business, too.

Not much happened in Chilton's 'lo' Dunbar Street colored section
that *some*body didn't see, and that self-same somebody didn't tell somebody else. And so on, until sooner or later what was told or what was
heard, or what was said to have been seen, got around to Vienna in as
close proximity as she was in the beauty shop, where talk, usually about
other people's business, was the lifeblood of daily communication.

Vienna. Vienna Minnifee. Future Mrs. Peck Morgan.
First chair beautician in
The Colored House of Beauty, Potluck's beauty salon.
Marcel Waving, Hair Dying, Facial and Scalp Treatments,

Shampooing, Manicuring, Eyebrow Shaping,
Always courteous treatment.
Closed on Mondays and Tuesdays
Except by appointment.

Now Pearl and Son's arrival in Chilton, that was one occurrence that others had to hear from Vienna, because she was there when they arrived. Standing that evening after work on the corner of Everett and Chilton, where she crossed to head home to 560, the rooming house where she lived. Owned by Chap, run by his wife Potluck. A Wednesday it was, which meant it had been a light day for doing heads. Hardly worth being open. A day consisting mostly of a little light cleaning up, getting ready for the rest of the week. It was the day when stories and hearsay were sorted and sifted through most thoroughly to be set for the coming late week and weekend rush.

So any telling of Pearl and Son's road weary arrival in Chilton, to be accurate, had to start with Vienna's version of it.

Standing there were she, who they'd come to know as Pearl Moon, with a satchel in one hand, a note in the other, and Son, holding on to her sleeve with his free hand, his satchel in the other. Both of them, after what looked like some hard traveling, were as dusty and scuffed as two bundles dropped off some shinny man's wagon.

Everybody in motion but the two of them. Women doing their last evening shopping before stores closed, men and women just rushing home after work, or men moving to the bar or the pool hall—moving around the two like streams of water around two rocks. Many of them giving the woman and boy a quick studying appraisal as they moved past, but none stopped, except Vienna, asking can I help you, point you somewhere?

Pearl nodding with that just-about-impossible-to-read half-smile people would come to know and puzzle over, thanking Vienna for her kindness, looking at her with the direct look they would also come to know and note for its intensity, taking Vienna all in, assessing and calibrating like Schlaffer the pawnbroker looking through his loupe at a trinket professed to be an heirloom with a pedigreed provenance, the final appraisal filed away to be referenced in all future evaluations and advisements.

Pearl held out the creased piece of paper. Did Vienna know this address?

Pulling her attention from the boy, Vienna looked at the paper. Not only did she know it, she said, it was where she was going. 560 Chilton. The boy nodded as if he knew it all along.

The three of them headed off, with Vienna a step or two in the lead, almost bumping into a light pole, listening and looking from Pearl to the boy as they were walking to 560. The boy clutching the woman's sleeve, his head in a slow bob and swing, rolling right or left like he was catching scents, or listening to a slow motion tennis match as he took in the sounds: voices, traffic, and footsteps.

Pearl was carrying on two conversations, one with Vienna, mostly asking questions about points of interest. At the same time, in a slightly lower voice with the boy, she was appraising everything in the sweep of her vision that might be an obstruction or of danger to her child.

It put Vienna in mind of the juggler in the amateur contest at King's Theater once, tossing balls and plates and a top hat, all at the same time. Pearl was way more amazing than that as she and her son moved together like two halves of something, some being, that was more than the sum of their two parts. Him like the tail on a kite as she wove, stopped, started through the shoppers and pedestrians on Chilton Street.

Vienna walked them along that block of two-or three-storied professional buildings with their awnings unfurled, which housed the offices of two colored doctors, the lawyer; the three-story hotel with the druggist, barbershop, and beauty parlor on the first floor; the pool hall, pawn shop, ice cream parlor, meat market, fruit stand, King's Colored movie theater, the café, the Baptist and Methodist churches (pointing to Reverend Leonard's Spain Street Zion A.M.E., where she sang in the choir); the grocery store, women's clothing and dry goods store, undertaker, insurance, and millinery; and the stoplights at the corners of Downing and Percival.

Vienna looked at the street from how the woman, a newcomer, must see it: the business district of 'lo' Dunbar. A street to be proud of. Almost 100% colored-owned and operated from one end to the other. Well kept. Clean windows. Fresh goods. Decent enough prices so that coloreds were satisfied or proud to do their shopping there. The merchants wheeling in their carts, sweeping down their sidewalks, cranking their awnings up, taking their aprons off. People speaking to Vienna, eyeing the couple with her, asking with scrunched-up eyebrows who the two new arrivers were, the woman with mouth going a mile a minute, the boy sniffing like a bloodhound. Vienna just smiling and nodding, as if she was too engrossed in what Pearl was saying to catch the meaning of their expressions, and them, thinking to themselves, Okay, don't tell us, we'll know anything worth knowing soon enough anyway.

The note with the address was from Mister R.W. Boone, the mother said.

"Royale & Rhymes," Vienna said.

"Royale & Rhymes' Minstrels All Colored All The Time!" The boy said.

Then they must know Peck Morgan.

The boy beamed up, "Peck the cornet player? Bums cigarettes."

Vienna laughed and clapped her hands.

"That's who you are," Vienna said. "Pearl and Son. He wrote me about you, maybe a year ago. Or more. You sew, and you sing."

Yes, mother and son said together.

"Peck is my boyfriend."

"You're Vienna," Pearl said. "He talked about you all the time."

"They were just here. You missed them by about two weeks. Peck wasn't with R.W. anymore either. Plays with Tate Dash now, first trumpet."

"Tate Dash?"

"Tate Dash."

Peck's in the big time.

The money was better too, Pearl bet.

They laughed. Peck Morgan. Small world. "They'll be back here at the end of November," Vienna said.

Pearl and Son. Honest to Jesus! Vienna couldn't get over it. What a small world. Just two weeks ago. She remembered he said they had had left the show—a while ago.

"And now here we are," Pearl said.

Pearl described 560 to Son.

A big old four-story brick house set back about thirty feet from the sidewalk. Eight columns and five big windows across the first two floors, with banisters between. Third floor was narrower. Four windows wide. Fourth floor was like a box or lookout space set right on the edge. A big green grass lawn all around the house. Like white folks' mansions they'd seen in various places. A high spiked fence with a double gate. Ironwork with scenes pictured in them. Look like somebody or something on fire on one side, and on this side something falling . . . She would tell him more about them later, she promised.

The house's white trim all painted nice. Clean front and big side yards. There's a small patch of flowers on either side of six sturdy wooden steps. No handrail. Then up the pavement to the house, with paths around both sides leading to the back.

Smells of supper met them on the porch; whispering through the screen door like Romeo calling to Juliet. Vienna called Luck, and introduced them. R.W. had sent them Pearl said, and they've been on the road a while, which was about as much as Vienna'd gotten out of Pearl on their short walk from the bus stop.

R.W. Boone said if they were ever up this way, Chap and Luck'd do right by them. R.W. had sent Chap a letter some months ago, Luck recalled.

"Luck?" The boy said. "Are you lucky, Ma'am?"

"Guess I am, for me," she said. "But it started as Potluck; from the way I cook sometimes."

"He's not shy about asking questions," his mother said. "He'll ask about anything. Won't stop until you quit answering. I prefer you not lie to him. But stop him when you want, or if he gets on your nerves."

"Children supposed to be curious," Luck said.

"He'll abuse it though," his mother said, stroking his head with a gentle gesture. "He'll ask a duck how many feathers it's got. Won't you?"

"Yes ma'am," he admitted slyly. "I can't help it."

Mama knows, she told him.

Luck called back into the house to Chap, who came with the easy, heavy-set flap-flap of his leather house slippers.

"I never looked for those that R.W. sent," Chap said looking Pearl and Son over. "They either showed the hell up, or they goddamned didn't."

"Oh, Chap," Potluck said with her gentle, disapproving way. "Maybe, now we got a child living here, you'll quit your cussing."

"He ain't no goddamned child," Chap told her, "look at him. His soul older than mine."

Potluck laughed. "What you know about somebody's soul, you old heathen?"

"Any goddamned way," Chap said, "If they were with R.W. long as he said in the letter, then this boy could probably tutor me on some cuss words. Right?" Putting his hand on Son's shoulder.

Showing no embarrassment, the boy smiled.

Chap, Vienna explained, cursed as natural as everybody else blinked or drew breath. It wasn't meant to be profane or offensive, it was just the way he talked, in front of a child, a preacher, the police, one of his tenants, or a widow woman. All white people and most Negroes *made* you curse, was how he explained it.

Son held his hand out and Chap grasped it and they shook.

Vienna could see Pearl did not know exactly how influential the woman and big Negro were that she was addressing. Just to look at them they would not seem, at first, even to Pearl's practiced eye, to be any more than a pretty well set colored couple, running a boarding house and a beauty parlor. But, throughout the 'lo' Dunbar colored community along the length and breadth of Chilton Street and the whole 'lo' Dunbar district, even on the west side across Anthony Avenue, it was rumored among the civic and law enforcement arms—in the middle-class White section of Henderson District, and as far uptown—that Chap owned property in his and Luck's names. How much was known only to a few in Chilton, most of them bankers above Dunbar Street. That, plus his side business of loans to 'lo' Dunbar Negroes who didn't trust or weren't trusted by the banks or credit unions. Therefore most of the money that came into 'lo' Dunbar at least touched Chap's hands before it got where it was going.

They'd seen and heard plenty, Pearl said, setting them straight right up front. Son'd taken it all in and remembered everything. He was going to do special before he was through.

Everybody was sizing everybody else up as Pearl asked about accommodations, house rules, mealtimes, and rent. Potluck gave her the rate and said they could settle all that up later, she wanted to get some food in them so they could go up and get some rest.

"No," Pearl told her. "I've learned to take care of business first, ma'am."

Chap didn't say anything but he took notice and approved. Chap was first of all about business.

Pearl, from somewhere quicker than they could spot, and, Honest to Jesus, faster than a card shark could produce an ace, or a snap-blade knife, pulled out that rubber band-wrapped roll of money. She thumb-licked off a month's rent, and without a word between them, passed it to Son. He moved to Chap and handed it to him without a missed cue or false step.

"We would like a receipt please," the boy said.

Chap laughed. "Luck, baby, would you feed this little Negro while I try to figure out how I'm going to keep him from taking over all my properties?"

Luck moved off to the kitchen, telling their new tenants to follow her.

Potluck was a school-trained, state-certified beautician who had originally come to Chilton from Chicago to take care of her dying mother, Barbara Ann McIntosh, who had grown up with Martha Jean, Chap's mama. Barbara Ann, ambitious as she was pleasant and charming, rented space from Tinhouse the barber in the back of his shop. Mama

McIntosh, poor thing, didn't last long—the cancer was cruel as a Mississippi prison guard. Barbara Ann, even in that short time, had built up a right nice clientele, being single and having no attachments back in Chicago, where she'd gone off to right after high school, mostly to get away from her daddy. She decided to stay on in Chilton and try to make the best of it.

She went to Chap for a loan to open her own shop. She had her eye on a storefront three blocks east on the northeast corner of Macy. It was, Barbara Ann explained, to be the first professional colored beauty parlor in Chilton. Not in somebody's parlor or back room, smelling of whatever was being cooked for dinner that evening, with children running all through the house; but three or four stations with trained, state-licensed cosmetologists, in clean uniforms: appointments on time, latest magazines, coffee or iced tea while you wait. Clean as a Mercy Hospital operating room. Just like Chap ran 560: linen changed Saturdays, meals on time, respectable boarders, prestigious address. She hadn't added the last part to flatter him but to let him know she had a business vision that was first rate.

Barbara Ann sold her family home soon after her mama died, refusing to live ever again within Big Walter's walls. She was a boarder at 560. Barbara Ann and Chap had eyed each other when they were in high school, but Big Walter, Barbara Ann's daddy, had wedged in between young Barbara Ann and young Chap and all of the rest of the young boys, and that was that. Chap offered her an option, a lease on the beauty parlor, or for Miss Barbara Jean McIntosh to become Mrs. Jasper Chap Metcalf.

For the longest time Potluck kept the beauty parlor, but finally, at Chap's urging, she semi-retired, as she called it, and put Vienna in charge at the shop. Potluck still occasionally did a few exclusive customers' hair on special occasions—weddings, proms—and by prior request, burials.

She didn't mention it to Peck in her letter, but thinking about the new roomers was exhausting, Vienna realized, just traveling the few little blocks getting to 560, and she thought about the toll it must take on the mother hour by hour, day after day. For a moment she had a little flash of fear at the thought of what would become of Son if something were to happen to his mother one day. The world would likely disappear. It was a sad and scary thought. She was sorry she'd had it and tried to not linger on it as she fell off to sleep.

May 7, 1938

. . . They haven't said where they've been since they left being with you guys. But some of it must have been pretty rough. They've been here a week now and have met everybody. Pearl watches everything & everybody like a mama lion. We all, including Chap & Luck, still kind of tiptoeing around her.

But everybody has taken to Son. Even Chap. It's hard not to. He's like a sponge & bright as a 500-watt bulb. All the men, Chap, Tinhouse, Cecile & String, they're like uncles to him. I'm starting to see already how he's using them all in different ways. The more he asks the more you want to answer. He's something.

Miss you,

Love

Your V

July 11, 1938

. . . Son couldn't ask for a better or more devoted mother.

Chap calls Son Butch, and keeps him busy when he's not doing something Pearl tells him to do. Son winds clocks, empties the pan under the icebox, helps Fletcher with emptying the ashbins, runs errands. The other morning he beat the rugs hung over the back fence, wailing on them with the baseball bat like Gosh Gibson.

Chap made it plain early on to everybody that Son is to come and go without being messed with from any sonofabitch out there. There is to be no running starts and bumps from behind, or cuffed hands to the back of Son's head to dislodge his cap, no outthrust legs meant to trip. No tight-packed snowballs, or water balloons, or soot-filled paper bag bombs. No bullying or they'd have to answer to Chap himself.

Potluck and I were wondering the other night just how he navigates like he does, mostly without stick or stumbling. Does he count steps, or is he like a bat, sending out silent signals? Does he have some kind of x-ray vision? Anyway—like I say, they're settled in and it's hard to remember a time when they weren't here.

Japan and China going to war

Bet that German still feels the Brown Bombers' right & lefts. That's the way you knock me out!

Miss you,

Love

Your V

P.S. It's hard

to remember

a time when

you were here.

Hurry up Nov.

X X X X

# 19

# Mr. Amalfi

## Spring through Fall 1939

Vienna'd just drug in one evening from being on her feet all day long. It had been busy because Tate Dash's band, with Peck now filling the first trumpet seat, was coming to town. Women wanted to look their best for the Dash band's Friday and Saturday night appearances. There was always a jumping time when Tate and his boys came blasting the blues.

Vienna sat there on the porch with Chap until she could get up enough strength for that last climb up to her room and to wash before dinner. When Mr. Amalfi, Carlo Amalfi, the produce man with the horse-drawn wagon, his hat tilted at the angle favored by the Negroes themselves as they angled against the walls and streetlamps along Dunbar Street, came walking up, whistling. During the winter he delivered coal and his wagon was for hire for moving and cartage.

He had on a suit jacket and clean shirt. His horse was nowhere to be seen. They spoke. Naturally, it was Chap he wanted to talk to. And Vienna wasn't about to get up to move. She wanted to see what had brought the *I*-talian, half-no-English speaking man who reminded her of somebody in the movies whose name she could not remember, late in the evening to talk to Chap.

He stopped whistling as he approached the porch, reminding Vienna of the way our colored men approached white men with say-so. The Italian was apologetic, humble, and respectful. Chap invited him up.

There were just the two chairs on the porch. Chap gave Vienna a look and she, over the protestations of the vegetable man, excused herself, but didn't go any further than just inside the screen door. The vegetable man took her vacated seat. He was very formal. He said, with obviously rehearsed language, how he had great admiration for Chap and his position on Dunbar Street. And he wanted to speak to him businessman to businessman. What it turned out to be was he wanted to ask permission for Son to come work for him. Ride along with him when he made his morning rounds. He had heard of the young man's singing from around the neighborhood and thought it might prove beneficial to all concerned if the young man—Son—did his singing to attract buyers for the grocery man, Mr. Carlos Amalfi's, produce. With the Italian's broken English and Chap's total lack of Italian, it took a while to get it all out.

Chap explained he wasn't the boy's father. Mr. Amalfi understood that. It was out of some kind of *I*-talian or old country courtesy to Chap, as the head of the house, that he was asking. Chap nodded.

Chap said he would speak to Son's mother on Mr. Amalfi's behalf. But there was one thing. For Chap to intercede on Mr. Amalfi's behalf, Mr. Amalfi would have to start his deliveries on Dunbar Street at least once a week, *before* he went uptown to Lewis Heights. What Chap was talking about was those on Dunbar getting the freshest vegetables first thing and not having to wait and end up with the picked-overs late in the afternoon. Mr. Amalfi didn't bristle. He didn't balk. Without missing a beat he had a counter offer. He said he would alternate his days. And, Chap added, Mr. Amalfi would charge no more on Dunbar Street than he did in Lewis Heights. A deal.

Standing in the foyer of 560, watching them on the porch, Vienna witnessed how Chap was his daddy's son. She had always known it. But again felt pride swell in her at witnessing once again the evidence of it. She thought of Peck and how she loved colored men who carried themselves like men.

Chap and Mr. Amalfi stood up together. They shook hands.

"*Rispetto per rispetto*," Mr. Amalfi said.

"Respect for respect," Chap said, understanding.

The first part was settled.

Now they had to convince Pearl. Chap asked Vienna if she would ask Pearl to come to the door.

Pearl joined them on the porch and Mr. Amalfi bowed from his waist as they shook hands. He told her how he wanted to offer Son a job. Pearl told him that Son had a job. She said Son had asked her back when they first arrived what he could do to help; what would his job be? She said she told him to listen and learn. She wasn't sending him to school, she said, and this was the way she was getting him to learn. Learn to talk like them, meaning President Roosevelt and most of the white men on the radio. Because that's how the educated talk. Listening is his job. Listening to everything they say, *they* being white folks, and how they say it. And learn what they think matters. Listen to the news and the soap operas and comedy programs and quiz shows and adventure shows. Learn that. That was his job she said.

Yes, Missus, Mr. Amalfi agreed. Being able to speak good was important. It was important to being a good American. But, he said, relaxing enough to make his first joke, earning money was important too. A good American was an American with an earned wage in his pocket. They laughed at his wisdom and wit. And being outside in the air, he added, rather than cooped up inside. That was good too.

What did he really want? Pearl asked him, direct. He could get any or a whole bunch of colored or Italian or white boys to ride with him. There were a plenty that could sing, and see. What did he really want with her son?"

"Your son is special, has *accortezza*," the vegetable man told her, shaking his head at not knowing the correct translation.

"*Oculato* . . ." Tapping his forehead with his index finger. "*Sagace*."

"Smart?" Chap asked. It wasn't exactly what Mr. Amalfi meant, but he didn't know a better word in English. He told her how he had not been able to speak any English when he arrived in American. How he had come with a dream of doing better.

"Good sense?" Vienna said.

"*Si!* Good sense," the vegetable peddler nodded. "*Oculato. Sagace. Graci.*"

"Shrewd," Chap volunteered, making a maneuvering motion with his hand.

"*Si, Si.*" That, Mr. Amalfi thought, was even closer to the word the Italian was looking for. *Accortezza.* Shrewd. Yes. And her too, he told Pearl. She was a wise lady, for she knew the value of speaking well.

He was, he said, too old and too busy to attend school. "I want your son to learn me to speak as he is learning to speak. Our true arrangement," he admitted, "will be that he will teach me to improve to speak good. And I will teach him what I have learned about the ways of my customers, and about music, and about—" He made a gesture indicating everything. "I will be his pupil. He will be mine."

"And," Son said, "If I teach you as I am learning, you will pay me—*si?*" They laughed.

"A smart man," Mr. Amalfi said, quoting from memory, "knows what to say. A wise man knows whether or not to say it. I say, *si.* I will pay you. Wages."

They laughed, acknowledging his wisdom.

"For what is in his head," Pearl said. She put her hand on Son's head, him not shying away. "This," she said, "is where he will do the work he does."

Mr. Amalfi left, whistling.

"Hear he likes a little dark meat," Chap said to Vienna and Luck after Pearl and Son had gone inside.

Vienna'd heard it too, said, "Mr. Amalfi'd be colored if he could."

"Would be if it didn't cost him," Luck said.

"Might be even if it did," Chap said.

Son started that next Monday morning.

In the early morning light, in the gateway of the writhe of metal of 560, Son stood at the curb. He was in his zipped jacket and wool cap, listening as Mr. Amalfi, in the seat of his produce-loaded wagon, rambled up Clinton. The sound of the man's whistling warbled dramatically above the steady pace of the horse's metal-shod hooves. Horse, man, and rig pulled to a halt.

"Good morning, Mister Amalfi."

"*Buongiorno, Senior Luna.*"

Giving the boy a hand up to the wagon seat beside him, and with a light flick of the reins, they began making their way up Clinton Street. The boy's heart rate much faster than Bellini, the horse's trod, which he would come to learn was *andante*. They crossed Dunbar, heading for the Lewis Heights district around North Clinton Avenue. Mister Amalfi, even that first morning, asking questions about phrases and punctuations, laughing when asking what something was called as he pointed to it, before remembering that Son couldn't see it.

*Stupido.*

Stupid.

It was the first instance of a lot of their time spent laughing at and about their handicaps with English and sight. Fun. Not like work.

> "Good morning, ladies,
>> ready or not . . ."

Daisy—the domestic, the girl, the help—who worked for Mrs. Jacob, who was the wife of Mr. Russell Jacob, who was the manager of First Chilton Bank, recognized the voice, but it took her a minute to place its owner.

> "Here comes the produce man
>> come see what Tony's got."

Then it came to her like sunshine breaking through a cloud. Son. Couldn't be nobody but that blind who'd won the last, she couldn't remember how many, amateur contests on Thursday nights at the King picture show.

> "Got sweet onions and salad greens,
>> peas and beans,
>> got carrots, turnips and beets,
>> 5 cents a bunch."

She heard him sing as she, wiping her hands on her apron, walked down the hall from the kitchen and looked out the parlor window.

"String beans, spinach, cooking apples,
    5 cents a pound."

Him, all right. Sitting beside the Dago Tony on the buckboard of the wagon.

Daisy saw the front curtains, upstairs and down, in the Boland house across the street pull back; Ruth Ann, old Mrs. Boland's girl, a fellow petitioner at Zion AME, likely downstairs; and Mrs. Boland, the wife of Mr. John Boland, a high-up, senior manager of something out to the plant, peeking out from the second floor.

Son's head held back at the same angle as when he was on stage, same joy in his voice, same smile on his face, singing out.

"Got sweet onions and got corn,
    tomatoes round and ripe,
    got string beans, pretty and green
    and the price is right, come see what I mean."

As she headed back down the hall for the back door, Daisy patted her apron pocket to make sure she had the seventy-five cents produce money she'd been given that morning.

"Miss Jacob," Daisy called, hoping the woman was having her after breakfast nap; "it's the vegetable man!"

Son was singing now, just like Bessie Smith,

"There ain't nothing I can do, or nothing I can say
    That folks don't criticize me,"

Just like Bessie Smith for the world,

"But I'm goin' to do just as I want to anyway
    And don't care if they all despise me."

Laughing she moved quickly back to the kitchen, pausing only to slip into her shoes, then grab the big woven-string shopping bag from the doorknob and through the back door, across the porch, around the side of the house toward the street.

In that bright spring to browning fall season along North Clinton Avenue and the wide, quiet, oak-lined streets of the surrounding Lewis Heights neighborhoods, there were occasional minor distractions that broke up the routine of Daisy's and the other domestic's monotonous day-work duties. Welcomed were the mailman, the door-to-door salesmen, the regular arrivals of the milkman and egg sellers, and shinny men. But their favorite diversion was the Tuesday and Saturday appearances of Son and the produce man. The sharp, slow clop-clop of the horse's hooves on the cobblestones, and the boy singing his chants about their produce and his other songs, popular and operatic, were the unquestioned highlights of those days.

Though they would not understand the opera songs' words, they marveled at how smooth, as the shimmering colors in the soap bubbles of her Monday morning wash, each note flowed out of and into the next, and how they rose from low to high and back like the call of a whippoorwill. Daisy longed to sing along with him, jealous to know the words the way the blind boy did, and to be able to speak Italian. She tried to imagine Horace and her sitting at a candle-lighted table in an Italian restaurant, with a strolling singer serenading them as they held hands.

That first morning Daisy was among the girls to gaggle and jockey good-naturedly to get the best of the items in bushels and baskets and boxes in the loaded wagon bed.

Tony, the not half-bad looking Italian man with the thick mustache, who reminded her of a rough-around-the-edges version of Warren William in *Imitation of Life*, answering, *Questo è il mio colore figliola.* His colored son, he translated, as he and the boy laughed, and he gestured for the women to keep it a secret from their employers.

Tony, as always, gracious to the colored women, young and old, as if they were *donna di casa*, women of the house, rich and positioned and white, white as the white women peering out at them from the windows of the stately houses they were mistresses of. Calling each by name with a tune whistle-trilled for each and a parting *Grazie e bona giornata, signora* (Thank you and good day, madam), as he added their coins to his four- barreled coin changer, and Bellini with a short nicker, neigh, or snort, clopped, shoe-hoofed forward, like an 80-stone winding-down windup toy. Windup toys being exactly what Mrs. Jacob thought all of them, their colored help, were, something mechanical to be wound up and ordered around until they finally ran down at the end of the day.

Even before they arrived, Daisy whisked the feather duster absent-mindedly at the menagerie of porcelain lords and ladies, as she imagined Son and Tony making their way among the other, just stirring, merchants at the farmers market, and maybe waving to Horace in the early light as they moved up Chilton Street and across Dunbar on the ride out each morning. Horace maybe saluting them with his nightstick, his badge number 79 shiny on his dark blue uniform in announcement of who he was: Chilton's first colored patrolman.

After they had purchased what their white women had instructed their girls to get and the wagon had moved up the street, their white women would come downstairs and sit in the way at the kitchen table, smoking and sipping at a cup of coffee, asking after the odd couple. Who was that colored boy sitting next to that Tony, singing? And was he blind?

Yes, and he had talent, he was smart and he was theirs, Daisy thought, and guessed all of the other colored maids and cooks, babysitters, and laundresses up and down the length of North Clinton Avenue were as possessive about Son as she, and would go through the same sort of interrogation. They too would know pretty much the same things about Son, but would parcel out bits of it in one-word answers like a miser doling ducats from his stash. Their employers wanting to know not only about Son but also about what went on down below Dunbar. It was as if the employers were striving to close the wide gap in the disparity between what their employees knew about them versus what they knew about those who worked for them.

Fat chance. It was one of the things the women and girls laughed out loud at as they waited at the bus stop or in the back of the public transportation as it rumbled them home in the evening. They swapped stories about how they had deflected inquiries about their business as they had picked up bits of gossip told directly, overheard during phone conversations, or the dozens of other ways the domestic cadre knew what they knew about the households and business lives of white folks in the North Clinton district.

Tony and Son went on up the street too busy tending to their own to think about them noisy women. Son singing and attracting the house-keepers like the Pied Piper, as if they were intoxicated by the fecund aroma of plump oranges, plums, apples, and melons to heft, sniff, thump, and then purr about in flirty tones, unnecessary to the trans-action but fun, like humming birds flitting around impatiens. Thinking the boy too green to understand the game as they teased the produce man in hushed, hussy-coded innuendos, inquiring about the firmness and juiciness of items in the tradesman's haul. All chirping at him at once as he tried to comprehend it all and answer in kind with rushing flourishes of tongue-stumbling English before having to resort to what, in their imaginations, were rutting yet romantic Italian expressions. Making him even more difficult to understand, and delighting them even more, until either the boy, humming and rocking slightly, secretly pulled the reins, or the horse's internal clock thought it time to move on, and with a snort took one clop step forward, causing the jingle of the traces, signaling it was time for the boy to sing out again above its *adagio* gait, in a tone as musky as a rotting onion—

> "Big fat berries been *plucked*,
>> peaches shook from the tree,
>> telling you the berries've been plucked,
>> sweet, juicy peaches
>> shook down from the tree.
>> Ladies, if you want you some,
>> run out here now and talk to me."

—and them covering their mouths to keep their screaming laughter at this twelve- year-old soul, sounding for the world like the bassist blues singer, from rippling across the lawn and through the windows for their boss women to hear, until then it was really time for them to scruff back to their dusting, scrubbing, diapering, or cooking.

Until soon one morning came a sudden summer downpour and they, man and boy, soaked to the skin, were given refuge by Daisy on Mrs. Jacob's back porch. It was on Daisy's own initiative to give them towels to dry their heads and she who double spread newspapers for them to stand on just inside by the kitchen door. Mr. Amalfi politely declined, but Son entered. He was given a cookie to nibble (and one wax paper-wrapped to put in his pocket for later), and a cup of milk from a quart delivered fresh that morning, cream on top, and if Mrs. Jacob didn't like it, then too black bad.

Daisy was asking about his mama, or Luck, Chap, or String, until Mrs. Jacob came to check on the commotion.

"He's dripping on your floor, Daisy," she said.

"Yes ma'am."

"Well, if you want to mop it again it's fine with me."

"Yes ma'am."

Well worth it, Daisy thought, in a way she didn't try to analyze or justify. She just knew it felt good to have him standing there, and if it meant mopping "her" floor again she'd do it and hum while she did.

What happened was Mrs. Jacobs pulled rank and the boy was kidnapped and ushered down the hall into the parlor and stationed by the door of the bright, dustless room while he was questioned about ways and things to do with Tony, or 'lo' Dunbar, including was his mama the woman who was the seamstress? Miss Pearl Moon, yes, ma'am she was. Well tell her I might be calling to speak with her about a garment, Mrs. Jacobs said, but it had to be kept a secret between the two of them. Yes, ma'am he would and he would deliver the message. Yes, she said, she could see that he was a young man of his word. And then, that bit of business out of the way, she went seeking verification of juicy bits of gossip gleaned from the tidbits overheard by her and the other mistresses from girls up or down the block, many of which he might have known but almost surely had little knowledge of and even less interest in, but which Daisy—probably eavesdropping from the kitchen—had claimed total ignorance of.

Until the rain stopped and it was time to go. Thanking them, and assuring them he'd pass the greetings along to Chap and Luck and his mother and Vienna and Branch Ottley, Son returned to his hawking—

> "Come look ladies, we got it all,
>> Tony's best produce for the fall.
>> Beets, carrots, cabbage, grapes,
>> okra, potatoes, collard greens,
>> pumpkins, peppers, pears,
>> lettuce, limes, Brussels sprouts,
>> come see our wares!—"

—and the planets and squirrels went through their cycle, and leaves greened and flamed and fell, and the wagon on the last day of the season rolled back down North Clinton Avenue toward Dunbar and below, Tony and Son together on the seat; the boy singing; Daisy, as she had come to do over time, humming, harmonizing her soprano with his tenor until they faded out of hearing.

They'd assigned each other homework, a radio program to listen to with an articulate speaker or a classical music or opera program, to be discussed the following day, clarifying points, defining, correcting grammar, notions.

Son had *buon orecchio*, a *good* ear, and *uccello beffardo*, mockingbird skills. He learned as much Italian as his boss learned English. It was still heavily accented, but grammatically correct. He had a steadily increasing English vocabulary. The boy had also learned about Italian opera and composers, and oratorios, *da capo arias*, trills, and accents that thrilled the listeners along North Clinton Avenue. If he had a voice, Tony said, never mind like Caruso, but like Son's, he would be happy as a lark. He would sing outside the windows of all the beautiful Negro women, *Tutte le belle donne di Negro*, while they flung roses down to him.

Until it was finally time, as Son, holding Bellini's reins, pulled up in front of 560. Mr. Amalfi helped Son down.

"Goodbye, Mister Moon. Thank you."

"*No, grazie, Mister Amalfi.*"

The boy moved through the iron gateway and up the walk as the horse's hoof beats faded down Clinton.

# 20

# Tinhouse

## Chilton, 1939

Those who knew Tinhouse knew they didn't really know him. They knew he did not run his mouth, and knew he took his time, but also knew what little they did know was enough to know if he'd wanted them to know more he would already, after all these years, have told them. That much they knew.

In the shop Tuesdays through Saturdays and after hours during weekend poker, cooncan, and tonk, while others around him were in rambling or heated discussions, Tinhouse was content to do what in his opinion was one of the two things he did best, play cards, and the other was to cut hair. To him neither activity required a whole lot of conversation.

His opinions on politics, news, sports, or music were not generally offered or sought, but the phrase "Ain't that right, Tin?" was often asked, as he was called upon to be the final arbiter in tangled matters of dispute. He was the man behind the first chair. It was his place of business. He was acknowledged and appreciated. They just didn't expect a lot of jawboning from him.

Tinhouse did not *mind* words, would listen as long as you wanted to talk, and you could always sense that he was paying attention, with interest, not just giving the *unhuh* or grunt at the appropriate time. You were never conscious of his having posed a question, but he must have asked you something, you would think later, otherwise why had you opened up to him like that, not that you were sorry you had, having felt good getting whatever it happened to be out. Furthermore, you never had to worry that what he was told was subject to judgment or in danger of being spread. The one thing everybody knew was, Tinhouse did not run his mouth.

That was part of what made it as hard to read him as a clean black-board. That, and that he was so deliberate. Steady. Working, eating, walking; what little talking he did was *slow*. They didn't mean slug-slow, or stupid slow, not dawdling but measured. He was always on time. He just took his time and yours too if you let him. No hurry, no worry, he'd've said if he had put it into words. But he didn't.

In poker, for instance, raking in the big pots wasn't what made him a frequent overall winner when, in the wee small hours, the game broke up. Chasing Lady Luck's whims down dark alleys with blind trust was not his way. Studied and steady was his game. So deliberate was he that it was hard to figure if his strategy was focused solely on the hand in play, or if he was thinking ahead four or five games, or five or six sessions. Either way, the general consensus was that Tinhouse was the turtle to bet on in the race with a hare.

Griff, the second barber, could cut almost two heads to Tinhouse's one, but being in Tinhouse's barber chair was a time you could close your eyes and, as he was giving you a hot lather shave, or washing your hair, or massaging your scalp, or hand clipping and scissor snipping and razor edging away, look like Lena Horne was humming some lullaby you first heard from your mama when you were still in her belly. You forgot all about your job and your bills and squabbles and the general jinx that was white folks. So when he tapped you on the shoulder and turned you so you could look at your newly shorn self in the mirror, you were nine times out of ten disappointed that he had finished and you had to be dusted off, powdered, and sent back out into the world.

Where was he from? Son, in Tinhouse's chair, asked, as Griff was finishing with Maxwell, and Haworth was getting in the other barber's chair for his every-two-weeks cut.

Alabama was Tinhouse's answer.

Him too, Son said.

A couple of them missed it, but a couple of the others turned their sudden attention toward what was really a private conversation between barber and his young customer, their ears perked up like a stream-lapping deer hearing a twig snap.

"Was Alabama where you came here to Chilton from?"

Naw, not directly, Tinhouse said, he'd traveled all over.

"Me too."

The blind boy, who before landing in Chilton had spent time traveling throughout the south with his mama leading him, was just asking with the kind of deep curiosity that was his way. And in those two questions he had already gotten more background on Tinhouse than any of them had in all the time they'd known him.

They generally thought the handicap of the boy losing one capacity, eyesight, was balanced off by the gaining of another, insight. Mother Nature's way of caring for her own. But even more than that the general thinking was he was like the rebirth of somebody who'd been around before, maybe two or three times prior. He was, like his mama Miss Pearl claimed, special. He felt the emotions of the people around him like an animal sensed the weather, like a cat or a chicken getting skittish when a tornado was brewing. It was an instinct to help alert the one-way-or-another disabled to the unseen dangers around them.

In the midst of his clipping Tinhouse was answering yes or no to place names that the boy was asking if he'd been to.

"*Got cha!*" Hughes shouted from his chair along the wall.

The shop went quiet. Tinhouse even looked up.

"Goddamn, I knew it!" Hughes said. He had stood, his finger pointing at Tinhouse like a redheaded woodpecker at a chestnut tree.

Knew *what?* Somebody asked, his tone as much as telling Hughes to cool it because they were finally finding out something about Tinhouse, but Hughes, excited as if he had just discovered fire, said, "I *knew* I'd seen you before!"

"Who?"

"Tinhouse."

"Where?"

"Fighting."

"What?" Haworth laughed. "Tinhouse? Fighting?"

A couple of the others added their disbelieving snickers.

Berks told Hughes to sit down.

"That's right, fighting," he said as he sat. "I saw you. Him."

Tinhouse didn't say anything.

"Fighting what?"

"Who?"

"When?"

"I'm fixing to tell you. About 19 twentysomething--I don't remember when right now." Hughes waited for Tinhouse to confirm it or call him a liar. Tinhouse did neither.

"I been coming in here eight or nine years," Hughes said, "and I knew I remembered you from *some*where." He started to rise again but looked at Berks and kept his seat.

Haworth confirmed that he remembered Hughes saying that to him, way back, that Hughes remembered Tinhouse from somewhere, long time ago.

"Yeah," Hughes said, "'28, '28, and when you just now said them places you were, I could think of you somewhere other than in this shop, and it come to me, just now. I saw you fight. Deny it."

"How he going to deny something didn't happen?" Berks asked.

"It was in Blythe, Tennessee. That boy you beat, the first one—"

"First one?" Berks got in while Hughes was trying to remember the name.

"Axe!"

"How many he fight?"

"Acts?"

"You say *first* one."

"Asks?"

"*Axe*—like a hatchet."

"Oh, Axe."

"His name was Axe. Axe. Like a hatchet. That was what they called him. And it was 'Come one, come all,'" Hughes remembered.

"And this was Tinhouse fighting this Axe?" Berks asked.

"Axe was the *bad*-est nigger in Blythe at that time."

"Was he?" Berks asked as if he was just humoring Hughes and it was all he could do to keep from laughing at him.

"I lost thirty-five cents on you," Hughes said to Tinhouse. "This was nineteen, twenty years ago, had to be, maybe longer ago than that." He shook his head like he didn't have time to figure it out, "but round in there, had to be," Hughes said, as Haworth said, "Thirty-five cents was a day or two's meal-money back then."

"Two or three, and you mighty well told right it was. And much as I hated that job. Working on the front line in a slaughterhouse, mopping blood and cleaning up cow shit. And they had fights every Saturday night in the stock pen stalls out behind the train depot. And I know you was the most—hardest—you know what I'm trying to say? Most *relentless* fighter I ever saw," as he stood, ignoring Berks. "Like a guard dog had snapped its chain." Showing them: "Come in low. Jab like a jackhammer, crosses, hooks, and uppercuts. All the tricks. It was winner take all. And you did. Had beat down two before Axe. Didn't a one of them go more than three rounds." He sat, winded from his demonstration. "Next thing anybody knew you was off in the night. Gone. Had everybody's money. You a little heavier now, aged of course, but it was you, Negro, no*body* but you."

"What you want?" Berks asked, "your thirty-five cents back?" Everybody laughed. "What you get for betting against Tinhouse in the first place." Berks looked to Tinhouse for confirmation that it was him, as Hughes turned to Haworth, "You remember I told you way back I knew Tinhouse from somewhere."

Yeah, Haworth remembered.

"It wasn't no-body *but* you! I remember because I hadn't ever seen no-body fight like that—that hard. And *nothing* you say going change my mind. It was *you*," Hughes concluded, folding his arms and crossing his legs.

"Was it?" Son asked.

"Not likely."

They were surprised it wasn't a full denial from Tinhouse.

It got quiet again before Hughes, pleased with himself, said, "Wasn't no could've been. Was. Was you."

"You talking about a long time ago," Tinhouse said. "I might not even remember."

Hughes said he remembered, and told it. "Tinhouse was like a bad boss, was one of them fighters the other guy didn't have to look for because he was *quick and nasty*, and always up in the other guy's face, like it was personal."

"Where did you say this was?" Tinhouse asked in a monotone that betrayed real interest.

"Blythe. Blythe, Tennessee."

"Blythe? I think I did come through Blythe once."

Now they were getting somewhere.

"Blythe. Yeah. I think that's where I met that boy. Can't remember his name right now."

Drawing it out, like he was spoon-feeding a sick child. "Blythe. Train run by a stockyard there."

"That's right," Hughes said.

"I was moving around a bit back around then. Had fights there, right?"

"Bare knuckle. Winner take all."

"This boy I'm trying to remember—we left about the same time. If I remember correctly he was a fighter," Tinhouse said, not missing a snip of cutting Son's hair.

"It was a long time ago," Hughes said. "It was a long time ago, and it took me a long time to remember, but I didn't forget. It wasn't no boy. It was *you.*"

"Was it?" Son asked.

Griff, who had known Tinhouse the whole twenty or so years he was in Chilton, waited with the others.

Tinhouse was edging around Son's right ear with the razor, wiping the shaven hairs and foam on a towel over his left wrist.

"Well?" Griff asked, after a long-time silence even for Tinhouse, "You going to tell it or not?"

Tinhouse, satisfied, moved to the left ear. "I cannot remember his name for the life of me. Can't even remember what he looked like. Remember he said he was on the run. Remember that. I had run away from home not long before then, so we traveled along together for a while. And trying to remember the story he told," his concentration still on cutting Son's hair.

Clifford, usually the last one to come in, came in then, smiling and glad to see everybody, wanting, as usual, to talk about something in the news that any other time would have, as usual, already been discussed. Its possibilities thoroughly sifted through and everybody with a position in place on all points of the issue, but by the short hushed greetings and sharp gestures they indicated for him to shut up, be still, and listen. Not insulted by their dismissive attitude toward his entrance, he did. He leaned, shoulder to the wall near the door, although there was an empty chair at the far end, concentrating, trying to catch on and catch up.

When they had settled again like a flock of birds that had in a sudden flurry swooped, circled, and reroosted, Tinhouse, as if he was unaware of any of it, continued.

"The boy—hell, let's say Willie—"

Fine with them. They were willing to concede the name; the point was to keep Tinhouse going.

"He said they accused him of thieving. Hadn't stole a thing," Tinhouse said.

"Next thing he knew he was under a shotgun. Free labor for the county, chopping weeds side the road, or fieldwork, or picking up dead animals, whatever bent-back slog they needed done."

"This is this boy *Willie* you talking about," Hughes, said, sarcasm dripping off his tone like rain off a rusty roof.

"Working off a seventy-five-dollar fine, he said," Tinhouse continued, not directly answering Hughes or his accusation, "plus twenty-five for court fees."

Whew.

"It had started at fifty, the boy said, which was the going vagrancy rate around there at that time, till he called the sheriff a lying motherfucker and the judge took offense."

*Mumph.*

"He, this boy, said he knew better, but patience wasn't one of his virtues then. One hundred dollars at the rate of fifteen cents a day, coming to seventy-five cents a week. Though he was only getting credit for five days, they had him working Saturdays too, off the books, the crew boss, or whatever they called him, pocketing the difference, feeding him wormy stew meat and moldy potatoes, sleeping on a bug-infested pallet on that hot tin house floor."

Tinhouse leaned away from Son to inspect the backs of both ears. Approved, he lowered his arms to his sides, inhaled and exhaled, then raised them and started on the line at his nape.

"Willie said most of the others were older than him, more tame to the treatment, better suited to put up with that old plantation shit. Anyway, he say he bristled, but so that it didn't show, and did what he was told, grinning the whole time." Son's hairline was level across the bottom as if he had used a straight edge, "Grinned them crackers into relaxing, grinned till that one evening it was just falling dark and they escaped."

Tinhouse stopped. Was he trying to remember or had he quit telling it?

"Now I don't even remember if he told me how or what," he said finally. "Had something to do with hanging from a Loblolly pine limb and stuffing a leafy mud ball in the chimney pipe, and in the smoky confusion he got his hands on a rifle—anyway, he escaped." He went quiet.

Was that it?

Had he now tapped out?

No wonder he didn't talk much. He couldn't tell a story worth nothing.

Somebody had to say something. Something. Somebody.

Son said, "And I guess it wasn't too long after that you met up with him? Did you and him become partners?"

That was the right thing to ask. The boy's mama, Miss Pearl, was right. Was something special about him. It was that little bit of a jigger that set the delicate contraption that was Tinhouse back into operation.

"A little while we did. I was fresh to the road and he'd been at it longer. It was him wised me to the ways to maneuver and snake through the twists and tights of being out of the ordinary confines. Ways of thinking about who I was and how I had to be. Ways my daddy would've been scared to even dream about."

"And this boy Willie, looked exactly like you, taught you all this?" Hughes said.

Tinhouse didn't answer.

"Willie the one," Hughes continued, "fought like a crazy man?"

"Wasn't crazy," Tinhouse said. "Fought the way you had to fight in his situation."

"Nigger on the run," Berks said, "in Alabama, them times."

Tinhouse agreed without acknowledging what Berks had said. "It wasn't about who you was fighting. Whoever they were, they were just standing between you and getting a meal without stealing. That meant fighting him like he was that white man you'd waited your whole life to whup."

Okay, then.

It was quiet for a moment, as if they had just heard the opening lines of Lincoln giving the Gettysburg Address, before Griff said, "The white man what had insulted your mama and belittled your daddy with you standing there looking."

"And always cheated you out of your share on the settling crop count," Berks added.

Everybody nodding except Son, Tinhouse, and Haworth, who, with his chin on his chest, was getting razor-edged by Griff, but nobody spoke.

How come, Haworth wondered half-mumbling, Willie didn't just serve out his time?

"And what?" Berks snapped, indignant on Tinhouse's behalf.

"His debt would've been paid—" Haworth said, turning to see why Berks'd asked like he had. "And he'd've been free to go back to—" Just that quickly it had turned to sound ridiculous even to him as he heard himself saying it.

"Down there our debt wasn't never paid," Berks said, stubbing his cigarette out in the ashtray in the arm on his chair.

Their silence was in agreement.

"Ain't that right, Tin?"

They waited. They had questions, but didn't want to press for details and miss out on what else he might be willing to tell. They didn't even turn from him when Reba, the coffee-colored girl with the neck-breaking Coke bottle shape, went switching her way by there from her part-time job at the confectionary. Scared any distraction might irk him and shut off the flow of the story, and they wouldn't get another drop out of him for another twenty or so years.

By that time almost a half hour had passed since the boy had sat down in the chair.

"All right then," Tinhouse said as he handed Son his dark glasses. "If you don't win that talent contest coming up it won't be because you didn't get the best haircut can be had in Chilton."

Griff was not insulted.

"Willie, my ass," Hughes said as the boy got up and Tinhouse was shaking out the barber cloth with a snap.

"Make up all the stories you want to. It was you."

Without leaning forward to look at Hughes, Berks, lighting another Lucky, said, "You think whoever it was was the only nigger down there fighting his way out of the south ten, fifteen, twenty years ago?" It got even quieter than it had been before. "Tin said it wasn't him. What he have to lie to you for?"

Nobody had an additional comment.

"Yeah," Tinhouse said, as if trying to reestablish good graces in the shop's congregation. "There was a lot out there like me."

They looked at Hughes, then away.

Tinhouse asked who was next.

Hughes raised his hand like he was in school.

"Get in the chair," Tinhouse told him, "while I get me a bottle of pop."

They knew Nehi Orange was his favorite, but they knew he'd settle for Grape. They knew he needed it because they knew he had run his mouth dry.

# 21

# Frocks

## 1939

Pearl had asked, "What's a fancy word for dresses?"

"Frocks."

"I'm smiling," his mother said. "You're so smart. Thank you, that's good."

"Pearl's Custom Frocks," Son said. "Smart dresses of distinction, tailored to the particular dimensions of her special clientele."

When Pearl started out the dresses she sewed were still kind of country, but it wasn't too long, what with seeing women on the street, in moving pictures at the King, and in magazines at the beauty parlor, before she caught on to the way it was done in Chilton and elsewhere. She reckoned who the colored women thought they were, what their place was, and who they wanted to be or appear to be. She made dresses that reflected her vision or what she thought their vision of themselves was. To show they were free to be themselves and stylish as white women without copying them, and so their men would see them anew. Her time at Mr. Fong's was at the base of much of what she was able to bring to her process.

Her range of creations, made with or without a pattern, could be flirty or formal. For dancing or church. Social or business—such business as they had. She had a knack of somehow putting some extra material in the back across the hips so the dress tails of her colored customers did not rise up in the back the way they did when they wore store-bought dresses, and their behinds, when walking or standing, engirdled or not, did not look like a pair of pumpkins rolling around in the rear of Mr. Amalfi's wagon. Pretty soon, what with Vienna and Potluck getting the girls in the shop to talk Pearl up, and with a couple of her samples hung on display in the shop, as well as down at the dry cleaners, Pearl was doing okay to fair, just fine.

She charged $2.50 to $3.00 a dress, fifty cents to a dollar more to white women. For coloreds they were over the price of store-bought, off-the-rack ones of the same quality, but worth it for the service, the fit, and having a custom-made garment.

Pretty soon women all over 'lo' Dunbar were ordering dresses for themselves, at half more than the off-the-rack price, but worth it, and Pearl Moon was in business full time for herself.

Then, slowly, Pearl picked up a client or two from the wealthy matrons above Dunbar, from when the domestics wore one of her garments to work to show off before changing in the bathroom into their work uniforms. For the wealthy Lewis Heights women, Pearl did both copies of her own designs and copies of pictures brought to her.

She went at first dressed as a maid, to do private fittings to camouflage that extra girth through the white women's middles, or across the hips, to add or subtract through the bosom. Then after she had reached favored seamstress status with a couple of the Lewis Heights white women, to save time, she went to being picked up by the chauffer, or the lady herself, considering it an adventure to drive to 'lo' Dunbar and park in front of Pearl's Custom Frocks, opposite the King Colored Theater, motor running, windows up, to pick Pearl up and drive her to Lewis Heights. The more adventurous were fitted in the rear of the little shop Pearl had set up in a space rented to her by Chap.

Son was telling her of the news humming in over the wires of the world news.

From as far back as '36, Hitler, greedy baby, his fist balled up and screaming, demanding other people's stuff, first the Jews, then nearby Europe, collecting pieces of property like he had the dice and a stay-out-of-jail-free card in a game of Monopoly.

Mussolini ran Salassie out of Ethiopia, the Spanish went to war with themselves, and Edward VIII wanted Mrs. Simpson more than he wanted to be king. The Olympics switched from Japan to Helsinki after the Japanese declared war on China.

A third shift, with some women included, was added at Glass and Metal to fill the government orders for war-related materials.

Joe Louis showed Schmeling, Hitler's boy, the canvas in the first round of the rematch, avenging the first fight mishap that had sucked the life of colored and white America.

Son listened, his eyes squeezed shut, as Martians invaded Earth in the "War of the Worlds" on the night before Halloween.

Jazz news came from Peck's letters: "From Spiritual to Swing" at Carnegie Hall with a mixed lineup of musicians and Bennie Goodman with Lionel Hampton and Teddy Wilson, both colored; everybody singing Chick Webb's tune "A Tisket A Tasket" with young Ella Fitzgerald, skipping through the nonsense lyrics, and Count Basie making everybody feel better about everything.

# 22

# Branch

## 1939

Sept 1, 1939

A short one tonight, babe. No news. Sneaking into NY without me, huh? Don't let those Harlem girls turn your head. The music you heard hasn't reach here yet. Sound like it knocked you out. I'm kind of knocked out myself. Sleepy.

Kisses.

V

Vienna was years too young, she told herself, so it wasn't The Change that woke her up soaking wet past the middle of the night. No. Years too young. It was her nature. Sleeping single she reckoned was at the root of it. The strain of restraint of her half-empty bed until Tate Dash and his boys were back in town and Peck was back in her arms. Peck with his jazzman gypsy-foot self, off who knows where, playing music and what all else with the rest of the fellas wild themselves as buck rabbits. The sweats got so regular she took to sleeping with towels atop the sheets and an extra nightgown laid out to change into in the night.

She went to church every Sunday, wrote Peck on Mondays, choir rehearsal Wednesdays, picture show some Thursdays, and worked her jigsaw puzzles in the winter months. She enjoyed it and it helped fill up the time left over after work and secretarial duties for Chap and Potluck, and that was her intention. Movies, though, were her favorite form of wiling away the idle hours until Peck showed up in town again full of vim and vinegar. In that way she was about the movies the way Son was about the radio. It was a means of learning about the world beyond her knowing otherwise. Like seeing what hairstyles the white stars were sporting, which she was going to be asked, through her tonsorial magic, to duplicate for her colored clientele. But her absolute favorites were the rooting tooting riding shooting westerns. It thrilled her to see evil eye to eye with a force superior to its own. Six-gun justice swift and sure.

She went every first Thursday night of the month when the pictures changed at the King Theater for Colored People, where they finally showed the feature picture that had played most likely months earlier at one of the white theaters above Dunbar. A double feature at the King usually consisted of a Hollywood offering and a B-level, often all-Negro cast second feature.

Some nights Pearl would tag along if there were a Laurel and Hardy comedy, unless she had a rush order. For Pearl work was always before pleasure, and she'd even miss a Bette Davis feature if she had a deadline. Lately she had gotten busy making custom dresses and had fallen out of the habit of accompanying Vienna.

One night at dinner Vienna had asked on a whim if anyone wanted to join her. It was Twin Collins, the Supreme Moving Pictures cowboy star, playing in *Showdown at Bar X Ranch*. Branch had laughed, something he seldom did, and said to everybody's surprise that yes, thanks, he believed he would.

Branch Ottley had arrived in the summer, July, when the back and front doors of the beauty shop were kept open in the pretense that there actually was a cross draft for the clicking fans rotating to and forth to catch and offer as a few seconds of relief—but it was just a pretense amongst the flutter of hand fans, pieces of pasteboard, magazines, and folded newspapers fluttering like monarchs' wings in a whirlwind.

The only thing hotter than the interior of the shop was the conversation about who he was, where he'd come from, and why he was in Chilton. Everyone contributed to the speculation. The most prevalent guesses were that he was an ex-cowboy who'd been in the army, or he was an ex-con, or that he was on the run from something or someone, and was only lying low until whatever it was blew over and he'd move on.

From 9:30 until closing there was a running chorus of cowboy clichés—in the saddle, bucking bronco. Some giggled about what horse-breaking tricks they dreamed about him showing them until they were lathered but "tamed."

His hands, they said, calloused from lasso ropes and reins, looked strong and capable as the grip of a pair of pliers. They giggled about the possibilities of his long, slightly bowed legs.

Peck's legs were short and bowed, now that Vienna thought about it, trying not to, but thinking anyway, what with the shop full of smutty-talking, rutty-smelling women chatting about her fellow border like he was Clark Gable or Twin Collins.

They'd drift off to another topic for a few beats, those being sham-pooed or under the dryer or being hot-combed falling silent, fanning, or absentmindedly humming to the tune of the radio, or gazing blankly at the mirrored wall, or out the window to the comings and goings on the street, and then one of them would, without warning, say "*Ye-haw! Ride 'em cowboy!*" And they'd all go limp with laughter, humidity rising off them like steam from the hot soapy sink.

One of them Oklahoma Negroes that every one of them, Vienna or anyone else, ever knew was of a breed apart. Appeared part Indian even if they weren't. Had ways regular Negroes didn't. A cowboy kind of swaggering independence like was as uncommon in your average Negro as purring was in a dog. Like they somehow hadn't had the same experiences with white folks as everybody else. West Indians were the only ones close to expressing the same sort of public disinterest for whites that colored Oklahomans had and didn't much care who knew it.

There's probably a word for him, Vienna thought, and an army word. Some term involving leather, or steel, or grit, or something that majors and captains use to describe the best soldiers. One that they know can be counted on when things get hot and would fight to the finish.

Branch Ottley was between sugar brown and nutmeg with a dash of cayenne, had straightish black hair and Indian cheekbones, and under his Negro nose wore a thick droopy mustache. Vienna had never seen a live rattlesnake ready to strike, but that was what he brought to mind by the smooth way he moved, and in the coiled way he stood, but with a sharp edge too, like you could shave your legs with him.

With his eyes set deep above his high cheekbones, half-hooded, he never looked like he was paying any particular attention, but like he was sitting in the sun after lunch and was about to doze off. When he spoke beyond a cordial greeting, it was mostly when spoken to. When he did look at you, you knew you were being looked at. His expression didn't change much more than the difference between sunset at 7:00 and 7:05, but there was a difference and you could feel it.

In the meanwhile he lived at 560.

Being with him on their walk from 560 to and from the King picture show made her walk different than when she was alone, or even with Peck. Walking beside Branch Ottley she was aware men and women looked at her different. It was because she was with him and looked to be under his protection, which in turn loosened up her stride and carriage. She was almost ashamed to feel so unencumbered by the regular everyday burden of having to be proper and self-protective. More than once she thought it must be how white women felt.

There was, though, something *off* about him. All Negro men were crazy in some way or other, she thought. It was a form of defense forced on them by white folks. For all of their craziness, of all of them she knew she couldn't imagine anyone more worthy of love or exciting to her soul than Peck, or more worthy of her respect than Chap, or more able to trigger snake-quick 3:30 a.m. flashes of heart-pounding tremors and trickling cold sweat than Branch Ottley.

Prior to their movie nights, Branch, when he did not go out with or on some business for Chap, tended to stay in his room reading Oscar Micheaux novels and history books.

None of the women in the shop admitted to seeing him out or about in the evening. There was speculation he might patronize the various dark delights of the gambling and girls of Mahogany Alley down in the district, but there was no confirmation of that.

For some reason that Vienna did not analyze, it was several Mondays after Branch arrived before she mentioned to Peck that Chap had somebody new doing what Sonny Bob used to do. Collecting rents from businesses and making "deliveries."

She did not specify that what he was delivering were sealed numbered envelopes with no names to policemen, councilmen, the tax assessor, building inspectors, and various others on Chap's under-the-counter, off-the-books payroll.

She also did not say that the reason Sonny Bob needed to be replaced was that he had disappeared with a stack of envelopes one Friday and wasn't heard from again. There was a whole lot more to it than Vienna knew. Whatever it was, it was something to do with something she didn't need to know.

It was a couple of weeks into their routine when Branch told her he used to be in the movies. Just as a horse wrangler and occasional stunt man in Twin Collins movies.

As surprising as his saying it was, she didn't doubt it for a second. They had been sitting in Drake's Drug Store, having stopped for coffee and the night's last cigarette.

He had been raised, he told her, from age nine or ten, in the town of Malone, Oklahoma—Yeah, it's famous as an all-colored town.

His adoptive father's brother was a lawman, a man hunter with a badge. The man Branch called his father was a stable owner with a contract with the army at Fort Levi Thomas near Malone. His daddy saw to the breaking and breeding of horses and the training of mules for use by the Calvary.

His mother was headmistress for the Malone Orphans' School.

How he got in the movies was, he and Twin Collins, yes, the big-named western star in Hollywood, were classmates at the orphan school. Vienna knew all about Twin Collins, his career and his world-famous horse Dakota. She knew from fan magazine columnists whose job it was know and report. Twin Collins' life was flashed in laudatory articles in *Photoplay*, *Movie Mirror*, *Modern Screen*, and the other movie magazines they kept for the customers in the shop.

Collins got his start with small, independent film companies making silent westerns in Oklahoma. He caught the first wave of movie making, working both sides of the camera, as stuntman and mechanic, then writer, director, and actor, rising to be one of the two reigning western stars of talkies. Tom Mix being the other.

Feeling as if she was being let in on behind-the-scenes secrets, Vienna got the real story from Branch.

Branch's mother had also taught Twin, who worked for a while for his father, Haskell, right alongside Branch. A Hollywood crew'd come to Malone scouting locations and stuntmen to shoot one-reel silent movies, back in around 1919, 19-20. Branch and Twin'd been among the company wranglers who taught horses to take tumbles during Indian chases, cattle stampedes, and the like. It was fun, Branch said. Twin had found his calling and caught several breaks and ended up in a mansion on the side of a Hollywood hill and was known all over the world, so flamboyantly rich and famous that his multitude of fans assumed unconsciously and without contradiction that everything they could ever hope to know about their symbol of common decency and champion of underdog redemptive justice and the American dream was true.

"No, he was good," Branch said.

"But I bet you were better," she insisted.

After he told of the time Twin cracked a rib near the end of a picture, they had put Branch in makeup, and he did the final stunts for Twin, all she could think to say was, Twin Collins makes $15,000 a week. It was in *Photoplay*.

He smiled at her nit-witty fan response. He had an investment in Twin, was his response, and, we still stay in touch some.

That, she thought, explained the envelopes Branch received at the beginning of the month postmarked from Los Angeles, California.

A week later, coming from the show after attending their regular Thursday night double feature, Vienna paused in the shadows on the side porch, which was their habit, it being the least obtrusive and closest to each of their rooms at the rear of 560. Nervous as a cat passing the dog pound, eyes on his, she turned to him. She could smell him, the Lava soap. "You tired?" she asked, her hand touching him, letting him know she wasn't.

He eased her against him. Strong. Sure. Full contact from chest to hips. Before he answered she felt him tense slightly and he gripped her shoulders, his hands hot, strong. He made a quick soft *Ssh* sound. It was a moment before she heard what he had. They stood pressed against each other. There was a line of perspiration napping her hair at the scalp line and nape, and ice snakes of it, trickling down, down the middle of her chest and the insides of her thighs. His right hand left her shoulder and eased his jacket back, giving him easier access to his pistol off his right hip toward the middle of his back.

What they heard was Arthur. Nobody but Arthur coming up the same path they had just used. Walking with the overcompensated posture and stride of a practiced drunk.

She knew Branch was probably armed as he usually was, whether alone or when he accompanied Chap to one of his business meetings in 'lo' Dunbar. Whether he was officially Chap's bodyguard, or if officially Chap needed a bodyguard, she wasn't sure.

Arthur mounted the steps like a sleepwalker. He reeked of Old Spice and the reason for his semiconscious state. With a gruff grunt he softly cursed his phantom companion or something behind him, as he either did not notice them or did not acknowledge their presence. He expertly inserted his key in the lock and opened the door and entered, closing it quietly behind him.

They stood for a moment still pressed together but silent, as if wondering if Arthur had really just passed them.

"Listen, girl," he whispered at last, "I'm trouble."

Who was he telling? She knew he could feel there was a trembling on her, like the spirit creeping in on one of the old sisters during Sunday sermon.

"More than you know," he said, "So it sure isn't you. But if we do what nature tells us, Peck will find out about it. I wouldn't tell him and you might or might not, but he'd know. That would hurt him, and put him in the position of whether or not to confront me. That's not a position he, or you, or I want him to be in. Do you understand?"

Hearing Branch say Peck's name made her wish that at that moment Peck was with some fan-tailed heifer, her hose rolled down and her hem hiked up. That was all that could forgive her for what she was thinking regarding the lean Lava soap-smelling man with his body against hers, her shoulders in his hands.

Even in the faint light she could see him make the decision to say in a flat, controlled voice, "I don't know how much Luck or Chap might've told you—"

"Nothing," she said before he was finished, hearing the tremble in her whisper.

"I was in a hospital mental ward. They say I had a breakdown."

She wanted to stop him, but she knew shaking her head wasn't enough.

"They give me treatments for the better part of a year."

Wanted to put her hand over her ears, or over his mouth.

"You know about me and horses. There was a white man who'd mistreated a bunch and I called him on it. He came at me with bad intentions."

Vienna wanted to ask, Oh god, did you kill him, but she knew he had.

"But because of my father and my uncle and Twin Collins' prominence in the area I got off with self-defense. But you know how it is, they had to give me some time so they sent me to an asylum.

"I say my father and uncle, but they weren't really. I was adopted from the orphan school, where my uncle took me. Mother was the headmistress. I was eleven. Pa ran the stable. That's where I learned horses."

He's just talking to let me cool down, she thought, not yet cool.

"Twin Collins worked for Pa there."

She nodded, connecting it all.

"So, see," he said, "I was released, but I'm easily provoked, and prone to violence when I am." It was a confession, not easily or proudly admitted, and she wished he had just pushed her away. Told her to go. She wanted to cover his mouth with her trembling hand, apologize to him for having heard it, and assure him that if she could she would sear the words from her memory. He said, "I don't know if trouble follows me, or I look for it. But sooner or later something will happen. And I do not want you to be a part of it."

Vienna had long ago decided she was less afraid *of* Negro men than she was afraid *for* them, for they were all capable of some degree of white-hot-as-a-poker-in-a-forge violence at their constant provocation. She wanted then to hold him, wanted to assure him that he had her solemn word that she would never breathe a word of what he had told her to a living soul. Hold less like a lover, then, and more like a sister would, a brother or a friend would. But all she could do was touch the side of his face as gently as she could. It was all she could do. It was what she did.

Without saying goodnight he kissed her forehead and moved down the steps and off into the darkness.

She stood in the quiet for a few moments thinking about Branch and Arthur, Chap and Son and Peck, before going up wacky-kneed to her own room, wondering where Branch was heading. To Mahoney Alley most likely. Where else was there to go in Chilton at that time of night? See one of them Mahoney Alley heifers?

When she closed her bedroom door behind her all she wanted was to get that girdle off and get over in her lonely bed and not think about cowboys or galloping stallions, burning beds, walking time bombs, trust, jazz band-stalking heifers, orphans, or hurt, but just to dream about Peck with his roving self.

Vienna wondered, if it wasn't for Peck, if she would be fool enough to take on the task of jumping down in that volcano in the heart of Branch Ottley, and leading him out, like a fireman rescuing a victim from a burning building.

That burning building was what Reverend Leonard talked and shouted about in his sermons. What it was was a burning place for 99 and 44/100% of the colored men she knew anything 'bout. Need for redemption, or self-forgiveness for something that wasn't their fault, was as close in words as a woman could get trying to describe what it was to be one of their men. Most men couldn't say it in words either. But it was on them.

Peck, with his trumpet-blowing self, didn't know just what a lucky, bowlegged, cleft-chinned, brown-skinned Negro he was. If he did he'd be on his knees somewhere at that minute thanking something on High, instead of where he probably was, on his knees trying to make his point on a pair of spotted bones, bless him. But he had freed himself from it, and his expression of it he put in notes squeezed nightly through his little brass horn. That was what made him so able to give love, and why it was such a joy to give it back to him.

Branch Ottley hadn't found his way of expressing, have mercy on him. Unless it was through dispensing pain when he was provoked. And if that was it and he didn't find a way to temper it, there would be a heap of Old Testament suffering before it was done.

And it was going to take more than just him alone looking to find it.

Then, her mind skipping around like a pinball, she thought about the bond between Pearl and Son. For the entire time she had known them, she had never been less than fascinated by them, separately or together. She was also amazed by how much of what the world was to him was shaped by his mother's view of it, and yet how independent he was. Was that because of how Pearl didn't encourage him to cling to her, or because of his personality?

Vienna wondered again what kind of mother—or even wife—would she be, what would she give? It made her admire Pearl all the more and think what it must be like to be her. And laying there in the dark, a wave of love for Peck lit her up like sunshine. She realized again that what Pearl had been telling Son on that first day and every day since was what he needed to know if he was to ever have to do without her.

It was into the early a.m. before she quit her tossing, her pulse settled, her mind regulated again into its normal reliability of the milkman's horse, and with the first rays of the morning sun, alone in her bed, she thought to herself with a smile that it was a good thing at least one of them had come to their senses. And after a fitful half hour or forty-five minutes of sleep, she rose, bathed, ate, and straightened her usual number of heads of hair.

Peck was steady as the insurance man coming to collect, she told herself, and she wasn't going to let herself forget it.

After that night she and Branch still went to the pictures on Thursday evenings and didn't change their seats at Potluck's table. They partnered at bid whist for match sticks, but they avoided being alone otherwise and they never spoke of that moment on the side porch, though it followed Vienna, whining on the back stoop of her nerves like a not yet weaned pup.

But it was many a day standing, doing a head of hair, that her mind wandered to what kind of woman he needed, biblical-big as his burden was. It sure wasn't some young girl who'd come directly into and up in the church from her mama and daddy's house. He needed somebody who'd traveled some of the by-ways, even a few back alleys on her journey before she'd settled her hips into a regular routine of every Sunday morning in the same pew. At best that heavy lifting job would be undertaken, if he was lucky—and why would that be assumed—by some woman, a woman who had Job's patience and Solomon's wisdom. Any woman short of that he'd melt down and scorch like a marshmallow charred by a blowtorch.

Heaven help them both.

# 23

# Ada

## 1941

July 8, '40

. . . Another new arrivee. A girl named Ada Mayhew. Pretty.
She had problems somewhere and somebody sent her here.

V

Ada was a pretty girl. A woman-child, oil-black hair, curly as a Brillo pad,
but fine as cobwebs. Like one of those Filipina or Polynesian women, or
one of them in one of those Technicolor places with fruit everywhere
that you see in the *National Geographic*, where it was all right, according
to them, to show the women bare-breasted like they was something in
a zoo or something. Ada showed up with a note from somebody, and
Potluck put her on the third floor in the room next to Vienna's. There
was no explanation of where she came from. "She'll be staying here,"
Potluck said at dinner. "She'll be going to school and helping out with
the cleaning, cooking, washing and all that. Her name is Ada Mayhew."

She was sixteen, with a slight squint that gave her a look of almost sad-
ness, but interest too. When the sun hit her just right she was the color
of a brand-new penny. Or she might have been a gypsy for that matter.
Kind of stocky, but built up nice. Men and women were well aware of how
nicely she was built. She would one day, way before her forties, go to fat,
women thought when they saw her. Some of that was wishful thinking.
There was a silence about her, but she liked bracelets and necklaces with
little charms that made tiny tinkling sounds when she moved.

"Men like me," Ada apologized to Vienna one Thursday when Ada
was in the shop, and Vienna was washing her hair. She couldn't help
how they felt, Ada said. And neither could they, Vienna thought. Just

by being Ada she made men wipe at their mouths because they wanted to taste her—for a start. There were certain women who wanted to hold her, stroke her in a motherly, or other, way.

Turned out Ada didn't help Potluck around the house all that long because Pearl discovered Ada had a hand for sewing, and she became Pearl's assistant seamstress and apprentice. Pearl had, by that time, opened a little, narrow shop in a space that Chap owned. Vienna thought Potluck turned Ada over to Pearl as much to keep the boys and men of 560 off her as anything.

Ada and Son took to one another right away. Maybe it was that quiet thing in them that attracted people to them that attracted them to each other. Maybe it was their being young and closer in age than anybody else in the house. Maybe it was their being something in them that neither of them could explain, or help, that they hoped the other could help them put a name to. Maybe it was just male and female.

Ada watched Son. Saw he was smart. Smart in what he knew and in how he got to know it. Every radio program he listened to raised questions and he'd figured the trick of asking two people who would likely have different opinions the same questions and listen to them discuss it to get a wider view. Son especially liked the quiz programs. He deflected any praise or wonder at his ability to quickly and accurately answer the more difficult questions, but was self-critical when he did not know. It became apparent to Ada that he was in competition only with himself.

The other thing he could do, and what she liked best, was he was very good at imitating anyone he heard broadcast during the day. Pearl's favorites were Orson Welles and Eleanor Roosevelt. Ada liked Mortimer Snerd and Charlie McCarthy.

That especially tickled Tinhouse too. That and the best jokes and songs Son reported on at the dinner table.

Aug 12, '40
. . . Son has somebody his own age to be with, not that he
considers himself a teenager . .

V

Ada was a pretty child and not nearly as innocent as she might look, and Pot and Chap knew prevention was better than cure. Separately, without one knowing the other was doing it, they had had a word with all the men in 560 about Ada. Each one they talked to gave assurance that they had better sense than that.

Chap was told more than once that Son was the one needed watching when it came to Ada. He was beating everybody's time as far as she went. They laughed, acknowledging the truthfulness of it. They also all watched how Pearl was watching her son and Ada.

Oct 23, '40

. . . Over the course of the fall they've gone from playing brother and sister to becoming fast friends. Everybody is watching Pearl watch them. We were sitting on the porch the other night trying to catch the last of the good weather and she said to me how she wasn't any fool who believed she was going to live forever. And she knew he was going to need somebody. It was the first time she's ever said anything like that—to me anyway.

You know me. It just made me think about you, and how much I love you. Enough of that for now . . .

Ada watches Son as he listens, absorbed in the radio.

Sometimes he sits close to it with his hand on its side. He touches it the way he lays his hand on his mama's arm when they walk—the way it lays on Ada's too. I guess it is because of the warmth from the orange tubes, or maybe the smoothness of the lacquered finish.

Hitler is a stark raving fool. I hope they can stop him over there and we don't have to get into it.

Enough of THAT for now . . .

I guess the shocking news is that Reverend Leonard suddenly announced his retirement. Surprised everybody. He hasn't given a real explanation, just said it was time.

V

"I wrote something," Ada said.

"What?" Son asked. "Homework?"

"No. Something for you. Want to hear it?"

He could hear her straightening out the sheets of paper on her lap and her bangles.

"It's silly," she said.

"Read it."

"I changed my mind."

"Please."

"Okay. You said please." She read, "'I like the way we can just sit and touch each other and breath in sequence.' See, I told you it was silly."

"It's not. Is there more?"

"'I like that you know everything, and that you are so gentle. And when we talk that I just lose myself and I can be like I used to be. You are my escape. When you're with me you aren't with anybody else. And there isn't anybody but me and you.'"

> Dec 28, 1940
>
> The year is almost gone and you've only been gone two days and it feels like six months . . . Everything is just rushing so fast and that fool Hitler is determined to horn in on everybody's territory.
>
> Listening to Shaw's "Frenesi." Nice arrangement by your boy Grant Still. Makes me think about us wandering down to old Mexico with the moon shining bright. Don't let any of these American señoritas catch your eye—you're mine all mine.
>
> Love,
>
> V

"You make me smile," Son said.

Yes, she could see him, she told him.

Son and Ada in her room with the door closed. It wasn't that unusual to hear them in her room or his. They might be listening to the radio, or whispering and laughing, or her reading to him, or him telling her stories of what he'd heard on the radio that day.

"Men like me," she said.

He liked her, he told her.

"You're just a boy."

"Am I?"

"It's a curse," she said, her bangles ting-tinkling.

"Don't be stupid."

"Don't call me stupid. You don't know as much as you think you do," she said.

"About what?"

"What people do."

"I know what men and women do if that's what you're talking about."

"How?"

"When I was little. A place. Where men came for the women."

"Was your mama one of them?"

"She took care of the women. Saw after them. I helped."

"Doing what?"

"Emptying pans, fetching."

"You might've *heard* about it, but *I* did it. It was *done to* me. Because there's a *curse* on me."

"There's no such thing."

"He told me I was pretty."

"I told you that."

"You can't even see me," she said, knowing better. She said, "He liked to touch me, and liked me to touch him."

"And you let him?"

Her charms went quiet.

"You're the one who's stupid. I didn't *let* him. He *did* it."

"Did he hurt you?"

"No."

"Yes he did."

"How do you know?"

"I just do."

"He didn't beat me or anything if that's what you think."

"I didn't say that."

"You want to know one thing I did?"

"You want me to?"

"Let me show you," she said.

"Why?"

"To see if *you* like it."

"I don't count."

"Yes you do—Okay?"

The sound was of their fumbling and making small sounds as her bangles ting-tinkled. Then he said, "We better stop."

The ting tinkling continued.

She said, "See? He said it gave him pleasure—You like it?"

"You?"

She sniffled. "Not with him." She sniffled again, several times. Sucking back tears and snot. "Did you do it before?"

"Yes," he said.

"With who?"

"A long time ago."

"One of the women?"

His not saying that it wasn't was saying that it was.

"Did you tell?"

"I'm telling you."

"Does your mama know?"

"It's okay if you liked it too," he said.

She asked, "But did you like it too?"

There was a long silence before he said in a voice like he was smoothing the wrinkles from a bedspread, "Your tears are salty."

Her light laugh echoed her bangles. "So is your sweat," she said, almost singing.

"I wanted to give you pleasure," she said.

He didn't say anything for a minute, and then he said—"Don't you see me smiling?"

June 16, 1941
Ada is Pearl's sewing assistant. She's real handy with a needle and thread. She's real helpful, but I think Pearl does it some to keep an eye on her and to keep her away from Son. But it's too late for that, if you know what I mean.

V

Another time Ada said, "You know what else?"

"What?"

"I had a baby."

He touched her shoulder, then her cheek.

"And I only gave it titty one time. It has already forgot me. I know it."

He waited through her pause as he wiped away a tear.

"It's going to be out in the world and won't even know its mama. They won't even tell it my name. So it can't ever find me."

"It doesn't need to know your name to think about you, though."

"Yes it does."

"I think about lots of stuff I don't know the name of."

"That's not the same. What you're talking about is things. I'm talking about a flesh and blood baby, come out of me. Soft and sucking, but that I couldn't give titty but one time. It won't ever think of me."

"Don't you think I think about my daddy that I don't know."

"You said he was dead."

"She said, but I'm not sure."

"Why?"

He shrugged. "And if he isn't he doesn't even know my name. I think about him all the time. Wouldn't know his touch or his smell if he was right here right now."

"Maybe that's why I think about my baby. Even more than I would if I knew all about him."

. . . The Reverend Cook Richardson & company arrived. He's going to be the new preacher at church. He reminds me of Cab Calloway. A big time showman . . .

Things are changing so fast . . .

V

"Miss Pearl knows," Ada said.
"Knows what?" Son asked.
"That you're not just hers anymore."
He found her hand. Held it.

. . . Son is growing up so it's hard to remember the little boy he was when they got here. You won't recognize him next time you see him.

Don't forget that I Love You Peck Morris.

V

# 24

# An Official Part of History

"What kind of boy were you?" Son asked.

Branch said, "My mother said she saw will and determination in the way I learned my lessons and shied away from the other children, except for one boy there. At the start that friendship was as much a standoff as a friendship. But it was something we each recognized in the other. That and we both loved animals—and fairness. So we could relax with each other."

Branch watched strangers meeting Son for the first time. Often they tried to talk to him like being blind meant that he didn't have good sense. Branch would see them thinking he was a fool, and then get put in their place. By the time Son got through with them their mouths would be hanging open and they'd be scratching their heads, wondering what just happened. But one thing for sure, they had learned something, something about the world, or themselves, or *something*. After, they were some ways different, that was guaranteed.

That, Branch knew, was because Son had so much common sense, more even than most old, grizzled people. Probably Branch included.

Neither Son nor Pearl thought being blind had any bearing on what the boy could do. If he didn't do it, his attitude said, it was because he didn't want to, didn't need to, didn't have to, or just hadn't gotten around to it. Not that different than Branch's adopted family had made him feel about himself.

His mama, Pearl, was a handsome woman and a good mother. Among the three best Branch'd ever seen, including his two. But good as she was she was a woman and a mother and the boy needed a man to fill in the other parts of him. Son knew it and spent as much time as he could with the other men of the house, sopping up what he could from them as he did with everything. The boy was like a cactus in that. And was as curious as a cat. He demanded information. There wasn't anything he wouldn't ask, and he took it all to heart, which was why Branch took time with and had serious interest in the boy.

Son asked what he thought about Hitler.

"He's a bully. I do not abide bullies," Branch said. "They're only strong because they make you think they are. And the longer you believe it the stronger they get."

"Who taught you that?"

"My Uncle. He taught me a great many things."

"Did your father teach you things too?"

"I had two fathers, and that uncle."

"Two fathers?

My first, my real father, died."

"Like mine."

Branch told Son of a saying from his uncle: " 'Only say what you mean, mean what you say, be true to your word, and people will respect your strength.' Do you understand?"

"Even from a boy?"

"Yep."

"Even from me?"

"You too. But you won't be a boy much longer."

That was what he wanted to know most about. Being a man. Asked Branch about his father. What had his father taught him?

"To treat people with respect, and they were more likely to treat you the same way."

"Even white people?"

Branch thought about it, allowed, "Even *some* white people." Thought about it some more. "And horses." That, Branch said, was why he most often preferred horses to people. Horses didn't discriminate. They didn't have the capacity for being cruel based on race hatred. "You ever been on a horse?"

"Just behind one, in the wagon with Mr. Amalfi. He let me guide sometimes—but mostly the horse knew the route. I was in an airplane one time," Son said.

"I grew up around horses. Fact, I learned about respect from horses."

"How?"

"When I was a little older than you my father got possession of a horse everybody thought ought to be put down. It had been mistreated and was so skittish nobody could get near it—nobody but my father."

"And you?"

"Not at first."

His (second) father, Haskell, showed him to approach the horse without fear, showing respect, expecting it. Over time, with gentle treatment, and respect for who the horse was, and the troubles it had had, his father won the horse's trust and was able to bring it back to health and usefulness.

It was from his uncle that he learned about the book *American Notes* by Charles Dickens. Had Son heard of it?

Nope. *Christmas Carol, Oliver Twist, A Tale of Two Cities*, which he'd heard adaptations of on the radio, but not that one.

"It was about Dickens' trip to a place, I don't remember the name, in Boston. He told stories to the boys and girls there, who were blind, like you, but also couldn't speak or hear."

"What happened to them?"

"They were taught to make things and use a signing language to communicate."

He thought for a moment. His silence gave no hint as to his thoughts.

"We have an advantage," Branch said, "and a disadvantage. When people don't know us, and what we're capable of—who we are—then they underestimate us. That's the advantage part. But if they know us they try twice as hard because of who they think we are—how good we are."

Son felt two jabs from Branch's fingertip: one to his chest, the second to his forehead. "What they don't know is that they don't matter. It's about us, not them. We're not trying to beat them, or be smarter than them. Being the best at what we've been taught—that's what drives us. Only we can know how good we can be."

The boy said nothing. Only slightly nodded.

He knew how to be quiet. He would be good on a hunt.

Another night. The Lone Ranger had said his final *A-wayyy*! Tonto by his side, they had galloped off at the end of another episode brought to them from WXYZ.

"He's for justice," Son said.

"What is justice?" Branch asked.

"Things coming out right. Right?"

"Right."

"Where in the old west did you grow up?"

"Malone, Oklahoma. An all-colored town."

"Wow."

"Till then it was the first big town I was ever in."

"Mama and I were in lots of towns, big, little, middle sized. Where were you before you were in Malone, Oklahoma?"

"It's a long story."

"Tell me?"


Old Miller's Allotment, Oklahoma. 1910.

Knew, the boy did, he was the first to see the approaching figure, floating from far as his eye could reach, forward on the flat of the Oklahoma prairie, as if through waves of water. Not that he'd ever seen any more water than down a well or in a creek wider than a running leap at its width. A man, it was sure, rising over the eastern edge of the world like in the beginning of the dream of his. Coming beeline straight, but as deliberate as Bossie at her cud.

Being the first to rise it was his privilege to be the first to espy the figure. And thought, who first must he tell? The two asleep in the barn he had just emerged from, who had arrived in a like manner two days ago? They had specifically told him to tell them in the event of another's coming. Or tell Niall, likely still asleep in the mud house behind him?

Or tell the woman, who'd be by now at her first morning stirrings? Let her tell Niall, their boss.

What he had an impulse to do was not let on at all to any of them. His knowing, and their ignorance, was two things of his own to hoard. Though he knew that if he did not tell at all, or delayed too long in the telling, it too would cost him. He weighed the worth of what pleasure there was of having the secret knowledge of the approaching man— what in the name of thunder was taking him so long—that none of the other of them did, against the certainty of reprisal from some or all concerned. Deciding that although being buoyed on the raft of his secret was like hurtling toward an impending falls, the thrill of even the limited time of his ride was worth it.

His reentering the barn where they were sleeping awakened the men.

"Somebody's coming."

They started as if dowsed with cold water. Pelting him with questions and curses they scrambled about, struggling to their feet, wiping at their eyes with the heels of their hands, brushing straw from their hair, stomping into their boots, strapping on their gun belts.

"How many?"

"How far off?"

"Why the hell'd you wait so long to tell us?" the younger one asked, gripping the boy hard by his upper arm before shoving him stumbling, cross-footed, through horseshit and against the stable wall.

"Was whoever it was close enough to tell who it was?" the older one asked.

As if none of it was of any matter to him, he didn't answer as he moved methodically about his horse dung-shoveling chore.

They, unshaven, ash blond and hazel-eyed, had come in like coyotes two nights before. He'd overheard them tell Niall they were willing to pay for sip and sup and a place to lay their heads. Niall had greedily agreed without explanation of where they'd left or were headed. Didn't care as long as they paid in advance and gave assurance they'd tarry no more than the time they'd paid for.

They offered the boy the payment of a nickel for keeping an eye out for approaching strangers, again with no explanation for their request.

The men, brothers, scurrying like ants at a drop of rain, were considering contingencies. Arguing about what they should do and who should do what and when and how.

The younger one, undercover, weaseled around to the sod house; the other stayed out in the barn. The boy was delegated to go out and greet whoever the hell it was.

Standing in the yard, the pitchfork tines resting in the dirt when the man halted his horse. He dismounted, horse between him and the barn. He was lean and average tall. Somewhere between a town man and a cowboy. A wide-brimmed, flat-topped straw hat shaded his bronze brown face, about the same color, the boy thought, as me. The man was Negro with the look of some Cherokee. He was not mustached or bearded but needed a shave.

He wore a trail-soiled white linen shirt, buttoned at the wrists and neck under a dark, dusty vest, and dark, ribbed-textured pants tucked into calf-high brown boots. Cartridge-filled belt with what looked to be a Colt Dragoon revolver on his right hip. He held his lever-action carbine, its blue barrel up against his left shoulder. But most notable was a round, gold lawman's badge centered with a five-point star pinned two or three inches above the top left-hand pocket of his vest.

The boy felt the man slowly and totally surveying the layout of the sorry allotment for signs of movement near the various clumps and implements that could hide a man. Foremost being the soddy house, like a dauber's nest of mud, stacked stone, buffalo grass, and castoff canvas, burrowed in a small hillock. All of it old, old when first taken up by its present owner, and now in even greater state of misuse, at the hands of one ill-suited for its care.

Then the man turned his inspecting gaze on him. He felt his heart double pump, leap like a hard-spurred horse, like it did during a hundred nights with the dream that startled him to waking among the stable's chorus of nights sounds: scurry and squeak of rats, pouncing of cats, screech of owls, horses' clipped whinnies and snores as they flinched through their dreams. His awakening always so sudden and disquieting that he could not remember what it was that came immediately before the snatch from one mind to the other. He stood not skittish but straight, flat-footed, braced as if for a blow or lash. Wanted the man, who looked like he had come to wake snakes, to know something of him, whatever might come after. That he was not of these people, only subject to their maltreatment, same as the other things in Niall, the squatter's seeing.

"There strangers here?" the man asked him quietly, his tone and look expecting nothing but the truth.

Looking him in the eye, the boy nodded once.

"House or the barn?"

The boy nodded to the barn and then to the house.

The man took the pitchfork from the boy and drove its tines into the ground.

"Walk my horse to the trough and give him water," the lawman said. "Then fill the canteens and stay at the well until I'm through with my business here."

He took the reins, leading the horse away.

The lawman announced, loud enough to be heard in both structures, "I am Cochrane Utterbach, deputy marshal, and officer of the court of Malone County, Oklahoma. I have an affidavit for the apprehension of Gideon and Zachariah Turlock. Turlocks, show your selves and submit to arrest, or suffer the consequences."

On seeing the way the lawman had taken the measure of his surroundings, the boy had thought him a man of caution. Where, the boy wondered with building anger at the man's recklessness, is the caution in standing unprotected in the line of fire from both places, and I already told him where they at?

Niall Burleson, the boss, ruddy, red-headed, came out like he was mad as a peeled rattler, his attention on the lawman, but cussing the boy as he crossed the yard, the pistol in the waistband of his pants, his hand on the handle. Niall saying in his sing-songy way of speaking around what was likely a new chaw of tobacco, "I'm Niall Burleson. Owner of the place. Did you bloody ask me if you could be watering his fucking harse?"

Niall, tough as Old Testament vengeance on a boy and a woman, didn't drink to get mean, the boy thought. He could quickly get that way without drinking a drop. Just come on him like a fever. And when on him it was deep as it was wide. See how, the boy thought, he fares with this man in the flat straw hat, star badge on his vest, carbine leaned on his shoulder.

Niall nearly across the yard saying now to the man, "Did you ask for my water?"

The lawman repeating, "I am Cochrane Utterbach, deputy marshal, and officer of the court of Malone County, Oklahoma. I have an affidavit for the apprehension of Gideon and Zachariah Turlock. Unhand the weapon."

Niall drawing up short then, them within three strides of one another.

"Unhand the weapon," the lawman said. "My business is not with you."

"Any business here starts with me," Burleson said, adjusting the chaw until it was in place. "This is my bloody property."

"You are harboring fugitives, Gideon and Zachariah Turlock by name. Send them out and I'll have them off your property before you know it."

"Get, goddamn you!"

His tone the same as when he first spoke to the boy, the lawman said, "Lay that firearm down, and if you jump funny I'll knock you cockeyed."

Niall Burleson didn't move.

Neither did the lawman. Instead he asked, "What is that boy to you?"

Without looking back Niall said, "He's nothing." And spit a skeet of tobacco near the man's boots. "Drug in about a year ago like a wet cat out of the rain."

"Are you are the cause of his condition?"

"He ain't complained," Niall said, his hand, well-practiced at beating the boy and woman to blisters, still on the weapon. "He's working off the debt of my taking him in. I treat him 'cording to his worth . . ." was as much as Niall could say before Utterbach stove in his nose and mouth with the brass-trimmed butt of his rifle. The spattering of bone, teeth, and blood sounded, even to where the boy stood, like a bundle of dry kindling was snapped.

The lawman's started, like he said he would, the boy thought, standing still and silent beside the lapping horse.

Niall slumped to his knees, moaning into the blood in his cupped hands. The lawman knelt in front of Niall, partially blocking him from view from the house. He pulled the handgun from the groaning man's belt and stuck it into his own. He raised his rifle and aimed it at the slowly opening door of the barn and the owl-like complaint of its rusty hinges.

"Gideon Turlock in the shed, you are in my sights."

The words froze Turlock like the unexpected sound of a snake's rattle.

The lawman said, "I come to deliver you to the justice you deserve. The manner of that delivery will be of your choosing. Throw your weapon out and follow it. Am I clear?"

Across the yard the penned hogs paid no mind as Turlock stepped out the barn entrance, his pistol half raised.

"You broke his god-damned face."

"Turlock, drop the pistol. Come to me, or go to God."

"Fuck you, you black son of a bitch."

"I take your words as resistance to my intention."

"Right, goddamn you," he said, raising the pistol.

Gideon Turlock, shot in the chest by the lawman, dropped to the dirt like a hay bale kicked from a cloud.

The pigs squealed at the sound of the shot and then their snouts in the slop returned to their rut and snuffle.

The lawman stood and moved quickly by Niall, still kneeling in the dirt and moaning in his hands. He ran to the windowless soddy wall and stood with his back against it, his carbine newly cocked.

From inside, Zachariah, with a howl like a coyote's, wailed his brother's name.

"Zachariah," the lawman called out, "Gideon, by his resistance, has forced me to shoot him."

"Did you kill him, you son of a bitch?"

"I give you the option I gave him. This is a sorry place to die."

"Maybe I won't."

"You will. Surrender or suffer the consequences. Do you understand?"

"I want to see my brother."

"Step out."

"Gideon!" Zachariah called from inside to no answer. "All this over some old nigger?"

"That you killed," the lawman said.

"Did you kill my brother, you son of a bitch? Is he dead?"

"You understand my terms. I await your decision."

"You think you can kill my brother, and I'm going to surrender back to your nigger town?"

"Either way it's likely your last day in the sunshine."

Zachariah burst from the weathered canvas-covered doorway, cursing and shooting, but not knowing where his target was. He realized too late.

And now the lawman's done, thought the boy who had observed it all as steadily as he did each evening, watching the sun's slow bleed, red as a reopened wound, over the western edge. Not, as in that instance, squinting, eyes slightly averted, but looking directly into the heart of the lawman's doings. Wanted to yell for him to kill them! Kill them all . . . her too, still in the house, who had stood, watching in taciturn disinterest when Niall had been teaching him with a stick of wood to properly mind . . . Kill them in a flood of Hell fire, but the words stacked against his voice box like rocks damming stream waters, and he stood mute.

Through it all the lawman's horse had kept lapping water, like it was deaf, or had seen it all before.

The woman came out then, her face white as milled flour, her hands up, and like a cur trained by the boot, cautiously approached Niall still kneeling in the dirt, rocking, moaning, and muttering. She was not cautious enough, for in his pain and anger Niall swung a bloody backhand fist, striking her weakly on her leg as he sputtered a profanity, but for his effort paid the price of additional pain. The woman cringed away. Niall then waved a searching, bloody-palmed hand in her direction and she stepped forward again. His hand clenched her skirt, and crying and gurgling, he gingerly rested his forehead against her thighs.

The lawman told them, "I repeat, I am Cochran Utterbach, deputy marshal, and officer of the court of Malone County, Oklahoma. The purpose of my visit is completed. But when this boy tells me your parts in the nature of his condition I might return. Meanwhile we'll be in Malone. Now, you have seen what I do. If there is any part of what you have caused here you do not accept, we can continue. Is there any part of this that is not clear?"

The dog, sniffing about Zachariah's sprawled body, nipped at the circling flies.

"He understands," the woman said, helping the stumbling Niall to his feet.

"In addition," Utterbach continued, "if I see you in Malone I will assume, until I know otherwise, you have come with larceny in your heart, rather than an apology on your tongue. Is that clear also?"

Several chickens were pecking at the teeth in the dirt as if they were bloody kernels of corn. Niall attempted to kick at them and lost his balance, falling against the woman with a pained grunt. She cooed softly to the man who had maltreated her. "I know him," she said, leading Niall, half bent, waddling wide-legged, leaving a weaving trickle of blood, as if he were trailing a snake. "You explained it clear." Stopping to gently pat his back as he shook through his belly's wrenching discharge. "He understands," she said. She continued guiding him to the well.

He started it and now he is done, the boy thought, as he led the watered horse back to the lawman. He wondered how many men over time the brown-skinned man had killed.

"You saw it all?"

The boy nodded. Knew these were not his first.

"You had breakfast?"

The boy shook his head, indicating he wasn't hungry.

"Get what belongs to you and a horse. You're coming with me."

The boy took the bay Gideon Turlock had ridden in on, and the tack and trail gear with it. He had nothing of his own to take, not even the nickel from the Turlocks he was owed.

## To Malone

As noon was approaching and they had been riding for four hours or so, moving across the terrain like two ants on a tabletop, the lawman said, "Telling each other stories is how people get to know one another. I'll start."

For the three days of their journey, riding deeper into the empty terrain, he told a sluice of tales, breaking the boring sameness of the skillet bottom-flat western high plains: short grass, dry lakes, the occasional sagebrush: coyotes, deer, antelope, quail, prairie dogs, or small herds of cattle watering themselves in a stream near the occasional distant homestead of sod brick dwelling, outhouse, barn, or shed—the family pausing from their toil to stare and wave, their yelling children and yapping dog running along after, until ordered to halt and scuff back to their chores and sentry duty. For the boy these lasted only however long it took for them to appear and then for them to pass from his view. He did not look back, as if assuming they would not be there if he did. Only later did it occur to him that the lawman's wave to the distant people had not solely been a polite gesture of acknowledgement but of thanks for their assisting him in his search for the Turlocks.

Meanwhile the lawman told of the sorrowful history of how Cherokee, Chickasaw, Seminole, Creek came at gunpoint, staggering and bedraggled to Oklahoma. How it was cruelty in its most treacherous form. Told of the history of coloreds there, escaping new forms of after-Reconstruction slavery. Told too, on that first day and evening, of his family, of his father's place, as an Indian-fighting soldier from seventeen, good man that he was, in Oklahoma's story. Told of his brother Haskell, who ran a stable, feed, and transport business in Malone, and his sister-in-law Florine Bell, the schoolmistress.

They stopped that first evening, as would be their pattern, while there was still light to read by after a simple supper. The lawman reading aloud by last daylight and then campfire from *American Notes* by Charles Dickens, detailing the Englishman's travels by rail, coach, and steamship during his trip to America, mostly way out east. The boy slept a tossed, grunting sleep.

The man said the morning of the second day, "I must be telling it well, since there have been no interruptions for events to be clarified or people to be explained." Then for much of that day he told about the land, its ways, and the secrets of surviving it.

The boy listened, deep. Not missing a word of the stories, or readings, or the way Cochrane Utterbach did all he did. The way he walked, talked, was aware of where he was, as he had been in the yard.

"My daddy used to say you let a man know that you hold him in respect and it's likely he will rise to your expectations," the lawman said on the third evening. "Said, Make no enemies by mistake."

It was too dark to read under the cloudless, twinkling night canopy, them stretched out beside a trickling spring, propped against their saddles, the winking flames of the ticking twig fire licking at the blackness. As his goodnight, Utterbach said, "We get to Malone in the morning. If you want, no matter what went on before, your new life can start right now. Do you understand?"

It was then the boy spoke. Told him, a word at a time:

Everybody had died but him. Sister got an achy, vomiting cold, believed to have been the Spanish flu. Mother thought if looked after proper it would be gone in three days. Instead, by the fourth, it was Sister who was gone. Buried among the patch of primroses she so loved. Three weeks later Mother went down with the same symptoms. He and Father, at Mother's insistence, had slept in the barn, and therefore thought that explained their survival. Then Father contracted it, with the same result.

He, for who else was there, had buried them, as best he could, in shallow, stone- topped graves by the flowerbed. And then with what he could carry on horseback wandered until near death to, if it was called anything, Old Miller's Place. Wondered why Niall Burleson, who already had a dog and a woman to fetch and beat, didn't run him off, or, just let him die.

Said he had thought about running away but had feared there was no escape across the flat of the ever-same emptiness.

Said that much and then quit, though there was still so much he couldn't make himself tell.

That night he slept through moonset without dreaming.

The next forenoon, after having passed the increasing scatter of farms and ranches, Utterbach halted his horse, handed a pair of binoculars to the boy, and pointed ahead of them.

He saw the train off to their right crawling along the far horizon like a linked line of ants inching its way toward a point right-angle to their route, and its whistle that he had heard some nights back, stealing in on eastern night winds faint as a mouse's heartbeat. That had made him hug himself as he trembled nearly to weeping.

The boy had already seen the town, had watched it grow, as it was rising from the ditch where the dusty flat of the earth met the expanse of rain-gray sky.

Two circles hot against his sockets, unfocused at first at his memory of his recurring dream on waking, then converging to one circle, and with a last slight adjustment of the binoculars' knob there it was, the town in sharper detail. Buildings, and smoke, but still too far distanced to make out people or horses.

Utterbach, in that moment, quiet as the boy had been over their time together.

The boy handed the device back. He told himself he had known this day was coming. It was the final seen but unseen part of what he had dreamed.

The lawman hayed his horse and the boy hayed his. The lawman picked up his story where he had left off, the boy watching, trying to control his breathing, as they approached Malone. A place with colors and no hateful people, a place he had wanted so hard he thought maybe that he had willed it with each body clench, lip bite, and fist clutch against stinging blows from Niall's lash across his back, hinny, and thighs.

When they reached Malone the train had arrived before them and was being readied for departure. The engine was a shiny black, steam-snorting bull, hunkered, ready to heave up and roar forth. The depot on the left at the end of the main street was empty of passengers and freight that had been on board. The lumberyard was on their right.

As much time as he had spent—multiple days dreaming and fitful, half-awake a.m. hours—constructing detail by detail the world over the gray horizon, nothing had prepared him for the sudden whirl storm of unimagined things that swept across the flat gray plains of his vision and limited experience. It was a swirling whirl of eye-popping new. Two-story-building tall poles strung together with wire running down the length of both sides of the main street and alongside the railroad tracks from way, way back until way, way off where they met at a dot.

Machines, horseless carriages that he had only heard spoken about. They seemed smaller versions of the train engine, self-powered and of shiny metal, with room for two or four. The horses didn't take notice or shy away at the loud chug and honk of them as he did.

They crossed the railroad tracks, and were on Malone's main street, lined on both sides with commercial establishments. Buildings with specific purposes—bank, hotel, restaurants, stores, and others, including the stable—none of which had been detailed in his dream.

The thing his dream or the binoculars had helped him foresee was the color in the town, the surprise of the stunning-hued signs, facades, products, their containers, and the cheerful clothing of the townspeople. It was like a dream garden. He had not seen colors to match since the primroses and petunias where he had put his people.

Malone on first impression was a place of laughter and high chins and postures like iron poles on the townspeople—mostly, it seemed, people of color and Seminoles and Creeks in broad-brimmed hats—who spoke, nodded, hunched one another, and stared, questions on their faces. Pointing.

He and Deputy Marshall Cochrane Utterbach reached the stable, harness, saddlery, and horseshoeing establishment on the main street near the edge of town. A small crew of coloreds serviced customers on horseback and in wagons. And a man in a derby, a leather apron over his clothes, came out grinning. He featured the lawman except for his drooping mustaches. The brother, the boy figured. Haskell Utterbach. They embraced and expressed their genuine joy at seeing each other. After their greeting they spoke softly below the conversations of the customers and clang of horseshoeing, the stable man nodding before slapping Cochran on his shoulder and reentering the stable.

Cochran motioned to the boy to dismount, and a young man came from inside the stable and took charge of their horses.

They stepped up onto the long boardwalk that ran the length of the block of buildings, the lawman's treads echoing with each step.

"Is the judge about?" Utterbach asked, as he stopped in front of the U.S. Land Office to converse with the three men lounging, laughing, whittling, chewing, smoking there, who proved to be lawmen like him.

Teasing the lawman: "See you brought in a desperado."

"Looks like he put up quite a fight."

Laughter.

"There a price on his head, Cochran?"

"Price? Or lice?" someone asked.

Laughter.

The lawman cussed them good-naturedly, and once their joviality faded one asked, "You find the Turlocks?"

The boy wandered a few steps off, head swimming in the blazing of sights and smells, sawdust, paint, food odors, perfume, liquor, and sounds, layers of conversations, wondering if he would ever be able to go to sleep among all the bustle and confusion. He moved up the plank sidewalk to the general store to look in though the polished glass. Saw instead a skinny scarecrow in tatters in front of a boy in city clothes. He turned quickly and the city boy was there. Wearing a cloth cap, store-bought jacket with too-short sleeves, knee britches, long socks, and ankle high shoes. There was no scarecrow behind the town boy. They stared at each other until the town boy held his nose, crossed his eyes, and stuck out his tongue before he raced off laughing as if in tickled terror toward the train as it whistled, bellowed, and churned into motion.

The boy turned quickly back to the reflection in the window glass to see the scarecrow turn as he turned to face it. He was the scarecrow in filthy tatters. He stared in wonder at the grimy bundle of rags he was clothed in. That was the condition the marshal had referred to and held Niall responsible for back in the yard! He began to itch, as if the lack of awareness of how he must look to others had protected him from realization of the filthiness that covered him.

His stare was broken by the lawman's whistle and motion for him to come.

The Turlocks will maraud no more, was how the lawman put it to the man he introduced as Judge Cleve Chitwood. Asked by the judge why had he not brought the bodies as usual, the lawman said for one thing he left an ignorant, heavy-handed Irish son-of-a-bitch some chores to do while he healed.

"And?"

"Brought a reliable eyewitness instead," Utterbach said.

"That?" The judge asked.

"My witness."

The boy stared at the shelves of what he guessed to be law books in the back room of the U. S. Land Office. They were the first books of any kind he had seen since he wandered from his home.

Called by the judge, the thin man on crutches they had passed in the outer office hobbled in, propped his crutches against the wall, and sat at the side desk. They gave him time to get ready. When he nodded the lawman spoke his deposition, as the judge called it, and the thin man wrote.

"I, Cochran Utterbach, Deputy Marshal of Randolph County, Oklahoma, am speaking in the matter of the deaths of fugitives Gideon

Turlock and Zachariah Turlock, brothers, wanted in the county of Monroe, state of Oklahoma, for the crime of murder."

The boy watched the ink pen dipping, lifting, soaring like a hawk on the wind, flowing the words onto the paper, as Utterbach told how it had been back there outside in the yard. His part in it, how he had cooperated in the apprehension by volunteering the whereabouts of the felons, was included. The lawman then looked the paper over and signed it.

"And as my witness," Utterbach said and turned to him.

"Are you of sound mind?" Judge Chitwood asked.

"Yes, sir," he answered, although he was not totally sure.

"Can you read and cipher?" the judge asked.

"I learned some—before," was as honest as he could be.

"Do you know who the president of the United States of American is?"

"It was President Taft."

"Still is."

"Yes sir. William Howard."

The judge nodded. Did he know the year?

That he was certain of. "1910."

"Right you are. Place your left hand on the bible," the judge said to him.

He did, raising his right as the lawman Cochran Utterbach had done.

"Repeat after me," the judge said. "I . . ."

"I . . ."

"State your name," the thin man said, not looking up.

"Your name," the boy said.

"Tell *your* name."

"Branch Ottley." He felt foolish.

"I, Branch Ottley."

"I, Branch Ottley."

"Do swear . . ."

"Do swear . . ." Trying at the same time to watch the pen writing his words, and to keep his hand from trembling like an anxious dog due a whipping. The pen dipping, gliding along the paper.

"That the foresaid facts relating to Deputy Cochran Utterbach's attempt to arrest Zachariah and Gideon Turlock for the crime of murder, and their subsequent actions of resistance that resulted in the deaths of the Turlock brothers . . ."

He repeated the judge's words.

"Are exact as you witnessed them?"

"Are exact as I witnessed them."

The judge nodded, moving the bible away. "Anything to add to this account, Master Ottley?"

"No sir."

"Thank you very much sir."

The writing man blotted the white paper with a smaller square of green and handed it to the judge, who looked over as the thin man dipped the pen, tapped off the excess, and offered it to the boy. The boy took it, his hand trembling.

"Affix your signature or mark," the judge said.

Branch Ottley feared he had forgotten his letters and how to sign his name. Willing himself not to look at either of them, and with a heavy hand, he scratched his shaky signature into the paper. He laid the pen down and stepped back, sweating, smelling the stink of his clothes and himself, and studied the grain in the floor.

The judge picked up the pen and signed the document, blew on it, and handed it back to the thin man. "Mr. Ottley, you are now an official part of the history of the town of Malone, Oklahoma territory."

On meeting Branch Ottley, Haskell's wife Florine Belle, smiling her sunrise smile, asked, "Should we feed him before we bathe him, or you think we might lose him in the deluge of resulting mud?"

"How did you feel all that time, before that lawman came to save you?" Son asked.

"He didn't *come* to save me," Branch said.

"But he *did*."

"He didn't even know I was going to be there."

"But you *were*."

"I was."

"And you thought it was your fault?"

"What? That he killed them?"

"No. Before he came. Your fault that you couldn't do anything?"

"Like what?"

"Get away."

"Maybe. You ask tough questions. At first I was a little mad at him."

"Who? That Irishman Niall? I would have been too. A lot."

"At the lawman, my uncle—"

Son knew to wait.

"—for taking so long to come."

"But you didn't know he was coming."

"Not him, but somebody."

"Oh? Why?"

"Sometimes I knew somebody would come because I wished it so hard. But sometimes I knew Niall would kill me, or I would just die, before anybody came."

"Were you scared when he came and started fighting with Niall and the Turlocks?"

"I don't remember. I just remember watching him."

"Was he scared?"

"He told me later that all he focused on was what he was doing."

"Not even that they might shoot him?"

"Nope. That's what he said."

"Just what he was doing?"

"Yep."

Son asked, "Did you ever think about going back and hurting Niall some more?"

"Yes. A lot. Every time I got scared—or mad."

"Did you?"

"No. Not him."

"Do you still think about it?"

"Sometimes."

"You were lucky."

"I was."

And they were both silent. Tired.

"It's a good story," Son said finally. "It has a good ending."

# 25

# Spain Street Zion A.M.E.

Reverend Cook Richmond was already there. He was one fine-looking specimen of a colored man, keen-creased and crisp in his tailored, camel-colored, double-breasted suit. In the guest speaker's high-backed chair, in the pulpit of Spain Street Zion A.M.E., sitting easy as a fat cat lying on a sunny window sill. His arms resting on the oak arms, legs crossed, the toe of his shiny brown oxfords tapping slightly to some tune in his brain. His gaze was fixed over their heads somewhere at the bottom of the balcony. There were no deacons fussing around him trying to look important. And a close, crane-neck survey by nearly every sister in the church gave evidence that there was no unfamiliar woman of elegance equal to his who might have been Missus Richmond. Interesting.

It was getting close to the time. The assembling congregation was starting to settle down, anxious for it to start, but they were probably going to be in for an extended service so they were still not prepared just yet to get in their sermon-ready frames of mind.

Ushers were shuttling up and down, greeting, seating. There was a harmonious hum to the greetings: polite recognition and proper respect for the deserving to the degree that either was appropriate. Special salutations for Old Mother Johnson, bless her heart, Don't she look good. And Elder Leonard, and how well he was holding up.

Young Brother Jefferies (Junie) on the organ, bless him, noodling an improvised medley of hymns. He was in their secret prayers in the hope it would help him—heal his—wasn't no way to say it but to say it—heal his swishy, sissy ways.

Looking like satin angels for the world, the choir, at Junie Jefferies' signal, entered in formation from the rear of the pulpit, strutting proud in their shiny new robes.

Vienna among them as they got settled, double-checking their hymnals, clearing their throats, saw Branch enter and refuse the offer of being ushered to a seat. He indicated he would stand, and as against custom as that was, he was allowed to remain at the rear corner of the right-hand aisle.

Scanning the church Vienna saw that by some mystery of group perception Branch's presence was almost instantly noticed. His entrance was the only thing, she thought, that could have diverted attention from Reverend Richmond. It ran through the church as if a horsefly had buzzed it and moved ear to ear through the church. Women began puffing themselves up at the unexpected sight of him.

"Ain't them robes something!"

"*Girrrlll*, how you doing?" Church Mother Daniels said. "You looking *goooood*."

"You too. And I *like* that *hat*," Mother Johnson praised in her rough-edged purr.

"Aw, thank you. Look like it took me forever to get going this morning."

"Well it certainly doesn't show."

"Thank you. I wasn't going to miss this for the world."

"Me neither, you know—" Cut off in mid-sentence as Junie gave the downbeat and the choir began to hum "*Oh Ship of Zion*."

There now, see, Junie's jumping the gun, lots of folks still to be seated and . . . and then that blind boy got up and started singing, bless his heart. Mother Johnson whispering how his mama had designed and made all the robes. His mama, Pearl. The two senior women nodding to each other how that Pearl Moon was a real go-getter.

Her son singing, "*What ship is this that's landed at the shore?*"

Looking at the watch her son Chepheus gave her last Christmas, Mother Johnson whispered, "Eleven o'clock sharp."

"On the dot!"

Maybe Junie just following instructions, they thought, as they *a-men*-ed with reconsidered admiration and approval. The tone of it said just the fact of Reverend Richmond starting on time was a whole sermon in itself.

"Oh, Glory hallelujah!" Son sang.
"It's the old ship of Zion, hallelujah!
It's the old ship of Zion, hallelujah!"

And the choir coming in with the chorus,

"Don't you see that ship a-sailing,
Going over to the Promised Land?"

The boy singing,

"What kind of Captain does she have on board?
Oh, Glory Hallelujah."

"Don't he sing *good*?"

"Mummm," Mother Daniels half approved, "but it ain't like Sister Ryder."

"No, Lord. That was *her* song."

Unannounced Reverend Richmond eased into position at the pulpit as smooth as oiled silk. He gave the text and topic of his upcoming sermon.

They looked at each other. Hadn't never seen it done like that. Raised their eyebrows, being patient. Must be the way they do it up in Riverton. Drum-patted the back of one hand with the fingers of the other. Waited to see.

"My theme," he said, "is a brand new day and a brand new time."

Hallelujah.

Simply by being punctual, Vienna thought, Richmond is saying he's professional. Not like any of the other of those old-timey Chilton jack-legged preachers. Operating on colored people's time like they still did, with their services starting anywhere from a half hour to forty-five minutes late was like the attitude of doing just enough to satisfy the white man. That might have been all right in its day, but not anymore. The whole world was changing—war in Europe, A. Philip Randolph and Walter White meeting with Roosevelt to get rid of government discrimination and let colored boys get a fair fight in the army—and this Reverend Richmond's starting on time was like saying, what he say his theme was, Hallelujah, a brand new day and a brand new time? Well, the white man didn't get rich and powerful by showing up late. Reverend Richmond was showing by his manner, attire, and punctuality how to go about it in a brand new way. That was just what Zion A.M.E. needed, Hallelujah.

"She has landed many thousands," the boy sang.

"She can land as many more."

Surprised latecomers whose usual habit was to make an entrance, nodding and being noticed, were unceremoniously being rushed to seats by composed but impatient ushers. *Is this saved?* Excusing themselves, squeezing by the already seated, who gave them smug, less than Christian looks, as if to say, it was time to put behind them those old ignorant ways of showing up late because you assume things going to start late, amen. Let that be a lesson to them.

Reverend Richmond saying just above the singing, "There was a time for plowing and planting and plucking. A stone gathering and a stone throwing time."

Oh, glory Hallelujah!

"A time for tearing down, and building back up . . ."
 "She sails like she is heavy-ladened . . ."
 "A time for laughing and crying, dancing and mourning . . ."
 "But she's a-sailing mighty steady
 She's neither reeling or rocking."
 "A time to be born and . . ."
 "But she's a-sailing mighty steady
 She's neither reeling nor rocking."

"Time for tearing, and sewing, and hating, and loving, and a time for moving on, crossing over from the old to the new," he said, enunciating in his crooner's voice like an English professor.

Professional. That was what his starting on time said to any with sense enough to hear it and take it to heart.

Junie Jefferies, his robe sleeves flapping like butterfly wings whipping the choir to an upbeat finish.

"Oh is your bundle ready? Hallelujah.
Oh is your bundle ready? Hallelujah.
A-men!"

Reverend Richmond turning to watch Son as he moved a few steps back, wiping at his forehead with the back of his hand.

"Isn't he a *blessing*," Richmond said.

"A-men," agreed the church.

"Isn't *he* a blessing," Richmond said again.

"A-men," agreed the church.

"Amen!"

"*Isn't* he a blessing?" Richmond repeated.

"*A-men*," agreed the church.

The reverend then said he wanted Son to stay right there to help him because he was going to dispense with the usual way he conducted a sermon. He was going to get right to it, because he didn't have much time to get to all he had to do.

They encouraged him to get to it.

That was when Mother Johnson, in her raspy bulldog growl with the same indignant inflection that she said most things, always making even her most damning accusations sound like questions from the Old Testament God, said, "What you doing with that gun in here, Mister?"

At the same time the first shot went off like a car backfiring, and the pandemonium began.

Chap had strongly suspected that Sunny Bob's disappearance wasn't about the payoff money Sunny Bob was delivering to the local officials and police for Chap. Sunny Bob did not work just for Chap. He also did distribution, or was a bagman in the employ of a legitimate syndicate of Chilton businessmen with semi-legitimate silent partners outside the city. Those partners, Chap suspected, were the Finkleman mob. They ruled part of the underworld activities in Riverton. The Finklemans, who had money and muscle, had been making overtures to Chap and white real businesses and estate owners about partnering with or buying up some Chilton properties. Chap's having to guess at whom and why told him the outcome would likely not be in his best interest.

Another possibility was Rudolph Lyons, aka, Ruddy the Lion. He was the head of the biggest Negro numbers racket in Riverton. The Finklemans were his backers. Reverend Richmond's big church in Riverton was one of the venues used by Ruddy the Lion to launder money. Whether it was the Finklemans directly or Lyons through them it meant trouble for Chap. That was why he had sent for Branch.

The bullet hit the reverend in his torso. He took a step back, not even raising his hands to the ballooning red wound. The second shot, from a different point in the church than the first, was also to his chest already leaking blood. He didn't stagger, he just tilted straight back like an axed tree, falling back against Son.

Branch knew the two out-of-place-looking Negroes were together, damn it. Same type and quality topcoats, suits, and fedoras, their right hand in their coat pockets. He had spotted and tracked them from the time they entered about four or five minutes apart a couple of minutes earlier. They had muscled their way into aisle seats on opposite sides of the church. They didn't look nervous but they did look out of place. They were there for a reason, all right, and it wasn't for coming to Jesus. But because it was his first time in the church, he hadn't known whom to ask about the two men.

Too late. Richmond was down. Branch's gun already out of his under-the-arm holster and aimed at the first shooter standing halfway down the aisle to his left above those crouched down in the pews around him. The man had turned to move back up the aisle. Branch's shot entered his center chest a couple inches below the four-in-hand knot of the shooter's tie, splattering tissue, blood, and spine bone.

Satisfied without checking that his first shot had inflicted sufficient damage to the shooter on his left, he swung his Colt around to his right. Amid the rush of scrambling, screaming congregants, the second shooter, perhaps aware that his partner had been shot, perhaps not, was trying to make his exit by, through, or over the panicked crowd who were doing their best in the confused press of bodies to back away from him and the pistol still in his hand. Branch whistled a loud, sharp single note. It pierced the air like an eagle's cry.

Still fighting his way out, the man heard the whistled note above the noises echoing through the church. He turned to look over his shoulder. The bullet entered his temple, snapped his head back, and he spun around and crumbled sideways, his arms thrown up as if signaling a touchdown. His errant shot, squeezed off in a death spasm, angled into the ceiling. A shower of plaster chips and dust sprinkled down on the confusion like snow.

In the basement Pearl had already stopped picking up after the choir members, having heard the upstairs commotion of people and chairs. Ada, picking up the strewn hangars and tissue paper and delivery boxes the robes were brought in, stopped too, having heard what sounded like a big branch snapping off a tree, and three more. Pearl knew they were pistol shots and was looking for her purse.

"Purse?!" she said to Ada, who had dropped her handful of wire hangers. The girl pointed to the floor by the long table near where Pearl was standing. Pearl stooped, picked it up, unsnapping open the large plastic tortoiseshell clasp handle and had one foot up on the bottom step as she pulled the blue steel snubbed-nosed pistol from it, and dropped the purse, its contents of folding money, change purse, receipts, identification, compact and lipstick, hair comb, everything raining and rattling, clattering to the floor. Her skirt pulled up with her free left hand. She was taking the steps two at a time and rushed up to and through the door at the rear of the pulpit into the screaming and scrambling.

Outside on Spain Street Horace Bradshaw, Horse, the colored dayshift foot patrolman, with his night stick, pistol, handcuffs, whistle, and badge 79, exited Kellwood's Restaurant and stood under the canopy, watching

Arthur Fuller hurrying across the street through the unexpected rain that had turned the day cement gray. The fool was gesturing behind him, to the church, Bradshaw guessed. What now?

Arthur stopped at the curb, not even enough damned sense to step up under the canopy, Bradshaw thought. "Get out of the street," he told him. Arthur did, but still stood in the rain. The smell of liquor leapt from him like a shout. He just stood there dripping. Waiting. Bradshaw exhaled gray smoke at him. It evaporated in the distance between them like a rabbit under a magician's cape.

"What?"

Without looking behind him Arthur pointed and spoke in a loud, conspiratorial whisper. "Horse," he said, "The devil in there claiming souls."

So sick of sorry Arthur Fuller, the only white man that Bradshaw almost felt pity for, he didn't know what to do.

"Who, fool?" he bothered to ask.

Then several men and women came, exiting Spain Street Zion A.M.E., and shouting to Horse, and anyone, that they were shooting and killing inside. He threw down his cigarette as a few more rushed out of the church. The cigarette sparked, sputtered, and hissed to death on the wet street. Some reverend had been shot as far as he could make out.

Bradshaw hoped it was a white gunman. He didn't have time to reckon why white men would be shooting up a church chucked with colored people any more than he had time to reckon why a Negro would. He just hoped it, and started running toward the gray- stoned structure, his service revolver in his hand.

Bradshaw didn't mind rousting and occasionally cold-sapping a colored man when the situation called for it, but he wasn't that crazy about the prospect of having to shoot one.

Bradshaw, as he leapt to the church's top step ordered, "Call for help!"

Did he remember a car parked outside the church when moments ago he went in to Callwells? Was there a white or colored man at the wheel?

He heard screaming from inside as he eased the heavy front door open and entered the vestibule. A couple of elderly people were crouched in the small foyer, hiding or scrunched down praying. With his left hand he gestured for them to remain silent and with the sharp gesture of his gun hand he motioned them to git, angry with them for their old cowering attitudes.

No more shots had been fired. A short couple of minutes ago he'd been standing out of the rain under the awning of the restaurant, picking fried pork chop from his teeth with his fingernail. Now with his back against the wall he took a short snort of air, collecting himself, his pistol gripped chest-high. It was the first time in two years on the force his gun had left his holster in the line of duty. With his left hand he pulled the inner door left open.

Vienna wondered if this was the trouble Branch had predicted on the side porch that night. Whether or not it was, he was in the middle of it, brought to him without his seeking it. She did not think to scream, or to duck. She watched as if she was seated next to him in the dark at the King picture show, eating popcorn and watching him on the silent screen. He was different from Twin Collins, fancy-dressed in jingling and shiny outfits, silver, and silk bandana. Branch, his arm extended, pistol in his hand, was more like a vengeful William S. Hart. She saw the pistol kick but she did not hear it fire, did not hear any of the sounds around her, had not since Mother Johnson shouted. She saw the gun steadied as it swept to Branch's right and stop, seemingly without its being aimed and kicked again as it fired, and she watched him move then through the scramble as easily as if she were on his arm as they were leaving the King after a Thursday night double feature. He moved through a dusting of plaster floating from the ceiling, like dandruff on his brown suit.

Then, as if someone had flicked a switch, Vienna heard the screaming again. And she felt the trembling throughout her body at the sight of the bedlam, Branch at the center of it, standing with his back to her and the choir that was still dissembling themselves from their hiding places.

Patrolman Horace 'Horse' Bradshaw opened the carved oak vestibule doors, his gun raised.

Branch, his right arm raised above his head with the .45 showing, let Patrolman Bradshaw see that he had it, and let him know he had done with it all that he intended to do at that time.

Pearl and Hughes reached Richmond and Son from different directions and at the same time knelt beside them. The reverend was face up, lying three-quarters on top of Son. The boy was saying he was all right. He was all right, mama, he was all right. Hughes rolled the dead preacher off the boy and Pearl lay down prone on top of her son, asking for additional reassurance that he was all right.

Upon his opening the door all went still and quiet in uncertain anticipation. It was like a children's game of Freeze. The congregation pressed, crouched, clinging, cringing against the floor, walls, corners, or each other, not knowing if Satan or salvation would enter. At the sight of Horse what passed among them was the slow realization that the first of it was over. The violent thundering storm had stopped and was being followed by what they hoped was a soft rain, like the gentle patter of drops spattering against the stained glass window, and sanity, or what had previously passed for it, was returning through the opened door in the form of the wet colored policeman, a gun in his hand.

Horse looked about the scattered space to the right-hand aisle at Branch Ottley, Chap's cowboy, his right arm up, what looked like a M 1911A1 Colt .45 Automatic in his right hand. A DOA Negro in an overcoat, his left temple oozing blood, lay next to a fedora, and what looked like a Smith & Wesson lay at the cowboy's feet.

It was all so quick, as Vienna and most of the others interviewed by the police said. It all just happened at once.

They began moving in two waves, one toward the widening circle around Reverend Richmond and Son, the other toward the door where Horse stood blocking the exit. Bradshaw had been handpicked by Police Chief Captain Francis Mahoney for what the chief thought was Bradshaw's guard dog-like loyalty, and allegiance to him over any ties he might have to the Negroes he was hired to keep guard of, and therefore he had the good sense to follow the orders of his superior officer.

Bradshaw, with only a slight tremor in his voice, told the cowboy to lay his pistol down. To Bradshaw's relief Ottley did.

Next, the young policeman announced, even though he was ordered to move by no less than Mother Johnson on the arms of two black-suited, white-gloved ushers, Deacons Hildebrand and Jenkins, that until reinforcements, meaning Chief Mahoney, arrived, and took official charge of the situation, no one was leaving.

And so it was, until, sirens screaming, tires screeching, Chief Mahoney in his rain slicker and plastic cover on his cap with the patent leather bill entered, the wedge at his phalanx of heavily-armed patrolmen to put down and straighten up the mess and supervise the cleaning up of the carnage and incarceration of the congregates.

Unnoticed in the confusion, Ada brought Pearl's purse up and got her pistol and with it under a robe hung over her arm she moved, unseen, back into the basement and out of the door there and took it home to tell Chap what had happened.

Big Horace Bradshaw was born and raised right on Evans Street. He had been All City center for the colored Lincoln High Panthers. Nicknamed Horse, who on offense was as protective of his quarterback as a mama bear of her cubs, and on defense was a nose-busting, head-cracking bruiser, who with a teeth-bared, red-eyed fury hunted and brought down ball carriers.

Horse Bradshaw knew the rage that boiled in the bellies above and within 'lo' Dunbar: fear of and anger at cursed, savage niggers; anger at and fear of damned hateful crackers. He also knew what was expected, no, demanded of him by Captain Mahoney, the mayor, and council and citizens above Dunbar. They made it plain enough.

They *thought* it was as simple as black and white, as them and us. He thought they had no idea, A, how wrong they were, or, B, how good he was at his job.

To keep its denizens in line was to keep them alive. And if it took the slight injustice of a lumped skull, or boot in the butt, a night or two in the tank to keep his flock safe, then so be it. Well worth the price, and everybody was better off for it, whether they were like children with stinging hands or burning butts too temporarily painful to understand the long-term benefits of a spanking. None of their hissing and spitting at him behind his back as he strolled his beat, his twirling nightstick whistling its little tune punctuated by its snapping rhythm as it hit his palm, mattered to him.

He was, he thought, whether they knew or appreciated it or not, their guardian and secret spokesman, negotiator and best friend. He saved them, he thought, from a bigger world of hurt in the long run. For he *knew* the depthless possibility of evil that lay in the tree line of the white folks' fear. He'd seen it at the bottom of the pile at a goal line stand. He saw it in the Captain's grease-soaked lunch bag each morning, heard it in the angry ring of the desk sergeant's phone with a white citizen's complaint about being bumped into on the street by some nigger bitch, or eye-balled by some young or old, big or little man or boy, felt it every-where. However rarely acknowledged and unappreciated his part in that was.

The more emotionally controlled were, with reassuring tones, calming children and weepers, patting the backs of hands, fanning the faint and frustrated who, under their hats, had sweated out their hot-combed hairdos, and whose mascara and skin-lightening face power was streaked despite their fanning. There were sprinklings of individual prayers, evident by closed eyes and silently-mouthed words. Some slumped in their pews looking upward. Grade school boys, squirming with their pent-up desire, eyed each other, trying to communicate with only their facial expressions their desire to whip out their pistols and have a running gun battle among the pews, or even better be out in the open of the playground; they were rehearsing their stories to tell in school. They squirmed and twisted their mouths and their eyebrows danced—until they were warned for the last time. Knowing better, they did not even protest their innocence but sighed and turned away from each other and tried to sit still.

After what Vienna would describe as the moments of pure pandemonium was the long wait to get out. Within about ten minutes every policeman in Chilton was there. It was announced everyone in the church were being detained until their statements could be taken and their contact information obtained.

Under the chief's command lines were formed, and like third graders at an assembly, the congregates were marched slowly forward to be interviewed one by one by uniformed policemen and plainclothes detectives.

They don't know what they're doing, an usher said to an usherette. They'd never had this kind of killing before. They were only used to a crap game razor fight, with a victim bleeding to death because of the perpetrator's indifference or medical neglect.

The three bodies, photographed from all angles before the coroner, in his golf clothes, had finally been found and had them declared dead, were bagged and hauled off to the morgue.

———

Daisy Wood, soprano who sang next to Vienna in the Zion AME choir, and did day work for Mr. Jacobs, the manager of First City Bank, and his wife, sat next to Vienna as they were waiting to be interviewed. Daisy listened to everybody complaining until she whispered to Vienna, "He's trying his best to do a good job."

"Who?"

"Horace Bradshaw."

"Oh."

Vienna found Bradshaw in the crowd, pointing parishioners to one of the four policemen taking names, addresses, and statements.

"He loves his job," Daisy said. "Being useful in his hometown."

Vienna could feel Daisy trying to hold herself back in her praise of Bradshaw.

"That's all he wants to do. Be useful, helpful to us."

Vienna nodded. Branch had been handcuffed and taken away.

"If it had been a white policeman first through that door," Daisy said, "no telling what would have happened."

Vienna smiled at Daisy. Honest to Jesus, she thought, there is some-body for everybody.

It was Horse Bradshaw, Daisy said, who had been the first law officer on the scene and was the other hero of the day.

Why him? Vienna wondered. To Daisy she said, "I wouldn't tell that to Mother Johnson I was you."

Mother Johnson, bless her feisty old soul—in her almost brand-new taffeta and chiffon dress that Pearl Moon had made especially for her—and Sister Durham, who was well traveled and therefore knew that Mother Johnson's dress was superior to anything women of taste were wearing in Chicago, Harlem, Detroit, or Riverton, were still giving Horace the side eye. It was Horace who had blocked her first attempt at an exit and had made her go and sit back down until the chief arrived to decide what was to be done. Whether everybody was to be taken down to the station or interviewed in the church was a decision the brass would have to make, Horace explained, but until then nobody was to leave.

He must have had her confused with sanctified country Negroes like them in that Reverend Prophet Riley Cook's so-called church that got happy and fell out, flopping like landed carp, or walleyed, snake-handling, red necked Southern Baptists who lay on the church floor. Mrs. Paul Johnson in Church Street Zion A.M.E. did not care how many people had been killed, or how many more had no home training, pistols or no pistols, she would not stand to be ordered around in that fashion.

Everybody agreed with her but his or her complaints were given no more weight than Mother Johnson's.

"Mysterious Father," Mother Johnson began, her usually raspy voice like a sharp handclap. It was as if the volume of a radio had suddenly been turned up on a conversation in progress. The others around her hushed, but most did not look her way for fear her wrathful gaze was focused on them. "You who have taught us not to argue with or question the hard lessons You teach. And once again shown us what the absence of Your presence in the hearts of men looks like."

There was an edge to her voice and a set to her countenance as if she were scolding a child who should have known better, especially after all of the talking-to's it had had. She paused. It was Pearl and Son she was focused on.

Pearl had her arm around his shoulder. The darkening red of the slain minister's blood on the boy's white shirt was like a splotched bull's-eye. She was whispering to him. He was nodding. Both of them were as calm as if they were watching butterflies on a sunny bench in Perkins Park.

Mother Johnson continued, "In our puny understanding of Your mysterious wisdom, and under the protection of Your loving, guiding hand, You allowed that cowboy man to defend us with his sure and steady aim, Mysterious Father."

"Amen."

"And we know we must thank You for nestling that child there to your bosom. Seeing fit to take his eyes, You have burdened him in one way, but giving him another kind of insight have gifted him in another. You spared him this day to carry forth with that gift."

"Amen."

She paused to swallow, one, two, three times, as if trying to get down a portion of graveyard dirt, then, eyes narrowed, focusing, Mother Johnson continued, the tone of her voice like a scythe slow-honed against a dry Arkansas grindstone. At the sound of it, children stopped their whining and squirming and bit their lips or sucked their thumbs. Clung closer. There was little doubt they would have regressed to the nipple had breasts been bared.

"—When You taught us through the bitter broth of experience we have sipped from the tarnished cup of injustice at the hands of the law, Mysterious Father—"

Mother Johnson stopped. Her voice had been ebbing lower and lower like a boat on receding floodwaters. It had fallen so low at the end they had to strain to hear her.

Unsure now if it had even been for those around her to hear, they wrinkled their noses as if they smelled smoke and kerosene, or brimstone. They listened to each other breathe.

—

Those who had been interviewed exited the church into the late gray afternoon. They grumbled but were relieved to see the crowd outside. There were husbands who'd come to meet their wives who'd gone to church without them. There were non-churchgoers who'd heard the news and came to see what was what.

Like a fire the word leapt from party line to party line, house to house, front porch to front porch, across back fences, domestic worker to domestic worker, factory worker to factory worker. That it was a Sunday made it easier. The businesses and the bars were closed. The weather even helped by it being gray and rainy, so few were out and about in the parks and such.

It wasn't long before somebody realized that the center of the action had shifted from the church to the police station. That was where they went.

It was 5:20 when Chap, with Hughes at the wheel, pulled up in front of headquarters. Chap had called ahead, leaving a message for the chief that he would see him at 5:35.

The rain had long ago stopped, the weak sun valiantly trying to dry things off. There were Son and Pearl and Mother Johnson sitting on one of the benches in Veteran's Square facing police headquarters. Son, with the fifteen-foot-or-so-high flagpole behind him, had dark blood on his shirt the same color as the stripes on the damp, dingy American flag hanging like an empty sleeve from the pole.

A car full of white street toughs, their complexions ruddied by the contents of the occasional flash of tilted flasks, parked on the west side of Veterans Square, across from colored boys from the plant slow-chewing sandwiches in Frank Parker's old green Hudson on the east side, both motors idling.

Greetings. Expressing their appreciation and relief for Chap's showing up, and their frustration with still having to be there.

Chap was still mad as a motherfucker.

Mad at the police for holding every goddamned body in the church for that long. Making him have to call up Lars Walton, a Negro lawyer, and have him call up a white lawyer that he trusted to meet him at the police station.

Mad too at the two dead motherfuckers who'd come to Chilton to shoot Richmond in the first goddamned place. Sons of bitches, served them right Branch'd shot their sorry asses to goddamn death. Last time they'd try some shit like that in Chilton.

Mad too at whomever had sent them.

Chap told Mother Johnson he was going to have Hughes take her and Pearl and Son home; he thanked them all.

He took the old woman's arm and walked her to the car. She nodded to him before he closed the door. Other than that she never said a word. They pulled off.

—

Branch sat on the kitchen stool with the lath-turned legs and spindles in the interrogation room in police headquarters.

The many chips, scars, nicks, and gouges revealed a dingy, money-green beneath the top coat of black enamel paint applied with thick slathering strokes streaked with bristle marks. The green was probably of the same vintage as shrouded the walls of the small windowless room. A sludge-gray beneath that, and where it was gouged, deepest evidence of the original stained pine. The rear left leg was at least an inch and a half shorter than the two it formed an equilateral triangle with, and two inches shorter than its kitty-corner opposite, causing Branch, his back to the door, to make an effort to sit straight so as not to titter. The stool was placed a couple of feet from the oak table with the matching chair behind it.

To calm himself he thought of the Oklahoma flatlands stretched quiet and tranquil, clear to the skyline laid out before him. He waited.

Horse Bradshaw, leaning back against the door, watched Branch Ottley's back.

"Branch Ottley," the chief said. He tapped the sheet of paper in front of him. "What the hell kind of name is that?"

Ottley didn't answer.

"We expect the occasional weekend incident in Low Dunbar," the chief continued. "It's expected. But murder?" He shook a cigarette from his Lucky Strike Green Label pack, hung it in the corner of his mouth, and struck a match, holding it as the flame crawled up the stick. "When they come three at a time"—he put the flame to the cigarette tip, inhaled, shook out the match, and dropped it into the jar top ashtray—"that's too much at once." He exhaled. "You a member of the church?"

"I was just there to hear the boy sing," Ottley said.

"What boy?"

Bradshaw told him about Son.

The chief asked, "What was Richmond to you?"

"We both roomed at 560."

"The boy lives there too," Bradshaw said.

"Does it seem funny to you, two Negroes with no identification would come in a church and shoot a preacher?"

"Strange. Not funny," Ottley said.

"Who were they?" the chief asked. The Lucky Strike was angled in the ashtray, burning down.

"Don't know."

"Do you know who sent them or why did they shoot the preacher?"

"I don't."

"Why'd you shoot them?"

"I had a choice to make. I could have backed off and got them coming out of the church, but I wasn't sure that Richmond was their only target."

"Who else you think it might have been?"

"Didn't think I could wait to find out."

You wouldn't tell me if you did know, would you?

"Why wouldn't I?"

"What are *you* doing in Chilton?"

"Working for Chap," Bradshaw said.

"Doing what?"

"Being around," Ottley said.

"For what?"

"In case."

"What?"

"I'm needed."

"Be careful," the chief said. "You want this to go rough it can go rough. Any more of this snake-hipping do-do bird shit I will let Horse do the questioning."

"And I know how to get the answers we want," Bradshaw said.

"Ordinarily," the chief said, "I'd have him beat the shit out of you, convict you of double homicide, and lock you away as a warning, and the mayor would give me a commendation."

Branch waited.

"But there's the slight smell of the hero on you. If only it hadn't happened in the church."

Branch waited.

"Why did you have a gun?"

"I always have one."

"Why?"

"In case."

The chief paused as he picked up the cigarette, inhaled, and stubbed it out. "Two dead center shots in a crowded church. That's pretty good shooting."

"I had a good teacher."

"Who? Annie Oakley?"

"My uncle."

"Who was he, Black Bart?"

"Peace officer."

"Your uncle is a lawman?"

"He was a marshal. It's in my statement."

The chief asked Bradshaw why he hadn't told him that.

"Sergeant Thomas interviewed him," Bradshaw said.

The chief asked, "Marshal where?"

"Malone, Oklahoma," Ottley said.

"You want me or Sergeant Thomas to check?" Bradshaw asked.

"I'll tell Thomas. You stay with him," indicating Ottley with a head gesture.

There was an urgent knock on the door.

"It had better be important," the chief called.

There was another series of knocks. "Chief?"

"What?"

The desk sergeant stuck his head in. "Talk with you a moment, Chief?"

The chief mumbled a curse under his breath, shook a cigarette from the pack; he rose and moved to the door.

The first thing the sergeant told the chief was about that little colored boy in the bloody shirt and two colored women sitting on the bench across in the square.

"What're they doing?"

"Nothing at first, then somebody brought them sandwiches."

The chief lighted the cigarette. "They litter, shoot them," he said, fatigue in his voice.

The sergeant noted the chief's tone and took a moment before he added about the several others, young bucks, and a bunch of white boys who'd showed up. Collected like crows on a wire, he said, wishing there was more to report, and thinking he hadn't explained it right.

"And?"

He had a ready answer for the chief on that one: Chap was there to see him.

"You should have told me that first," the chief said. "Put a man out front to watch them," he told the sergeant as he headed for his office.

"I'm here to get him," Chap greeted the chief where he was waiting in his office.

"Ain't that simple this time, Chap."

"Why the fuck not?"

"He killed two men."

"Who had killed a goddamned preacher in a fucking church full of people."

"That's a lot of shooting for a stranger."

"He's been rooming with me for damn near a year."

"I've had phone calls," the chief said.

"The mayor and his stooge, Councilman Bradley, and . . . ?"

"Members of the business community . . ."

"Them sons of bitches," Chap said.

". . . who don't like the idea of a sharp-shooting Negro being on the loose. They were questioning me about why we didn't go in guns blazing, because they'd heard there were snipers firing out of the church windows and from the bell tower. They were afraid of a full-scaled race riot."

"Did you explain to them that this is bigger shit than their nightmares about boogie-man Negroes? It was self-defense, Maloney. No telling how many lives of Chilton's finest colored citizens he saved. Tell me I'm fucking lying and I'll head on home, let you keep him."

"But his kind of killing is new for us, Chap. And when you get into new territory the safest thing is to be guided by the rules you already know."

"That sounds like a politician."

"I might not always want to be chief," Maloney said.

Well, you sonofabitch, Chap thought. The possibility of Maloney wanting to one day be mayor surprised Chap. He cursed himself for not having counted on that possibility sooner, and for therefore not figuring on it in his long-term dealings with the man.

"First things first," the chief said. "What we all know is that whoever he is that's not an ordinary nigger in there."

"He is from Malone, Oklahoma. His uncle was a famous lawman. I've talked with the people out there. They are going to call you to vouch for him, if they haven't already."

Maloney thought for a moment. "Yeah," he said. "I know about his connection to the marshal there, in Oklahoma."

"He is trouble in dark skin. And we cannot afford him in Chilton."

Chap didn't deny it.

"I have to think of my future same as you do yours," Mahoney said. "Either way it'll never be on my tombstone Francis J. Maloney was the chief when some outside gunslinger set off some kind of colored uprising."

Was that the policeman or the politician or both? Chap wondered.

They'd known each other all their lives. Chap had always thought Mahoney as even-tempered as they come. There were only two things upset him; one was his wife's relatives, and two, people telling him how to be chief of police.

"I don't write the laws, but I enforce them as they are, fair or not."

Chap's ability to read people was momentarily shaken. Mayor hell, Chap thought. Maloney, you son of a bitch, if you can sneak cheese by a fucking rat like me you might be sneaky enough to be the goddamn governor.

"Best way to keep this quiet and peaceful," Chap said, "is for Branch to disappear. I promised I'd either bring him out or have your guarantee he was all right now, and will be all right when you let him out."

Maloney, all business again, maybe fearing he'd revealed more than he'd intended, maybe rolling another wooden horse up to the door said, "I told the city fathers that the shooter is in custody, and I've got some more looking into it to see just who he is and how much of a threat he is. I'll hold the suspect and continue our investigation on Monday, until *I'm* satisfied."

"You could've said that up front," Chap said.

"I'm the law in Chilton," Maloney said. "I didn't have to say anything. I want you and the mayor and Harden and Bradley to know it. Now go out and tell them across the street I've got everything under control,

and I want them the hell away from in front of my station. And *if* I'm
satisfied after tomorrow, I'll let him go."

"By the end of business tomorrow," Chap said.

"You handle your business I'll handle mine."

"I'll see him before I go," Chap said.

—

The Oklahoma flatlands stretched quiet and tranquil, clear to the skyline. As his uncle Cochrane had taught him, Branch inventoried the
small room again for weapons: the bandy-legged stool, pencils on the
desk, the gooseenecked lamp with its iron stand, the electric cord on it,
in addition to his hands, fists, feet. Surprise would also be on his side.

He said, "I asked the white cop why you weren't taking my statement."

Bradshaw made a sound.

Ottley continued, "He said the chief wanted *him* to do it. I just thought
it should've been you. You were first on the scene. *You* arrested me.
Where was the other guy when you were controlling the crowd, keeping
order, while the sergeant was what? Getting coffee for the chief?"

Bradshaw made the sound again. It was part grunt part snort.

"You're the one out there being the guardian at the corral gate," Ottley
said, "heel-nipping, circling, barking, keeping the Dunbar Negroes
from straying, keeping the captain and the good white folks satisfied so
they can go about their daily business, sleep cozy at night."

"I should've done it because we're both *colored*? That what you're tipping around? Well it don't mean shit to me. And you know something
else? Don't think if I had interrogated you that you wouldn't've told me
everything I want to know."

"I do believe you'd try," Ottley said.

Bradshaw made the sound again.

"Being a lawman means straddling a shifting line," Ottley said as if
he knew what he was talking about. It was the way he said everything.

Bradshaw looked at the back of Ottley's head, waiting.

"Casting your lot with the chief as guard dog at the 'lo' Dunbar border must've seemed the safest bet when you took the job," Ottley said.

"I know my job."

Ottley said, "Like always with them it's use one to control another. You get along out there now because Chap and the 'lo' Dunbar Negroes tolerate you."

Horace, conceding nothing, said, "You got a point?"

Ottley said, "This might be new frontier for you. It's when a situation gets really desperate is when you find out something about your true self. Anything untoward happens to me in here it'll be *your* doing, that's the way the chief will tell it. How I leave this room will determine how the rest of your life goes in this town."

"You having a special opinion of yourself don't change my job."

"You ever tasted your own blood anywhere but a playing field, Officer Bradshaw?"

"Turn around," Ottley was told.

He did and said, "Just so you'll know, I'm not one of your 'lo' Dunbar Negroes that will take a lesson from a roughing up."

"You'll take what you're given."

"No. I won't," Ottley said.

Bradshaw tried not to blink but he did.

Ottley asked, "You killed for them yet?"

"It ain't come up."

"It has now," Ottley said.

They looked at each other.

Ottley said, "I took my last beatings when I was a boy. A hand raised to me now with intended harm will end in death. Do you hear me?"

Bradshaw glanced down to make sure the prisoner's handcuffs were still secure. He said, "I got my job to keep."

They left it at that.

Branch was facing forward, his back to Bradshaw, seeing cattle watering themselves, prairie dogs, quail, antelope, deer, sagebrush, short grass, and hardpan lakebeds, when the chief's return interrupted him.

The single knock on the interrogation room door gave Horse just enough time to step aside before the chief opened it and entered, leaving it open. "Turn around," the chief said to Ottley, who did. Chap was there one step back in the hall. The chief said to Chap, "You've seen him." As he closed the door he stepped back in the hall with Chap and said, "You go tell them you saw him and there's not a scratch on him."

Chap said, "I'll tell them you'll release his ass when you're satisfied that all he is is the motherfucker who saved a church full of people from probable bodily harm. I'll tell them you expect to complete your investigation by fucking end of business tomorrow."

"I'm going to tell the cop outside that within a half hour he is to clear everybody, colored and white, from the front of my station, or they will be arrested for loitering. The mayor and the good businesspeople of Chilton want everybody fit and ready for work in the morning."

Chap nodded and turned without a word and moved up the hall.

Chief Maloney knocked twice, opened the door, and said to Bradshaw, "I'm going home, have a shot or two of bourbon, and a piece of lemon pie. Thomas should have some word on him soon. Meanwhile you take him and lock him up. It's your responsibility to see he doesn't bump his head or stub his toe."

"Yes sir," Bradshaw said.

Before closing the door he said to Ottley, "You are one lucky black son of a bitch."

Branch sat astraddle the stool, looking at the closed door and thinking of the Oklahoma flatlands stretched quiet and tranquil, clear to the skyline.

—

"When there's blood spilt," Chief Maloney said to Branch Ottley the next afternoon, "we want to spill it. If some sharp-shooting, brown-skinned buckaroo is doing my job then they won't need me."

Bradshaw could see the chief had thought up the brown-skinned buckaroo last night and was pleased to get it in.

"We heard from the mayor and the head marshal in your home town. So here's what happens next," the chief continued. "You get your boots and saddle and ride the hell out of my town, no, make that my state."

"Wednesday soon enough for you?" Ottley asked.

———

First thing that morning Vienna had sent Peck a telegram. She did not want him to hear the news before she had a chance to reassure him that they were all okay.

> CHILTON 845AM MON NOV 30 1941
>
> MR. PECK MORGAN
>
> PALMS HOTEL 193 WALTON STREET GALLERT ILL
>
>    WE ARE FINE. DON'T WORRY WILL WRITE TONIGHT
>
> STOP
>
>                             VIENNA

"Or fucking what!" Chap asked Branch, laughing, so angry for so long that everything was funny now.

Branch was sitting in the back seat on the driver's side behind Hughes, who was driving. Chap was in the front passenger's seat, on their way to 560 from the police station.

"What the hell he think he's going to do, meet you in the goddamn street? Him and who? Horse?"

Branch was even smiling.

"Get out of town by Wednesday," Chap said, the laughter gone.

Son had been awake earlier that morning. He had heard Chap when he began making telephone calls, local and long distance. To the members of the Negro Businessmen's Association, following up on the calls he had made to them the evening before, to the two colored lawyers, and the ministers. He had talked to some people he knew in Riverton, and then to Reverend Richmond's people. Chap would make arrangements to claim the reverend's body. He would let the coroner worry about what happened to the two other bodies.

That evening, seated around the dinner table, they worked it out. Branch said he knew he had to go because he had turned into a lightning rod, and therefore he was a liability to Chap. It was decided that Branch would accompany Richmond's body to Riverton, and then see if he could pick up a lead on who sent the shooters. They'd had no ID on them; only the labels in their overcoats, suits, and hatbands were from Riverton stores. They had no keys in their pockets, not for an automobile or a residence. How had they gotten to the church? Where had they stayed before? Who? What? Why?

Chap had given Branch a list of names of people who might be of help in Riverton, including Reverend Richmond's guy—Erskine Churchill—who'd set up the arrangements, first for Richmond's visit, then relating to the transfer of the body.

The next morning Ada read to Son from the Extra edition of the *Chilton Daily*.

## TRIPLE KILLING IN NEGRO CHURCH

### Reverend Gunned Down in Colored Church

#### Killers Shot by Third Man

Two unidentified negro gunmen gunned down Reverend Cook Richmond during Sunday service at Zion A.M.E church. Minutes into his sermon two gunmen fired multiple shots into the minister, killing him. Richmond was a visiting minister from Riverton.

The police, led by Chief Frank J. Mahoney, detained negro Branch Ottley. Ottley shot and killed the gunmen during a gun battle in the church. None of the others in the church were hurt. Ottley is a resident of 560 Fuller, a boarding house in Lower Dunbar, owned by local businessman Chap Metcalf. The mayhem erupted with approximately 100 present in the church on Spain Street.

Branch Ottley is in custody at the police station pending further investigation.

Local negro Attorney Lars Walton, retained as counsel for Ottley, said he expects his client to be released on an undisclosed bond.

Chief Mahoney reports that the investigation into the identity of the deceased killers continues.

There were pictures of the church with the crowd outside and interviews with a few of those who been inside during the shooting.

Vienna wrote to Peck. She gave him a brief-as-she-could eyewitness report. Then,

> . . . Just in this little while I get the feeling that things are going to change because of this. I'm not even sure what it is but I think someday we're going to look back on this and point to it as a moment of change.

V

Wednesday morning Branch Ottley left for Riverton.

# Kin–The Nettles

# 26

# Kin

## c. 1960s

I'm Emmie. Emmie Mto wa moto Nettle. I was Flo's older sister, Page's great aunt. I'm gone now. Deceased at fifty-four. I've got my own headstone in the Nettle family's plot. I lay proud among the others so long gone.

Ezekiel Reason Nettle was the first after slavery to own land, this land, in Acorn, Alabama. He named himself Nettle to remind him and all that followed to be an irritant to the white folks. It was Emilia Nettle Dillon who started the colored school on this land. Noah and Sara Hicks Nettle who sent the first child to college off this land. Ella Nettle was that child. Nettles from before and after. Lives. Stories.

This is how it was for me:

I started working for the Kimbroughs when I went into my senior year of high school. Mister and Missus Ethen Kimbrough. The banker. Kimbrough Savings Bank and Loan. I was innocent as creek water.

"Good morning, Mister Kimbrough." Like Mama taught me. Mama was their "gal" during the week: cleaning, washing, and cooking, baby-sitting their two little hellions.

"Good morning, Mister Kimbrough." He wouldn't even grunt or look up. *Cracker.* Fine. They paid me my little money the same either way.

I cooked their breakfast and dinner Saturday and Sundays.

If he wanted something he'd tell Missus Kimbrough, off-handed, short, and she'd tell me. Hard to tell sometimes if he was being nasty to her, or just to me through her.

"Mister Kimbrough would like so and so, Emmie."

"Yes ma'am."

And I'd pour him some hot coffee, or get more grits. Fine. All the same to me. *Cracker.*

I was cleaning up the kitchen after their Sunday breakfast. Nobody there but me. And I hear the car crunch in their gravel side drive. And the motor cut off. *Humph!* They back early—no—just *his* footsteps. Crunching up the steps onto the front porch. That's strange. He had taken Missus Kimbrough and the children to church, Grove Baptist, and like usual he didn't stay. He always headed straight for his home office when he came back. He would work there til time to pick them up and come eat the dinner I'd cooked and left to warm in the oven. Ordinarily. But the front door opens and eases shut. He usually just let it slam.

Just another few minutes by the mantle clock, tick-tocking now like it's mocking, and I would have taken off my apron, folded it into my bag, and locked the door behind me. Now Mister Kimbrough is standing in the doorway, still hasn't announced himself.

Even in the kitchen smelling of roast, potatoes, string beans, she smelled his cigarette smoke, his aftershave. The warm summer morning air whistling in his nose as he slowly inhales and exhales. My back still to him, "You back, Mister Kimbrough?" He doesn't answer, like I'm not even in the world. But I am. I'm standing there, humming a made-up tune, halfway between a spiritual and a fox-trot. The noon-nearing sun is making lacey-rose patterns on the drying dishes and glasses and utensils as it streams through Missus Kimbrough's parted kitchen curtains.

I'm looking out at the river that runs along the back of the property, at the line of dead trees.

Soon as he took his first step I thought about those pictures.

Now I don't know what it was had made me start fooling with his Kimbrough family portraits. Hanging all over the house. A gallery of hard-eyed, tight-jawed, stiff- necked racist crackers, proud of looking like the hard-eyed, tight-jawed, stiff-necked racist crackers they had been, and were. Make me want to spit just talking about them.

*Crackers.*

Now the Kimbrough family ruled Acorn, Mardalwil County, and all through northern Alabama. From the statehouse down to the country stores, going back to when all this land was first settled, from slavery forward.

Tintypes, paintings, and photographs in the parlor, the hallways, up the stairs, and I reckon in his home office out back. That's where he spent most of his home time. Call his-self writing the history of the Kimbroughs. Had trunks of their stuff. Filled with their diaries, bibles, slavery logs and other business records, old newspapers, and books. Nobody allowed in, neither Missus Kimbrough nor their brats, not even Mama in there to clean it up.

I willed my trunks of Nettle's things to Page, my nephew. It is to be opened when he's twenty-one.

When the main house was built way back in slavery times, that was the kitchen, which was kept separate from the house because of the danger of fire. He had it fixed up. It stands there between the house and the river.

I don't know if it was foolish or childish or the devil in me, but every morning when I went in, and I'd speak and he wouldn't, *Cracker*, I took to tilting one or two of those pictures, just enough so it was out of lineup with the others, and go on about my business. If she knew it she never said anything. I knew he knew I was doing it, but he never said anything to me either. I knew it because I'd tilt one and sometime later I'd hear him pass that spot and stop, then when I'd look later it would be straight—and I'd tilt another one.

I would have been gone that morning if I hadn't been standing there looking, mindless, out that window over the sink. His office, and beyond it to the riverbank, lined with dead oak. Over the generations the river's floodwaters ebb and wane, eroding the land closer and closer to the house. The land where my people, the Nettles, and all the others once ploughed and plucked, slavery through sharecropping, for his people's profit. Here I am standing with my back to him in the doorway, with the dishrag still in my right hand wiping the dry lip of the sink. Looking out at the line of leafless, no-bark, ash-gray oak. They were leaning tipped over, roots showing where the water had washed the land away to there. The river creeping up toward the house like haints, or night bandits.

Except for that hall clock signifying, it is quiet as one of those dead trees.

My heart is thumping like a mangy dog's hind leg. And he clears his throat. Didn't even say my name then. Like it was his right not to. It was his kitchen, his back window I was looking out of at his office; his Oldsmobile with the motor cooling from driving his wife and brats to church; his back yard with the clothes line where my mama hung his drawers that she picked off the floor where he dropped them; and his uprooted oak trees, in his Cracker town, where he ran his business, and the council meetings; in his south, where it was his right to make nigger men lower their eyes and step aside; his right to write the history of the men who had given him that right, the way it was his Cracker right to clear his throat and not call my goddamned name . . .

All I can do is tense myself so that when he takes that second and third and fourth steps across the black and white linoleum tiles, I am nothing but a knot, looking out that back window.

But when he touches my shoulder I know right away he is even more afraid than I am . . .

In the space of those few moments, several things came to me, quicker than I could think them.

We have our little struggle. He got me to the floor, him fumbling and pawing . . . . We both knew he didn't want *me* so much as needed to prove something—to himself, to me maybe, or to those pictures, or his ancestors, but whatever nerve he had worked up wasn't enough to see him through to the conclusion of what he didn't have the capacity to prove—so he quit, without ever getting my hem up much past my knees.

"You *through*?" My saying that was better than killing him.

The hall clock mocking him now, because he looked pitiful as a dish-rag, sniffling something about his "wife" or his "life"—it didn't matter.

Standing with my back to the sink and the window, I said, "Your great great- granddaddy tried the same thing with my great great-grand-mama, Hattie. He put his hands on her." Looking him dead in the eye as I had the whole time. "He thought he got away with it."

He was leaning against Missus Kimbrough's kitchen table, like a tipped-over oak, roots bleached, dangling like dry bones after a lynching. "'Hattie, a negro,' he said, as if he was reciting his homework at the front of a class.

What he had tried, and then the way he said her name, like there was no life attached to it, and she was just another asset, like a bolt of calico listed in a yellowing ledger, was the last drop that caused the overflowing of a damn that had been building since maybe the first Nettle arrived in Mardalwil in chains.

I was seventeen going on eighteen, but in that minute or so that we tussled, I had got grown, because he had fooled around and let me know, for all his strut and assumptions, how deep our family roots went down, and what that meant, for each of us. I saw him lose his innocence while he was trying to take mine. And I knew his will wasn't any more stalwart than mine, and that had let me get as strong as Bette Davis in the movies. Mama and me watched her from upstairs in the Noland picture show on Foster Street.

Miss Bette Davis was one strong, grown white woman. The ones that came along later, on television, were just housewives, like Missus Kimbrough. But Miss Bette Davis was so grown she could shoot a man in the back, till her pistol clicked on empty, and swear it was self-defense.

I told him, "Used to be a garden out back, years ago, a great laurel bush in it. Fatal if you eat even a little of it. Hattie, my great great-grandmamma, she put a half pinch of it in his chicory for months, until he didn't wake up one morning in June."

I don't know if he took it as a threat, but for the first time he looked at me as if I had sense enough to know something besides just what he wanted me to know.

"1861," he said.

I nodded. "Summer. He didn't live to see harvest."

"Cameron Kimbrough," he said, "my great great-grandfather," his mind slowly ticking up to the minute. "June 13th. Heart attack."

I shook my head.

He waited, antsy.

"He had a stomachache in the afternoon, vomited, had the shakes, then his heart quit before sundown."

He took out his handkerchief and wiped at his face, as a long-dead colored woman rose up from a column of names in a slave log out in this office in the yard and became a presence.

The Kimbroughs' and Nettles' roots were tangled as tap roots. He knew *some* of his family history, but I knew *all of it*, and mine too.

Mama asked me, "Where you get the money for these tickets, Emmie?"

"Mister Kimbrough loaned it to me, Mama."

"Why?"

"It's an advance on my salary. He hired me to help him with his family book."

That he had been working on since even she could remember. What he needed me for was to type and like that, and fill him in on what I knew about the Nettles and what they knew about the Kimbroughs.

And I told Mama that while I was doing that I could live with our cousins, Antonia and Sipp. They had said it was okay. And that way Mama could go up north to where Aunt Harriet and Uncle Otis were. They were a couple of the first Nettles in the chain that had left Acorn. They were old and needed looking after. I would follow soon as I was graduated.

As it worked out I didn't get there until much later.

All that time him and me worked together he still didn't call me by my name—except that once—at the very end.

I'm Page.

Grams my grandmother is Florence Nettle Thompson. Emmie Nettles was my aunt, Grams' sister. My Grams is in hospice now. But I remember when they sent word to Grams from down south that Aunt Emmie was dying. Grams went down and got her.

I think it was right around the time that the man who ran Acorn, the town Aunt Emmie lived in, had burned up in a fire. In a place on his property I think.

Note to myself to look into that.

Aunt Emmie was almost gone by the time Grams got her up here.

One night I heard this sound. Coming from the back room where Aunt Emmie was. Where my Grams is now.

It was human, but—not words, or not that I can put into words. Two sounds: one a low-pitched steady moan-hum, so low I almost couldn't hear it. Like whale music, or the wind-carving mountains. It was Aunt Emmie's sound of pain. And Grams, she was on the bed, holding Aunt Emmie and rocking with her, the bed creaking, and Grams making her soothing, kind of sing-songy harmonic sound as she whispered to her sister—

And as hard as I listened I could only catch a word now and then . . . "Ishom . . ." "Crop . . . " I heard just enough to know Grams was soothing Aunt Emmie by anointing her in a home remedy of Nettle kinfolk stories.

And, at the same time, through her rocking and cradling, Grams was drawing the pain out of Aunt Emmie's body into her own.

The sound of them—I had never heard such love before in my life.

So—Time's running out, but I'm trying to get as much of the history of the Nettles as I can before—

My Grams has dementia.


# FLO

Flo is sorting through letters and photo albums. She is fighting confusion with flairs of frustration.

—The first crop a Nettle made after slavery on their own land, it was great-grandmama, Lena, and papa Spencer, and their six-year-old, Florence, toddling along, holding that plow steady as a grown woman, with her daddy and mama in harness, pulling it like two mules.

That's where—uh—uh—It was something I was saying about—

A mule?

I can remember a story from almost two hundred years ago and can't—can't even remember why I was telling it.

She pauses, calming herself.

—It's like the joke—uh—my—it'll come to me—daughter—my sister I mean, used to tell—or tells—

She considers it, then moves on, trying to be light.

—About the two morons who find a good fishing spot. Fish are practically jumping in their boat. And the two morons decide they want to come back the next day. Get some more. Fish. So one moron says he'll mark the spot. Only trouble was the way he marked the spot was to put an X on the side of the boat—did I tell it right?

—And what did I even tell it for? I had a point—

Damn it! It is so frustrating! I can't remember anything anymore. Names, people—

Emmie was my *sister*! My big sister Emmie. She told the joke.

It was something I was saying about Emmie.

Iron Emmie they called her in the paper and on TV. She had another name too. African name they gave her. Swahili. *Mto wa moto*. Isn't it funny I can remember that? It means River of Mosquitoes. They gave her that name. And that's how she was on them white folks down there.

She was tough and daring.

Emmie come by her stubborn from Aunt Mule. They didn't call Aunt Mule "Mule" because she let white folks work her like one, but because she was twice as hard- headed as two mules. Florence was her real name. I'm named for her, but Emmie should have been.

And Emmie's daring? That goes back at least to great-uncle Otis. He's the one they say put the copperhead snakes in the white folks' Jefferson Davis Day picnic baskets.

We always had a big laugh at that.

They say white folks were vacating out of old man Henry Robert's pasture squealing and squalling like they had wasps in their under-draws, leaving horses, wagons, buckboards, and babies behind.

They had a bigger shock than that some years later with "Emmie's Army," as TV and the newspapers called them. The newspapers and them got it wrong about when she got what they called militant. That flood started as a trickle right after Emmie sent Mama and me north.

I got the whole story because Emmie and me used to write each other at least two or three times a week, every week, regular.

Stamps were two cents. The mailman delivered twice a day, once on Saturday.

Her letters were always typed on Kimbrough letterhead stationary that she just turned over and used the other side. I remember her practicing typing when she was still in high school and I was a little girl. It sounded like hail on a tin roof. She could type a mile a minute. Think that's why he hired her.

Emmie said her fight for fair treatment was a slow tide rising from the trickle, traceable back to the way she started to carry herself when she went to work typing for Kimbrough. That's how she said it in one of her letters—I remember that.

In a way they couldn't name people started to notice how she went about her business—wasn't no pouting or uppity or hangdog or taking low in it—she was just Emmie Nettle. And she wasn't any more concerned with white people than the spider was with the rain.

She wasn't concerned about boys either. I knew before she even told me. We didn't tell Mama.

But as much as Emmie didn't care about them, I liked them twice as much.

I used to be sharp and fine and feisty, and there weren't that many didn't like me. Like when Winston first saw me.

He says, "You know you're fine as corn silk, don't you?"

I said, "I know what I know. What I don't know is what you think you know." Well, he told me. And I liked the sound of it. We were peaches and cream from then till the day he died.

I had on one of Mama's black hats. "Taps" was playing. Somebody in white gloves handed me a flag folded into a triangle.

Winston died in the Battle of Chipyong-ni. Chipyong-ni, Korea.

He was my first husband. You mother's daddy . . .

Korea wasn't even a war.

But I wasn't talking about that. Was it about Emmie's letters? She wrote long, beautiful, funny letters. She was good enough to be a writer. I mostly just wrote about my husbands, and asked questions.

We used to write each other at least two or three times a week, every week, regular.

Stamps were two cents. The mailman delivered twice a day, once on Saturday.

No. I remember.

Meetings at Emmie's.

They started meeting evenings at cousin Antonia and Sipp's house where Emmie was living. Could have been quilting bees, or parlor socials, for all the white people knew. Wednesday evenings after choir practice, Thursdays on their nights off . . .

First it was the young colored girls.

Emmie told them whatever way it was she walked it was because there were all those people walking right behind her. Blood. Kin. Pushing her forward. So, no, she didn't have time to be studying the little everyday slights and racist pettinesses of pitiful white people. And the girls listened and it woke them up to the same push behind and in them.

Then, seeing how the girls were carrying themselves caught the boys' attention. Put salt water in their veins, made them dream the dreams of men, which in turn got noticed by the old heads, the "aunties" and "uncles." They began questioning just grinning and bearing and enduring.

It was in full flow by the time white people noticed—*something*. The poor white people, them crackers, could not figure out what the hell was going on! Niggers still said "Yes sir" and "Yes ma'am." Still went around the back, still obeyed all the signs, the laws, knew their place and their jobs, but it looked like their negroes had—they didn't know—a new way they followed orders, or waited for their change to be counted, look like it took longer for water to boil, biscuits to bake, or hedges to get trimmed—not longer, but the water wasn't as hot, the biscuits didn't rise as high, there was a sharper snap when the blades came together . . . *Some*thing. It wasn't spite or even sass. But they all noticed it: white housewives, store people, mailmen, the insurance agents, ice men, business owners, police. Everybody who came into contact with them noticed it. Felt it. Whatever it was, it was beyond the old way both sides had come to accept. There started to be—they didn't know what to call it—if it was even anything—a difference.

Then coloreds would just not do something they had always done. Like not going into a particular store for a week or so. Just not even to buy whatever was being sold there. Emmie said it was like a test. And it would go on until the owner noticed and Emmie knew they had noticed.

Emmie said the white folks couldn't name their misgivings, but they were *spooked*. They started reacting without knowing what they were reacting to.

Even in the heat of dog days, they'd have sudden chill-shivers. The riddle of whatever it was, or wasn't, penetrated their sleep like the reek of mildew. Even in the daytime they thought they heard a faint, off-rhythmic leak from a rusty spigot in a closed off room, or the sigh of seepage from a cistern.

In bed at night they flopped about like fish out of water and in their dreams black gals were grinding maggots into cornmeal; there was the whisper of black boys' straight razors being stropped. They tossed and turned till dawn, when they woke, weary, fretful, sweat-damp, wondering who, what, when, where, and how?

There were cloud-gray doubts where there'd been sunshine.

Emmie said there's no stopping water once it starts.

Her letters would have me rolling.

I've got all the letters she wrote, stored in shoeboxes in my closet. They came twice a day, once on Saturdays.

That's what I was trying to talk about. Emmie—

My big sister is Emmie.

Mama Janie was my mama. My mama Janie used to say, "We got to remember, but we got to forgive so we can move on . . ."

That made all of the sense in the world. Then! But now I'm lost as an ice cube in the ocean. When I can remember it's never what I'm trying to remember—Where's my X mark? What spot does it even mark? Where the fishing was good? Or just the boat I'm adrift in? So I have to change with the time and tide. I can't be worried with what was. All that is, is what was.

These people around here are all morons! They don't know anything, and try to tell me anything—or nothing—they don't think I know what they're up to.

# FLO 2

"You, boy, who are you?"

"Page."

"Do you know who I am?"

"Do you?"

"Tell me."

"Essie Nettle Fuller Williams. You're my grandmother."

"Oh."

"That's okay if you don't know me, Grams."

"What was your name, Sweetnums?"

"Page. Page Nettle."

"—Was there a—Emmie Nettle—?"

"Yes, ma'am."

"—who—made a big name—?"

"Yes, ma'am."

"—somewhere down south?—Acorn!"

"Yes, ma'am."

"She here?"

"No ma'am."

"Sweetnums, don't you know anybody that's living?"

Laughing. "Yes, ma'am."

"This—It must be a movie or TV or something—or am I dreaming? Mama and—my sister used to like going to the movies. Emmie. We were colored. We had to sit upstairs. Was it a movie, is that what it is?"

"Yes ma'am. It's just a movie. That's all it is. Don't even worry about it."

"What makes you think I'm *worried* about it?"

"I don't think you are."

"Then why you say I was."

"My mistake."

"I remember I had men—but I don't remember their names."

"Bennie. My grandfather Bennie was one. Benjamin Fuller."

"It was love both ways—In bed when he rolled over I rolled over. Then he too soon was also taken."

"Yes ma'am."

"I could get *maaaaad!* You wouldn't think it now, huh? It wouldn't last but a minute, but I meant it while I was—at him especially—

"Most I was ever mad at him was when he had that heart attack—still mad at him for that—can't help it. Wasn't his fault, was it? He just worked so hard and loved so hard.

"He died before I was born."

"It is so goddamn frustrating. When people remind me of things they want me to remember—Like they're pointing out of a speeding train window, saying, 'See! See?' and all I can see is rushing darkness. Is their wanting me to remember for their sake or mine, I wonder?"

"I wonder."

"Me too."

"You taught me to forgive, but not forget."

"I forget everything. And who needs forgiving? Just get mad then get over it. I think I used to get mad at him just so we could make up. He still thought I was sweet as a sugar dumpling."

"You must've been."

"Must've been."

"Some things people tell me over and over—some things I don't tell—Emmie never did like boys—she told me but I already knew—people thought it was because—but it wasn't—that my mama and Emmie are dead—some things I think they don't tell me at all—what's the use, must be what they're thinking. Why put perishable in a refrigerator that won't keep anything? Or maybe they're there and I forget to look. And who am I anyway, a fine and feisty young woman, sweet as a sugar dumpling—? It's so goddamn frustrating—Where do I put the mark to know how to find myself? Tell me your name again, Sweetnums, and don't get mad at me if I forget it."

"No ma'am. I know. Page."

"Page—like in a book?"

"Yes, ma'am. Page Nettle."

"—Bennie—did you know him?"

"No ma'am. He died before I was born."

"I guess I don't know anybody but dead people either."

"You were telling me about Emmie. Remember?"

"Emmie was my big sister."

"Yes, ma'am."

"We took care of her, didn't we?"

"Yes ma'am."

"I held her in my arms. Crying. 'Tell me the stories, Flo,' she said. 'Tell me the stories again—'"

"Do you know what she was talking about? I don't."

"You knew it when it counted, Grams."

# AFTERWORD

The obvious criticism of course will be that it is not finished—that I have not seen the heroine to the end of her situation—that I have left her *en l'air.*—This is both true and false. The *whole* of anything is never told; you can only take what groups together. What I have done has that unity—it groups together. It is complete in itself—and the rest may be taken up or not, later.

Henry James notebook notation